THE WORKS OF LIANG YUCHUN

梁遇春

著译全集

6

第六卷

李力夫 商昌宝 主编

海峡出版发行集团 | 福建教育出版社

本卷总目

The Old Nurse's Story
老保姆的故事 ················· 1

In the Steppes
草原上 ······················ 87

Youth
青春 ······················· 165

The Constant Lover
忠心的爱人 ················· 289

The Old Nurse's Story

老保姆的故事
（英汉对照）

Mrs. Gaskell 著

梁遇春 译注

"英文小丛书"之一，上海北新书局，1931年4月付排，1931年5月初版

Mrs. Gaskell
(Elizabeth Stevenson)
(1810—1865)

这位女作家是英国小说家里第一个把穷人们的生活老老实实地描写出来。迭更司写下流社会时总是画出一幅闹哄哄的，怪有意思的图画，虽然有时也说得叫人辛酸流泪，但是他的滑稽口吻把穷神的单调的，死板板的，毫不容情的丑面目遮住了。这位女作家却敢大胆地将英国工业区里工人穷苦不堪的状况素朴地写出，而成为很妙的小说，从这点上我们可以猜出她的艺术手腕是多么高明，她的处女作 *Mary Barton* 和 *North and South*，是属于这类的长篇小说。

但是她又具有细腻的诙谐情调，曾经用极恬美的笔描状一个全是女人住着的僻乡里的生活。这本中篇小说 *Cranford* 可算做她的杰作。

她对于低微朴素的生活深有同情，能看出内中的种种意义。所以有人说她是英国第一个善说出保姆，管家婆，女仆的心情的人。这篇《老保姆的故事》是她在这方面最大的成功。

她不单会体贴平凡人们的心境，而且能看透许多人的动机。

她的长篇小说 *Ruth* 就是分析一个女子的动机的作品，可说后来心理小说派的前身。

总之，她知道怎样用女性特有的锐敏观察力和体贴能力，做平凡人和穷苦人的生活的舌人。这个功绩是值得钦仰的。

The Old Nurse's Story

You know, my dears[1], that your mother was an orphan, and an only child[2]; and I dare say you have heard that your grandfather[3] was a clergyman up[4] in Westmorland, where I come from[5]. I was just a girl in the village school, when, one day, your grandmother came in to ask the mistress if[6] there was any scholar there who would do for[7] a nursemaid; and mighty[8] proud I was, I can tell ye, when the mistress

---

1 dears: beloved ones 亲爱的人们。
2 only child: a child who has neither brother nor sister 独生子。
3 grandfather: 祖父或外祖父，这里是外祖父的意思，就是所谓 father of one's mother。
4 up: 因为 Westmorland 是高原，所以用 up 字。
5 where I come from: 我是从那里来的，就是说我本来是那里人。

老保姆的故事

你们知道,我的乖乖,你们母亲是一个孤儿,又是一个独生的孩子;我敢说你们听见过人们说你们的外祖父是卫斯特摩兰地方的一个牧师,我就是从那里来的。我刚是村里学堂的一个女学生,有一天,你们的外祖母来问女校长这里有什么学生可以当个保姆;我可以告诉你们,我是很得意的,当校长叫我上去,保证我是很会做针线的一个女孩子,一个靠得住的诚实

---

6 if:whether与否。
7 to do for:to answer the requirements of 具有做……的必要条件,可以当……。
8 mighty:very 很。

called me up, and spoke to[1] my being a good girl at my needle, and a steady honest girl, and one whose parents were very respectable, though they might be poor. I thought I should like nothing better than to serve the pretty young lady, who was blushing as deep as I was, as she spoke of the coming baby, and what I should have to do with it. However, I see you don't care so much for[2] this part of my story, as for what you think is to come, so I'll tell you at once. I was engaged and settled at the parsonage before Miss Rosamond(that was the baby, who is now your mother) was born. To be sure, I had little enough to do with her when she came, for she was never out of her mother's arms, and slept by her all night long[3]; and proud enough was I sometimes when miss is trusted her to me. There never was such a baby before or since, though you've all of you been fine enough in your turns; but for sweet, winning ways, you've none of you come up to[4] your mother. She took after[5] her mother, who was a real lady born; a Miss Furnivall, a granddaughter of Lord Furnivall's, in Northumberland. I believe she had neither brother nor sister, and had been brought up in my lord's family till she had married your grandfather, who was just a curate, son to a shopkeeper in Carlisle—

---

1 to speak to: to attest 保证。
2 to care for: to like 喜欢。
3 all night long: throughout all night 整夜里。
4 to come up to: to arise to 达到；赶得上。

孩子，而且父母都是值得尊敬的，虽然他们也许穷些。我当时以为服事这位美丽的年青太太真是我顶喜欢干的事情，她的脸羞红得正同我的一样，当她说起那将要来临的小孩，和我得怎样照料那小孩。但是，我看出对于这部分故事，你们不像对于你们所预测的下文那么注意，所以我就立刻向你们说出来罢。我被雇去，住在牧师寓所里，在洛沙萝德小姐（那个小孩就是你们现在的母亲）生下之前。真的，她来到世界以后，我并不忙于照料她，因为她绝没有离开她母亲的怀抱，整夜都同她母亲睡在一起；有时，我很得意，当太太肯托我照呼她。从来没有过这么好看的小孩子，此后也没有见到，虽然你们都曾经是够漂亮的孩子；但是说到甜蜜的，叫人喜欢的态度，你们没有一个赶得上你们的母亲。她像她的母亲，她的母亲的确生下来就是一个贵妇人，叫做斐妮发尔小姐，诺森伯兰地方斐妮发尔爵士的孙女。我相信她既没有兄弟，也没有姊妹，在爵士家养大，一直到她嫁给你们的外祖父，他只是一个副牧师，卡来儿

---

5 to take after: to resemble 相似；像。

but a clever, fine gentleman as ever was—and one who was a right-down[1] hard worker in his parish, which was very wide, and scattered all abroad over the Westmorland Fells[2]. When your mother, little Miss Rosamond, was about four or five years old, both her parents died in a fortnight—one after the other. Ah! that was a sad time. My pretty young mistress and me was looking for[3] another baby, when my master came home from one of his long rides, wet, and tired, and took the fever he died of; and then she never held up her head again, but just lived to see her dead baby, and have it laid on her breast before she sighed away her life. My mistress had asked me, on her death-bed, never to leave Miss Rosamond; but if she had never spoken a word, I would have gone with the little child to the end of the world.

The next thing, and before we had well stilled our sobs, the executors and guardians came to settle the affairs. They were my poor young mistress's own cousins, Lord Furnivall, and Mr. Esthwaite, my master's brother, a shopkeeper in Manchester; not so well-to-do then as he was afterwards, and with a large family rising about him. Well! I don't know if it were their settling, or because of a letter my mistress wrote on her death-bed to her cousin, my lord; but some-

---

1 right-down: downright 全然；真正。
2 Fell: mountain 山，用时多半同地名连在一起。
3 to look for: to be in a state of expectation 正在期待中。

地方一个店主的儿子——但是一个再聪明漂亮不过的士君子，在他教区里真是一个努力的工作者，他的教区很大，分布卫斯特摩兰·斐尔斯的全部。当你们母亲，洛沙萝德小姑娘，差不多四五岁大时候，她的父母在两星期之内相继死去。呀！那真是个凄凉时候。我美丽的年青主母同我正期待另一个小孩的出世，我的主人从他的一个长途骑行回来，淋湿的，疲倦的，得了致他死命的那个热病，此后她再也不抬起头了，刚好活到看见那产下就死的小孩，把他放在胸前，她就叹一口气死了。我的主母弥留时候请我永不要离开洛沙萝德小姐；但是假使她一个字也没有说，我也肯跟这小孩走到世界的尽头。

接着，在我们把呜咽完全压下之前，执行遗嘱人同遗族保护人来解决事情了。他们是我这位可怜的年青太太的表兄弟斐妮发尔爵士同我主人的兄弟，厄斯所威特先生，曼撒斯特地方的一个店主，那时候不像他后来那么富足，又有一个大家庭围他身边。呀！我不知道这是他们商量的结果，还是因为我的主母临终时写给她的表兄弟，这位爵士大人的那一封信；但是不

how it was settled that Miss Rosamond and me were to[1] go to Furnivall Manor House, in Northumberland, and my lord spoke as if it had been her mother's wish that she should live with his family, and as if he had no objections, for that one or two more or less could make no difference in so grand a household. So, though that was not the way in which I should have wished the coming of my bright and pretty pet to have been looked at—who was like a sunbeam in any family, be it never so grand—I was well pleased that all the folks in the Dale should stare and admire, when they heard I was going to be young lady's maid at my Lord Furnivall's at Furnivall Manor.

But I made a mistake in thinking we were to go and live where my lord did. It turned out[2] that the family had left Furnivall Manor House fifty years or more. I could not hear that my poor young mistress had ever been there, though she had been brought up in the family; and I was sorry for that, for I should have liked Miss Rosamond's youth to have passed where her mother's had been.

My lord's gentleman[3], from whom I asked as many questions as I durst, said that the Manor House was at the foot of the Cumberland Fells, and a very grand place; that an old Miss Furnivall, a great-aunt

---

1　be + infinitive 表 intention（意向）。
2　to turn out: to prove in the result 结果显出。
3　gentleman: servant 仆人，是指贵族的从者（valet or gentleman's gentleman）。

管是什么原因，最后的决定是洛沙萝德小姐同我到诺森伯兰地方斐妮发尔邸宅去住，爵士大人说时好像她母亲希望她将来同他家里人住在一起，好像他并不反对，因为在这么伟大的一个家庭里，多一两人，少一两人，并没有什么关系。然而，拿这种态度来看我这位聪明伶俐的小宝宝的来临虽然并不是我所希望的——我这小宝宝在任一个家庭里都好像一线阳光，无论那个家是多么伟大——可是我却很高兴，因为山谷里的人们会直着眼睛赞美，当他们听到我将做斐妮发尔爵邸里斐妮发尔爵士大人家中的小姐的保姆。

但是我错了，以为我们去住在爵士大人住的地方。其实他家里人离开斐妮发尔邸宅已经五十年了，或者还多些。我没有听见人们说过我这可怜的年青主母曾经住在那里，虽然她是在那家里养大的；我对于这一点心里觉得难过，因为我很希望洛沙萝德小姐的青春光阴会在她母亲的青春光阴所在的地方过去。

爵士大人的仆人，我敢向他提起的多少问题全说出了，说那爵邸是在昆布兰山的脚旁，是一个很壮伟的所在；一位年迈

of my lord's, lived there, with only a few servants; but that it was a very healthy place, and my lord had thought that it would suit Miss Rosamond very well for a few years, and that her being there might perhaps amuse his old aunt.

 I was bidden by my lord to have Miss Rosamond's things ready by a certain day. He was a stern, proud man, as they say all the Lords Furnivall were; and he never spoke a word more than was necessary. Folk did say he had loved my young mistress; but that, because she knew that his father would object, she would never listen to him, and married Mr. Esthwaite; but I don't know. He never married at any rate[1]. But he never took much notice of Miss Rosamond; which I thought he might have done if he had cared for her dead mother. He sent his gentleman with us to the Manor House, telling him to join him at Newcastle that same evening; so there was no great length of time for him to make us known to all the strangers before he, too, shook us off; and we were left, two lonely young things (I was not eighteen), in the great old Manor House. It seems like yesterday that we drove there. We had left our own dear parsonage very early, and we had both cried as if our hearts would break, though we were travelling in my lord's carriage, which I thought so much of[2] once. And

---

  1 at any rate: at all events; certainly 无论如何；的确。
  2 to think much of: to hold in high estimation 看重。

的斐妮发尔小姐，爵士大人的祖姑母，只跟几个仆人住在那里；但是那是个很合于卫生的地方，爵士大人以为洛沙萝德小姐这几年里住在那儿会很适宜，而且她也许可以替他的祖姑母解闷。

爵士大人嘱咐我某一日把洛沙萝德小姐的东西预备好。他是个冷酷骄傲的人，人们说斐妮发尔爵士们素来都是如此；他绝不说一句多余的话。人们的确说他从前爱上了我的年青主母；可是因为她知道他父亲会反对，她绝不肯听他的求婚，嫁给厄斯所威特先生了；然而这件事我并不知道。无论如何，他是绝没有结婚过的。但是他也绝不大注意洛沙萝德小姐；我想他会注意，若使他曾经倾心于她的已死的母亲。他派他仆人送我们到邸宅，叫他当天晚上到纽喀斯尔去找他；所以他没有多大时光可以把我们介绍给宅里一切生人，只好匆匆地也离我们去了；我们就剩下来在那壮大的老邸宅里，两个孤寂的小孩子（我还不到十八岁）。现在想起来，好像是昨天的事情，我们坐车子到那里去。清早我们离开我们自己的，亲爱的牧师住宅，我俩哭得好像我们的心会碎了，虽然我们是坐在爵士大人的车里旅行，

now it was long past noon on a September day, and we stopped to change horses for the last time at a little smoky town, all full of colliers and miners. Miss Rosamond had fallen asleep, but Mr. Henry told me to waken her, that she might see the park and the Manor House as we drove up. I thought it rather a pity; but I did what he bade me, for fear[1] he should complain of me to my lord. We had left all signs of a town, or even a village, and were then inside the gates of a large wild park—not like the parks here in the south, but with rocks, and the noise of running water, and gnarled thorn-trees, and old oaks, all white and peeled with age.

The road went up about two miles, and then we saw a great and stately house, with many trees close around it, so close that in some places their branches dragged against the walls when the wind blew; and some hung broken down; for no one seemed to take much charge of the place; —to lop the wood, or to keep the moss-covered carriage-way in order[2]. Only in front of the house all was clear. The great oval drive was without a weed; and neither tree nor creeper was allowed to grow over the long many-windowed front; at both sides of which a wing projected, which were each the ends of other

---

1 for fear: lest 怕的是。
2 to keep in order: to keep in tidiness 收拾干净。

那件事我曾经以为是这么光荣的。现在是十一月里一天中午过了许久的时候,我们最后一次停在一个烟雾弥漫的小镇换马,那里满是煤矿工人同坑夫。洛沙萝德小姐睡着了,但是亨利先生叫我把她喊醒,为的是那么她可以看见猎苑同邸宅,当我们车子快到的时候。我觉得这有些苦了小孩;但是我照他的话办,怕的是他将向爵士大人说我的坏话。我们离开了,市镇的,甚至于乡村的,一切标记,那时走进了一大片荒凉的猎苑的大门——不像我们南方这里的猎苑,却有岩石,流水的声音,错节的荆棘,同因为年代久而全白了,全脱皮了的橡树。

那条路延长了二哩左右,我们就看见一所高大壮丽的屋子,有许多树紧围在四旁,是这么紧近的,有些地方树枝拖曳碰着墙上,当风吹过时候;有些树中断了斜挂在那儿;因为好像没有人很注意去料理这地方;——去把树修剪好,或者把满盖着苍苔的马路修理完整。只是在屋子面前,一切都是干净的。椭圆形的宽大马路上连一根草都没有;那个长的,多窗户的正面墙也不许长有什么树或者爬藤;正面的两头有边屋凸出,这些

side fronts; for the house, although it was so desolate, was even grander than I expected. Behind it rose the Fells, which seemed unenclosed and bare enough; and on the left hand of the house, as you stood facing it, was a little, old-fashioned flower-garden, as I found out afterwards. A door opened out upon it from the west front; it had been scooped out of the thick dark wood for some old Lady Furnivall; but the branches of the great forest trees had grown and overshadowed it again, and there were very few flowers that would live there at that time.

When we drove up to the great front entrance, and went into the hall I thought we should be lost—it was so large, and vast, and grand. There was a chandelier all of bronze, hung down from the middle of the ceiling; and I had never seen one before, and looked at it all in amaze. Then, at one end of the hall, was a great fireplace, as large as the sides of the houses in my country, with massy andirons and dogs[1] to hold the wood; and by it were heavy old-fashioned sofas. At the opposite end of the hall, to the left as you went in—on the western side—was an organ built into the wall, and so large that it filled up the best[2] part of that end. Beyond it, on the same side, was a door; and opposite, on each side of the fire-place, were also doors leading to the east front; but those I never went through as long as I

---

1 dogs: metal supports for burning logs 靠燃烧的木头用的金属架子。
2 the best: most; largest 最大部分的。

边屋又是各边另面的正面的顶端；这所屋子，虽然是这么荒凉，却是大得甚至于超过我所预期的。屋子后面耸起一座荒山，那好像是没有围住，也没有什么森林；屋子的左边，当你对着屋子站着时候，有一个古式的小花园，这是我后来发现的。屋子的西面有一个门通过去；这座花园是为着某一位斐妮发尔老太太从深黑的丛林里挖出；但是大森林的树枝又长出来，把它遮住了，我们到的那个时候很少花能够活在里面。

当我们的车子到了正面的大门口，我们走进大厅，我想我们将遗失在这里面了——那屋子是这么宽，这么大，这么庄严。有一架全是青铜制成的有枝烛台从天花板的中间挂下；这是我从来没有看见过的，惊讶到极点地尽瞧着。在大厅的一头有一个大壁炉，大得像我们乡间屋子的边墙，有厚重的薪架预备放木头烧；旁边有几张沉重的旧式沙发。在大厅的那一头，你走进去时靠左的那一边——就是屋子的西部——有一架大风琴镶在墙里，大得几乎把那头全占满了。再走过些，也是在西边，有一个门；对面，火炉两旁，也有门引到屋子的东部；但是我

stayed in the house, so I can't tell you what lay beyond.

 The afternoon was closing in[1], and the hall, which had no fire lighted in it, looked dark and gloomy, but we did not stay there a moment. The old servant, who had opened the door for us, bowed to Mr. Henry, and took us in through the door at the further side of the great organ, and led us through several smaller halls and passages into the west drawing-room, where he said that Miss Furnivall was sitting. Poor little Miss Rosamond held very tight to me, as if she were scared and lost in that great place, and as for myself, I was not much better. The west drawing-room was very cheerful-looking, with a warm fire in it, and plenty of good, comfortable furniture about. Miss Furnivall was an old lady not far from eighty, I should think, but I do not know. She was thin and tall, and had a face as full of fine wrinkles as if they had been drawn all over it with a needle's point. Her eyes were very watchful, to make up[2], I suppose, for her being so deaf as to be obliged to use a trumpet[3]. Sitting with her, working at the same great piece of tapestry, was Mrs. Stark, her maid and companion[4], and almost as old as she was. She had lived

---

 1 to closs in: to enclose; to come nearer 围着；一步步走近一步。黄昏时候，黑暗从四面迫来，所以说"暮色四合"。
 2 to make up: to compensate 补偿。
 3 trumpet: 老年人耳聋，向他说话的人用喇叭向他耳边说。

住在那屋子里时候,绝没有走过那些门,所以我不能告诉你们再走过去还有什么。

暮色四合了,大厅里没有燃起火,现出黑暗忧郁的神气,但是我们在那里一会儿也没有停留。替我们开大门的那个老仆向亨利先生鞠躬,带我们走进大风琴过去的那个门,引我们穿过几个小厅同甬道,到西面的客厅,他说斐妮发尔小姐正坐在那里。可怜的洛沙萝德小姐紧靠着我,好像在这个大地方她吓住了,迷路了,至于我自己呢,也并不比她强多少。西客厅看起来很热闹,里面有温暖的火炉,排了许多坐着舒适的家具。斐妮发尔小姐我想是离八十岁不远的一位老太太,但是我知道不清楚。她是瘦长的,脸上满是精细的皱纹,好像用针尖画在上面的。她的眼睛很精灵,我想是补偿那聋得人们要用喇叭向她说话的耳朵。坐在她旁边,绣着同一个大帷帐,有一位斯塔克太太,她的女仆,又是她的陪伴,差不多同她一样的老。自

---

4 companion:英国老太太感到生活寂寞,常雇个人专同她做伴,这种人叫做companion,仿佛比女仆高一点儿。

with Miss Furnivall ever since they both were young, and now she seemed more like a friend than a servant; she looked so cold, and grey, and stony, as if she had never loved or cared for any one; and I don't suppose she did care for any one, except her mistress; and, owing to the great deafness of the latter, Mrs. Stark treated her very much as if she were a child. Mr. Henry gave some message from my lord, and then he bowed good-bye to us all—taking no notice of my sweet little Miss Rosamond's outstretched hand—and left us standing there, being looked at by the two old ladies through their spectacles.

I was right[1] glad when they rung for the old footman who had shown us in at first, and told him to take us to our rooms. So we went out of that great drawing-room, and into another sitting-room, and out of that, and then up[2] a great flight of stairs, and along a broad gallery—which was something like a library, having books all down one side, and windows and writing-tables all down the other—till we came to our rooms, which I was not sorry to hear were just over the kitchens; for I began to think I should be lost in that wilderness of a house. There was an old nursery, that had been used for all the little lords and ladies long ago, with a pleasant fire burning in the grate, and the kettle boiling on the hob, and tea-things spread out on

---

1 right: very; extremely 非常；极端。
2 into, out 同 up 都是接着前面 went 一字，就是 went in, went out, went up。

从她俩年青时候，她就同斐妮发尔小姐住在一起，现在她更像是个朋友，倒不像是个仆人；她是这么冷淡，灰色，和石头一样的不动情，好像她绝没有爱过或者关心过谁；我不相信她除开她的主子外还有关心谁；她的主子是这么聋，斯塔克太太待她真好像她是个小孩子。亨利先生传几句爵士大人的话，就向我们大家鞠躬告别了——也没有睬我这甜蜜的洛沙萝德小姑娘伸出来给他握的小手——让我们站在那里，给两位老太太从她们的眼镜瞧着。

我十分高兴，当她们按铃喊起先引我们到那里的那个老仆人进来，叫他带我们到我们房子去。我们就走出那大客厅，走进一间闲坐的房子，又走出来，上一个长的楼梯，经过一个宽阔的走廊——那有些像一间书房，一边全排了书，一边有窗子同写字桌——一直走到我们的房间，那刚好在厨房上面，这句话我听时觉得很高兴；因为我开始想在这个荒凉的屋子我将迷途了。屋里有一间旧育婴房，一切小爵爷小淑女历来都是用这个房间，炉格上的火快乐地燃烧着，烘物架上的壶子煮沸着，

the table; and out of that room was the night-nursery, with a little crib for Miss Rosamond close to my bed. And old James[1] called up Dorothy, his wife, to bid us welcome; and both he and she were so hospitable and kind, that by and by[2] Miss Rosamond and me felt quite at home[3]; and by the time tea was over, she was sitting on Dorothy's knee, and chattering away as fast as her little tongue could go. I soon found out that Dorothy was from Westmorland, and that bound her and me together, as it were[4]; and I would never wish to meet with kinder people than were old James and his wife. James had lived pretty nearly all his life in my lord's family, and thought there was no one so grand as they. He even looked down[5] a little on his wife; because, till he had married her, she had never lived in any but a farmer's household. But he was very fond of her, as well he might be. They had one servant under them, to do all the rough work. Agnes they called her; and she and me, and Jamse and Dorothy, with Miss Furnivall and Mrs. Stark, made up[6] the family; always remembering my sweet little Miss Rosamond! I used to wonder what they had done before she came, they thought so much of her

---

1 James: 前面所说的开门的老仆人的名字。

2 by and by: gradually 渐渐。

3 at home: at one's house; free from constrict 在自己家里；无拘束。

4 as it were: so to speak 可以说；仿佛。

5 to look down on: to despise 蔑视。

茶具已排在桌上了;从这房子走过去就是夜间育婴房,架给洛沙萝德小姐睡的有栏卧床紧挨着我的床边。老詹姆士叫他的妻子多罗塞上来欢迎我们;他同她都是这么殷勤,这么仁爱,洛沙萝德小姐同我渐渐觉得好像同在家里一样;喝完茶点后,她坐在多罗塞膝上,尽她小舌头的本领,顶快地说一大阵话。我不久就发现多罗塞也是从卫斯特摩兰地方来的,这一点好像把她同我连在一气了;我绝没有希望会碰到比老詹姆士同他的妻子更仁爱的人们。詹姆士几乎一生都是在爵士大人家里过去,以为天下没有别人像他们这么高贵。他甚至于有些瞧不起他的妻子;因为在他娶她之前,她除开农夫家里外没有在别个家里住过。但是他很爱她,这是他应当的。他们底下有一个仆人干一切粗事。他们叫她做阿格尼;她,我,詹姆士,多罗塞,斐妮发尔小姐,斯塔克太太,这些就是全家的人了;她们老是记着我那甜蜜蜜的洛沙萝德小姑娘!她们现在是这么注重她,我常纳罕在她来这里之前她们天天干什么事。厨房同客厅里面人

---

6 to make up:to compose 组成。

now. Kitchen and drawing-room, it was all the same. The hard, sad Miss Furnivall, and the cold Mrs. Stark, looked pleased when she came fluttering in like a bird, playing and pranking hither and thither, with a continual murmur, and pretty prattle of gladness. I am sure, they were sorry many a time when she flitted away into the kitchen, though they were too proud to[1] ask her to stay with them, and were a little surprised at her taste; though to be sure, as Mrs. Stark said, it was not to be wondered at, remenbering what stock her father had come of. The great, old rambling house was a famous place for little Miss Rosamond. She made expeditions all over it, with me at her heels[2]; all, except the east wing, which was never opened, and whither we never thought of going. But in the western and northern part was many a pleasant room; full of things that were curiosities to us, though they might not have been to people who had seen more. The windows were darkened by the sweeping boughs of the trees, and the ivy which had overgrown them; but, in the green gloom, we could manage to see old china jars and carved ivory boxes, and great heavy books, and, above all, the old pictures!

Once, I remenber, my darling would have Dorothy go with us to tell us who they all were; for they were all portraits of some of my

---

1 too + adjective + to: so + adjective + that + subject + cannot
2 at one's heels: close behind one 紧跟着他。

们都是一样地喜欢她。严酷的，愁闷的斐妮发尔小姐同冷淡的斯塔克太太都现出高兴的神气，当她像一只鸟地飞进来，跑这里跑那里玩耍瞎跳，口里不断地喃喃着，说出许多巧妙的欣欢话。我相信，有许多时候她们觉得难过，当她飞跳到厨房里去，虽然她们太骄傲了不肯请她滞在那里，同有些纳罕她这种下流的趣味；当然，斯塔克太太说，这是不足奇的，一想起她的父亲是从什么门第出身的。这个广大的，散漫的古屋对于洛沙萝德小姑娘简直是一个名胜之区。她在那屋里到处探险赏玩，我跟着她；到处都走遍了，除开东部，那是从来没有打开的，我们也绝不想到那边去。但是在西部同北部有许多有意思的房子；满是我们认为稀奇的东西，虽然在东西看得比我们多的人们眼里，那些是并不足奇的。窗子是被扫来扫去的树枝和窗外长的长春藤弄暗些；但是在绿的幽暗里我们能够设法瞧见旧瓷瓶，雕刻的象牙盒子，沉重的大本书，尤其旧画。

有一回，我记得，我的乖乖要多罗塞同我们去，告诉我们画在上面的人们是谁；因为他们都是爵士大人家里一些人们的画

lord's family, though Dorothy could not tell us the names of every one. We had gone through most of the rooms, when we came to the old state drawing-room over the hall, and there was a picture of Miss Furnivall; or, as she was called in those days, Miss Grace, for she was the younger sister.[1] Such a beauty she must have been! but with such a set, proud look, and such scorn looking out of her handsome eyes, with her eyebrows just a little raised, as if she wondered how anyone could have the impertinence to look at her; and her lip curled at us, as we stood there gazing. She had a dress on, the like of which I had never seen before, but it was all[2] the fashion when she was young; a hat of some soft white stuff like beaver, pulled a little over her brows, and a beautiful plume of feathers sweeping round it on one side; and her gown of blue satin was open in front to a quilted white stomacher.

"Well, to be sure!" said I, when I had gazed my fill. "Flesh is grass, they do say; but who would have thought that Miss Furnivall had been such an out-and-out[3] beauty to see her now?"

"Yes," said Dorothy. "Folks change sadly. But if what my master's father used to say was true, Miss Furnivall, the elder sister,

---

1 英国家庭里顶大的未出阁姑娘可以称姓，比如姓Lamb，就可以被人们喊做Miss Lamb，其余的大概称名，如名做Lucy，就叫Miss Lucy。

2 all: entirely quite 完全是。

3 out-and-out: thorough; surpassing.

像，虽然多罗塞不能说出个个人的名字。我们走过了许多房子，然后走到大厅上面的旧式大客厅，那里有一张斐妮发尔小姐的画像；或者，照当时人们对于她的称呼，可说是格累丝小姐的画像，因为她还有一个姊姊。她从前必定是这么一个美人！但是这么一种坚决的，骄傲的神气，她那明媚的双眸现出这么蔑视一切，她的眉毛稍微抬高一点儿，好像她纳罕有谁敢无礼到向她瞧一下；她的嘴唇是向我们卷起来，当我们站在对面凝视她。她穿有一套衣服，那种样子是我从来没有看见过的，然而那是顶时髦的，当她年青时候：一顶像海獭皮一样软的白色料子做的帽子戴得很低，把她的眉毛稍微遮一点儿，一片美丽的羽毛横镶在帽子的一边；她那蓝缎长袍胸前是打开的，露出里面夹绒的白色胸衣。

"呀，真的！"我说，当我看够时候。"人们说得不错，肌肉是同草一样地易萎；但是看到她现在的情形，谁能想斐发妮尔小姐从前是这么一个绝代佳人呢？"

"是的，"多罗塞说。"人们变更太可怕呀。但是假使我主人的父亲所常说的话是真的，那么她的姊姊斐妮发尔小姐是比格

was handsomer than Miss Grace. Her picture is here somewhere; but, if I show it you, you must never let on[1], even to James, that you have seen it. Can the little lady hold her tongue, think you?" asked she.

I was not so sure, for she was such a little sweet, bold, open-spoken child, so I set her to hide herself; and then I helped Dorothy to turn a great picture, that leaned with its face towards the wall, and was not hung up as the others were. To be sure, it beat Miss Grace for beauty; and, I think, for scornful pride, too, though in that matter it might be hard to choose. I could have looked at it an hour, but Dorothy seemed half frightened at having shown it to me, and hurried it back again, and bade me run and find Miss Rosamond, for that there were some ugly places[2] about the house, where she should like ill for the child to go. I was a brave, high-spirited girl, and thought little of what the old woman said, for I liked hide-and-seek as well as any child in the parish; so off I ran to find my little one.

As winter drew on[3], and the days grew shorter, I was sometimes almost certain that I heard a noise as if some one was playing on the great organ in the hall. I did not hear it every evening; but, certainly,

---

1 to let on: to reveal secret 漏泄秘密。
2 ugly places: haunted places 有鬼的地方。
3 to draw on: to approach 来临。

累丝小姐更美丽。她的画像是在这儿某地方；但是若使我指给你看，你千万不要告诉人，甚至于对詹姆士，你看见了那画像。你以为这位小姐能够禁得住她的舌头吗？"她问。

我不敢担保，因为她是这么一个甜蜜的，大胆的，直言无隐的小姑娘，所以我使她自己藏起来；然后我帮多罗塞把一大张画像翻过来，那是脸向着壁地靠在那里，不像别张那样挂起来。的确，这个在美丽方面是比格累丝小姐强得多；我想，在轻蔑别人的骄傲方面也比她妹妹厉害，虽然关于这一点，是比较难决定些。我能够瞧她整整瞧一个钟头，但是多罗塞好像因为指出给我看这东西有些吓住了，赶紧把它归还原位，叫我跑去找洛沙萝德小姐，因为这个屋子有几个不干净的地方，她不愿意小孩到那里去。我是个勇敢的，血气方盛的女孩子，不大睬这老太婆所说的话，因为我喜欢捉迷藏不下于教区里任一个小孩；我于是跑去找我的小宝宝了。

冬天来到，白天一天一天短促了，有时我几乎很的确我听到一种声音，好像有人在大厅里弹那大风琴。我不是夜夜听到；

I did very often; usually when I was sitting with Miss Rosamond, after I had put her to bed, and keeping quite still and silent in the bedroom. Then I used to hear it booming and swelling away in the distance. The first night, when I went down to my supper, I asked Dorothy who had been playing music, and James said very shortly that I was a gowk[1] to take the wind soughing among the trees for music; but I saw Dorothy look at him very fearfully, and Bessy, the kitchen-maid, said something beneath her breath[2], and went quite white[3]. I saw they did not like my question, so I held my peace till I was with Dorothy alone, when I knew I could get a good deal out of her. So, the next day, I watched my time, and I coaxed and asked her who it was that played the organ; for I knew that it was the organ and not the wind well enough, for all[4] I had kept silence before James. But Dorothy had had her lesson, I'll warrant, and never a word could I get from her. So then I tried Bessy, though I had always held my head rather above[5] her, as I was evened[6] to James and Dorothy, and she was little better than their servant. So she said I must never, never tell; and if I ever told, I was never to say she had told me; but

---

1 gowk: fool 傻子。
2 beneath one's breath: in low tones 低声。
3 to go: to become 变成。
4 for all: notwithstanding 虽然。
5 to hold one's head above: to look down 瞧不起。

但是的确很常听到；常当我把洛沙萝德小姐放在床上后，十分安静，不则一声地坐在卧室里陪她的时候，那时我常听到它在远处隆隆作响，声音渐渐大起来。第一次听到后，我当天下去用晚餐时，问多罗塞谁在那里弹风琴，詹姆士很简约地说道我是个傻子，把风过树梢的声音当做音乐；但是我看见多罗塞很惶恐地望着他，柏赛，厨下的女仆，极低声地说一句话，脸色变得很白了。我看出他们不喜欢我这个问话，所以我就不做声，等我同多罗塞独自在一起的时候，我知道那时候我一定可以从她听到许多话。所以，第二天，我等个合式的时候，用话诱她，问她谁去弹那风琴；因为我很知道那是风琴的声音，绝不是风声，虽然我并没有反驳詹姆士的话。但是我敢说多罗塞受过了教训，我从她那里绝不能听到一个字。所以我就去试一试柏赛，虽然平时我总是不大瞧得起她，因为我跟詹姆士多罗塞是平等的，她简直可说是他们的仆人。她就吩咐我千万不要告诉别人；若使我说出了，也绝不要讲是她告诉我的；但是这的确是个很

---

6 to be evened：to be made equal 居于平等地位。

it was a very strange noise, and she had heard it many a time, but most of all on winter nights, and before storms; and folks did say, it was the old lord playing on the great organ in the hall, just as he used to do when he was alive; but who the old lord was, or why he played, and why he played on stormy winter evenings in particular, she either could not or would not tell me. Well! I told you I had a brave heart; and I thought it was rather pleasant to have that grand music rolling about the house, let who would be the player; for now it rose above the great gusts of wind, and wailed and triumphed just like a living creature, and then it fell to a softness most complete; only it was always music, and tunes, so it was nonsense to call it the wind.

Thought at first that it might be Miss Furnivall who played, unknown to Bessy; but, one day when I was in the hall by myself, I opened the organ and peeped all about it and around it, as I had done to the organ in Crosthwaite Church once before, and I saw it was all broken and destroyed inside, though it looked so brave and fine; and then, though it was noonday, my flesh began to creep[1] a little, and I shut it up, and ran away pretty quickly to my own bright nursery; and I did not like hearing the music for some time after that, any

---

1 to creep: to experience nervous shivering sensation due to fear 因为恐惧而觉得发抖不宁。

奇怪的声音,她听到许多次了,多半是在冬夜,暴风雨之前;人们说这是老爵爷弹大厅里的大风琴,正如他活在人世时所弹的;但是这个老爵爷到底是谁,他为什么弹大风琴,为什么特别在冬天里暴风雨之夜弹,她是不晓得的,也许是不肯说。我不是对你们说过我有一颗勇敢的心;我觉得这也都还好玩,有这么庄严的音乐在屋里回响着,不管是谁弹的;那声音一下子比狂风还大声,怒号着,高呼着,正像一只活动物,一下子又沉到极完全的柔和声调;只是总是音乐,有调子的,所以把它叫做风是太无聊了。

我起先以为也许是斐妮发尔小姐弹琴,柏赛不知道;但是有一天当我独自在大厅里,我把大风琴打开,向里面同四周尽瞧,像我从前一次对于克洛斯威特礼拜堂的大风琴所干的,我看见里面完全破烂毁坏了,虽然外面看起来是这么漂亮华丽;那时,虽然是中午,我觉得有些毛发悚然,把它关起来,很快地跑回我自己光明的育婴房去;此后有些时我不喜欢听那音乐,正同詹姆士,多罗塞一样。这些时候里,洛沙萝德小姐使她自己更见爱

more than James and Dorothy did. All this time Miss Rosamond was making herself more and more beloved. The old ladies liked her to dine with them at their early dinner. James stood behind Miss Furnivall's chair, and I behind Miss Rosamond's all in state[1], and, after dinner, she would play about in a corner of the great drawing-room, as still as any mouse, while Miss Furnivall slept, and I had my dinner in the kitchen. But she was glad enough to come to me in the nursery afterwards; for, as she said, Miss Furnivall was so sad, and Mrs. Stark so dull; but she and I were merry enough; and, by-and-by, I got not to care for that weird rolling music, which did one no harm, if we did not know where it came from.

That winter was very cold. In the middle of October the frosts began, and lasted many, many weeks. I remember, one day at dinner, Miss Furnivall lifted up her sad, heavy eyes, and said to Mrs. Stark, "I am afraid we shall have a terrible winter," in a strange kind of meaning way. But Mrs. Stark pretended not to hear, and talked very loud of something else. My little lady and I did not care for the frost; not we! As long as it was dry we climbed up the steep brows, behind the house, and went up on the Fells, which were bleak, and bare enough, and there we ran races in the fresh, sharp air; and once we came down by a new path that took us past the two old gnarled

---

1 in state: in full ceremony 礼仪完备。

了。老太太们喜欢同她一起用她们的较早些的晚餐。詹姆士站在斐妮发尔小姐椅子后面，我站在洛沙萝德小姐椅子后面，都是很正式地；餐后，她在大客厅的一个角落上玩耍，静悄悄地宛如一只耗子，那时斐妮发尔小姐睡一会儿，我到厨房用我的晚餐。但是她后来回到育婴房来找我时心里很高兴；因为，她说，斐妮发尔小姐是这么悲哀样子，斯塔克太太是这么无精打采；但是她和我却是欣欢得很；渐渐，我也不去理那凄凉的大声音乐了，那并没有害了谁，虽然我们不知道那是从什么地方发出来的。

那年的冬天是很冷的。十月中旬就开始有霜了，一连好几个星期都有。我记得一天用餐时候，斐妮发尔小姐抬起她那悲哀的，沉重的眼睛，向斯塔克太太说道，"我恐怕我们将有个可怕的冬天，"用一种奇怪的，含有别种意义的口气。但是斯塔克太太假装没有听见，很大声地说到别的事情上去。我的小姑娘和我并不怕霜；我们绝不！只要天气是晴朗的，我们总是爬上屋后的峻岩，到山上去，那里是够荒凉萧条的，我们到了那里就在新鲜尖利的空气里乱跑；有一次我们从一条新路下来，那

holly-trees, which grew about halfway down by the east side of the house. But the days grew shorter and shorter; and the old lord, if it was he, played away more and more stormily and sadly on the great organ. One Sunday afternoon—it must have been towards the end of November—I asked Dorothy to take charge of little Missey[1] when she came out of the drawing-room, after Miss Furnivall had had her nap; for it was too cold to take her with me to church, and yet I wanted to go. And Dorothy was glad enough to promise, and was so fond of the child that all seemed well; and Bessy and I set off very briskly, though the sky hung heavy and black over the white earth, as if the night had never fully gone away; and the air, though still, was very biting and keen.

"We shall have a fall of snow," said Bessy to me. And sure enough, even while we were in church, it came down thick, in great large flakes, so thick it alomst darkened the windows. It had stopped snowing before we came out, but it lay soft, thick, and deep beneath our feet, as we tramped home. Before we got to the hall the moon rose, and I think it was lighter then—what with the moon, and what with the white dazzling snow—than it had been when we went to church, between two and three o'clock. I have not told you that Miss Furnivall and Mrs. Stark never went to church; they used to read the

---

1 Missey：把Miss念得好玩些，以表亲热的意思。

条路引我们走过两棵多节的老冬青树，都是长在屋子东边半山的地方。但是日子一天一天更短了；老爵爷，假如是他，弹大风琴也越弹越猖狂同凄切了。有一个星期日下午——那一定是十一月月底——我请多罗塞看护我的小姑娘，当斐妮发尔小姐睡过了，她从客厅里出来的时候；因为天气太冷了，不好带她到礼拜堂去，但是我自己又想去。多罗塞欣然允许，她是这么喜欢这小孩，一切好像都没有问题了；柏赛同我很活泼地出发，虽然天是沉闷的，黑色的，盖着这白色的大地，好像夜永没有完全走去；空气，虽然无风，又是尖利刺肌的。

"我们将碰到下雪了，"柏赛对我说。真的，我们还在礼拜堂时候，大片的雪花就落下来了，下得这么密，几乎把窗子都弄不透明了。在我们走出之前，雪已经停了，但是它软软地，厚深地铺在我们脚下，当我们步行回去。在我们走到大厅之前，月亮已出来了，我想那时天还更亮些——有了月亮和耀眼的白雪——比起我们去礼拜堂时候，那是下午二三点钟之间。我还没有告诉你们，斐妮发尔小姐同斯塔克太太素来绝不到礼

prayers together, in their quiet gloomy way; they seemed to feel the Sunday very long without their tapestry-work to be busy at. So when I went to Dorothy in the kitchen, to fetch Miss Rosamond and take her upsrairs with me, I did not much wonder when the old woman told me that the ladies had kept the child with them, and that she had never come to the kitchen, as I had bidden her, when she was tired of behaving pretty in the drawing-room. So I took off my things and went to find her, and bring her to her supper in the nursery. But when I went into the best drawing-room, there sat the two old ladies, very still and quiet, dropping out a word now and then[1], but looking as if nothing so bright and merry as Miss Rosamond had ever been near them. Still I thought she might be hiding from me; it was one of her pretty ways; and that she had persuaded them to look as if they knew nothing about her; so I went softly peeping under this sofa, and behind that chair, making believe[2] I was sadly frightened at not finding her.

"What's the matter, Hester[3]?" said Mrs. Stark, sharply. I don't know if Miss Furnivall had seen me, for, as I told you, she was very deaf, and she sat quite still, idly staring into the fire, with her hope-

---

1 now and then: occasionally 有时；间或。
2 to make believe: to pretend; to act as if 假装；做得好像。
3 Hester: 老保姆的名字。

拜堂去：她们常按着她们那种安详沉闷的样子一同念祈祷文；她们仿佛觉得星期日特别长，没有〈理〉由忙于她们的织绣工作。所以当我到厨房找多罗塞，去把洛沙萝德小姐带到楼上去，我并不觉得奇怪，当那老太婆告诉我太太们把小孩留着陪她们，她并没有像我所吩咐的到厨房来，当她不耐烦再规规矩矩地在客厅里玩的时候。我于是就把外面的衣服脱下，想去找她，带她到育婴房用晚餐。但是当我走进那顶好的客厅时候，两位老太太坐在那儿，很静默安详的，有时说一两个字，她们的样子好像从来没有过像洛沙萝德小姐这么漂亮高兴的人在她们身边。我还以为她也许躲着不让我看见；这是她的一种娇憨行为；也许她求她们装做好像她们全不知道她在那里；所以我轻轻地向沙发下，椅后细瞧，打扮出我害怕得很厉害，因为没有找到她。

"什么事，赫斯德？"斯塔克太太厉色问道。我不知道斐妮发尔小姐有没有看见我，因为，我不是告诉你们过，她是很聋的，她很静寂地坐在那儿，无聊赖地望着火，脸上老是现出失

less face. "I'm only looking for my little Rosy-Posy[1]," replied I, still thinking that the child was there, and near me, though I could not see her.

"Miss Rosamond is not here," said Mrs. Stark. "She went away more than an hour ago to find Dorothy." And she too turned and went on looking into the fire.

My heart sank at this, and I began to wish I had never left my darling. I went back to Dorothy and told her. James was gone out for the day, but she and me and Bessy took lights and went up into the nursery first, and then we roamed over the great large house, calling and entreating Miss Rosamond to come out of her hiding-place, and not frighten us to death in that way. But there was no answer; no sound.

"Oh!" said I at last, "Can she have got into the east wing and hidden there? "

But Dorothy said it was not possible, for that she herself had never been in there; that the doors were always locked, and my lord's steward had the keys, she believed; at any rate, neither she nor James had ever seen them; so I said I would go back, and see if, after all[2], she was not hidden in the drwaing-room, unknown to the old ladies; and if I found her there, I said, I would whip her well for the

---

1 Rosy-Posy：把Rosamond这个字改成好玩些，若使译成意思，就是"蔷薇花束"。

2 after all：in spite of what has been done or expected 毕竟；到底。

望的神气。"我只是找洛西普西小姐,"我答道,还以为那小孩子是在那里,就在我身旁,虽然我没有看见她。

"洛沙萝德小姐不在这儿,"斯塔克太太说。"她去找多罗塞已经有一点多钟了。"她也转过脸,去望着火。

听到这话,我沮丧极了,开始希望我起先不离开我的宝宝。我回去找多罗塞,告诉她。詹姆士那天出去了,〈但〉她,我同柏赛就拿着亮,先到育婴房里去,然后我们到这个广大的屋子各处,喊洛沙萝德小姐,求她从藏匿的地方出来,不要这样把我吓死。但是没有答话,没有声音。

"啊!"末了我说道,"她会不会到屋子的东部去,藏在那儿?"

但是多罗塞说这是不可能的,因为她自己就绝没有到那里过;那里的门总是锁着,她相信钥匙是在爵爷大人的管家那里;无论如何,她同詹姆士都没有看见那钥匙过;所以我说,我要回到客厅,看一看她究竟有没有藏在那里,也许太太们不知道;我还说,若使我在那里找到她,我要把她结结实实鞭打一阵,因为

fright she had given me; but I never meant to do it. Well, I went back to the west drawing-room, and I told Mrs. Stark we could not find her anywhere, and asked for leave[1] to look all about the furniture there, for I thought now, that she might have fallen asleep in some warm hidden corner; but no! we looked, Miss Furnivall got up and looked, trembling all over, and she was nowhere there; then we set off again, every one in the house, and looked in all the places we had searched before, but we could not find her. Miss Furnivall shivered and shook so much, that Mrs. Stark took her back into the warm drawing-room; but not before they had made me promise to bring her to them when she was found. Well-a-day! I began to think she never would be found, when I bethought me to look out into the great front court, all covered with snow. I was upstairs when I looked out; but, it was such clear moonlight, I could see, quite plain, two little footprints, which might be traced from the hall door, and round the corner of the east wing. I don't know how I got down, but I tugged open the great, stiff hall door; and, throwing the skirt of my gown over my head for a cloak, I ran out. I turned the east corner, and there a black shadow fell on the snow; but when I came again into the moonlight, there were the little footmarks going up—up to

---

1 to ask for leave: to beg to be permitted 请允许。

她使我受这个惊；但是我心里绝没有想打她。我就回到西部客厅，我向斯塔克太太说我们什么地方也找不到她，请允许我在房里家具旁边找一下，因为我现在想，她也许在一个温暖的，边〔偏〕僻的屋角睡着了；但是，不然！我们到处看，斐妮发尔小姐也起来寻觅，浑身颤抖着，我们还是不能在那里找到她；然后我们，屋里个个人，又出发，到我们已经找过的地方再找一遍，但是我们不能找到她。斐妮发尔小姐颤动发抖得这么厉害，斯塔克太太把她带到温暖的客厅里去；但是她们先同我约好，带她到她们那里，当找到她时候。天吓！我开始想恐怕永远找不到她了，那时我又想望一望前面全被雪盖住的大广场。当我向外望时，我已经登楼了；但是月亮是这么清明，我能够很明白地看出两个小脚的足印，那可以从大厅的门口，一直追踪到屋子东部的基角，然后转弯过去。我不知道我怎样从楼上下来，但是我拖开大厅那不易推动的大门；把我长袍的边缘翻上来盖在头上当外套，我就跑出去了。我到那东部的基角转弯，屋子的黑影子射到雪上；但是当我又走到月光照着的地面，又有那小脚印了——一直走上

the Fells. It was bitter cold; so cold that the air almost took the skin off my face as I ran, but I ran on, crying to think how my poor little darling must be perished, and frightened. I was within sight of the holly-trees when I saw a shepherd coming down the hill, bearing something in his arms wrapped in his maud. He shouted to me, and asked me if I had lost a bairn[1]; and, when I could not speak for crying, he bore towards me, and I saw my wee bairnie[2] lying still, and white, and stiff, in his arms, as if she had been dead. He told me he had been up the Fells to gather in[3] his sheep, before the deep cold of night came on, and that under the holly-trees (black marks on the hill-side, where no other bush was for miles around) he had found my little lady—my lamb—my queen—my darling—stiff and cold, in the terrible sleep which is frost-begotten. Oh! The joy, and the tears of having her in my arms once again! For I would not let him carry her; but took her, maud and all, into my own arms, and held her near my own warm neck and heart, and felt the life stealing slowly back again into her little gentle limbs. But she was still insensible when we reached the hall, and I had no breath for speech. We went in by the kitchen door.

---

1 bairn: child 这是乡下人用的字。
2 bairnie: 也是 child 的意思，加上 ie，无非表示亲爱之情。
3 to gather in: to collect 收集；收回。

屋后的山。外面的空气是苦冷了；冷得吹过的风好像把我脸皮扯去，当我望〔往〕前跑时候，但是我还是望〔往〕前跑，哭着想起我可怜的小乖乖必定快冻死了，吓得要命了。我看见那冬青树时，才看得见一个牧羊人下山来，怀里抱一个东西，那是用他的绒布肩挂包着。他向我大声喊，问我有没有失掉一个孩子；当我哭得说不出话时，他抱来给我，我看见躺在他怀里我的小姑娘，一点儿也不动，皮肤冷得发白，僵板板的，好像她已经死了。他告诉我他到山上去，打算在夜间的深冷来临之前，把他的羊群收到栏里，在冬青树底下（那是山旁黑色的标记，周围好几哩都没有别的灌木）他看见我这位小姑娘——我的小羊——我的皇后——我的宝宝——僵冷了，在那可怕的酣睡里，那是遇了霜的结果。啊！那种喜悦，那种又把她拥在我怀里时流下的眼泪！因为我不让他抱她；却把她接过来，人同肩挂一起，到我的怀里，将她靠近我自己温暖的颈项同心，觉得生命渐渐偷偷地回到她秀美的小四肢。但是她还是没有知觉，当我们走到大厅时候；我也喘不过气，不能说出话了。我们从厨房的门进去。

"Bring the warming-pan," said I; and I carried her upstairs and began undressing her by the nursery fire, which Bessy had kept up. I called my little lammie[1] all the sweet and playful names I could think of—even while my eyes were blinded by my tears; and at last, oh! at length[2] she opened her large blue eyes. Then I put her into her warm bed, and sent Dorothy down to tell Miss Furnivall that all was well; and I made up my mind[3] to sit by my darling's bedside the live-long[4] might. She fell away into a soft sleep as soon as her pretty head had touched the pillow, and I watched by her till morning light; when she wakened up bright and clear—or so I thought at first—and, my dears, so I think now.

She said that she had fancied that she should like to go to Dorothy, for that both the old ladies were asleep, and it was very dull in the drawing-room; and that, as she was going through the west lobby, she saw the snow through the high window falling—falling—soft and steady; but she wanted to see it lying pretty and white on the ground, so she made her way[5] into the great hall; and then, going to the window, she saw it bright and soft upon the drive; but while

---

1 lammie：就是lamb字。
2 at length：at last末了。
3 to make up one's mind：to determine决定。
4 live-long：the whole length of全部；整整一个。
5 to make one's way：to advance前进。

"拿暖壶来，"我说；我把她抱到楼上去，在育婴室的火旁开始解下她的衣服，那里的火柏赛起先添了燃料。我用我所想得起的一切甜蜜的，好玩的称呼喊我这小羔羊——甚至于当我们的眼睛还是哭得看不见东西时候；最后，啊！最后她睁开她那大的蓝眼睛了。于是我把她放在她那暖和的床上，派多罗塞下去告诉斐妮发尔小姐小姑娘已经没有危险了；我决定整晚坐在我乖乖的床边。她那可爱的头一碰到枕头，立刻就沉到微睡里去，我在旁边守她一直到天亮；当她醒来时候，活泼了，心里明白了——或者我起先以为是这样的——呀，我的乖乖们，我现在还以为是这样的。

她说她想她要到多罗塞那儿去，因为两位老太太都睡着了，在客厅里真是无聊极了；当她走过西穿堂时候，从高窗子她看见雪落下来——落下来——轻轻的，不断的；但是她想看见雪美丽洁白的躺在地面，所以她望〔往〕大厅走去；走到窗口时，她看见白雪光明柔软的铺在马路上；但是当她站在那里，她瞧见一个小姑娘，没有她这么大，"但是这么漂亮，"我乖乖说，

she stood there, she saw a little girl, not so old as she was, "but so pretty," said my darling, "and this little girl beckoned to me to come out; and oh, she was so pretty and so sweet, I could not choose but[1] go." And then this other little girl had taken her by the hand, and side by side the two had gone round the east corner.

"Now, you are a naughty little girl, and telling stories[2]," said I. "What would your good mamma, that is in heaven, and never told a story in her life, say to her little Rosamond, if she heard her—and I dare say she does—telling stories!"

"Indeed, Hester," sobbed out my child, "I'm telling you ture. Indeed I am."

"Don't tell me!" said I, very stern. "I tracked you by your footmarks through the snow; there were only yours to be seen; and if you had had a little girl to go hand-in-hand with you up the hill, don't you think the footprints would have gone along with yours?"

"I can't help[3] it, dear, dear Hester," said she, crying, "if they did not; I never looked at her feet, but she held my hand fast and tight in her little one, and it was very, very cold. She took me up the Fell-path, up to the holly trees; and there I saw a lady weeping and crying; but when she saw me, she hushed her weeping, and smiled very proud

---

1 cannot choose but: must necessarily 只得。
2 to tell stories: to tell lies 扯谎。
3 cannot help it: cannot remedy, prevent or avoid it 无能为力。

"这位小姑娘招手找我出去；啊，她是这么美丽，这么甜蜜，我不能不出去。"那时那个小姑娘拉着她的手，两个并肩一直走到东边基角转过去。

"吓，你现在是个顽皮的小姑娘，扯起谎来了，"我说。"你那在天的，生平从来不扯谎的好妈妈会对她的小洛沙萝德说多少教训的话，若使她听到她——我敢说她的确是——扯谎！"

"真的，赫斯忒，"我这小孩鸣咽说道，"我告诉你的是真话。我的确是说实话。"

"别同我说！"我很严厉地说道。"我追踪你从雪中走过的足迹；只看见你的；若使你有个小姑娘和你携手偕行到山上去，你以为她的足迹不会跟你的在一起吗？"

"我也无可如何，亲爱的，亲爱的赫斯忒，"她哭着说，"若使她的足迹不跟我的一起；我绝没有去看她的脚，但是她把我的手紧紧地拿在她的小手里，那是非常，非常冷的。她带我走上山路，走到冬青树旁；那里我看见一位太太流泪鸣咽着；但是当她看见我，她按下她的鸣咽，很骄傲自大地微

and grand, and took me on her knee, and began to lull me to sleep; and that's all, Hester—but that is true; and my dear mamma knows it is," said she, crying. So I thought the child was in a fever, and pretended to believe her, as she went over[1] her story—over and over again, and alwsys the same. At last Dorothy knocked at the door with Miss Rosamond's breakfast; and she told me the old ladies were down in the eating parlour, and that they wanted to speak to me. They had both been into the night-nursery the evening before, but it was after Miss Rosamond was asleep; so they had only looked at her—not asked me any questions.

"I shall catch it[2]," thought I to myself, as I went along the north gallery. "And yet," I thought, taking courage[3], "it was in their charge I left her; and it's they that's to blame[4] for letting her steal away unknown and unwatched." So I went in boldly, and told my story. I told it all to Miss Furnivall, shouting it close to her ear; but when I came to the mention of the other little girl out in the snow, coaxing and tempting her out, and wiling her up to the grand and beautiful lady by the holly-tree, she threw her arms up—her old and withered arms—and cried aloud, "Oh! Heaven, forgive! Have mercy!"

---

1 to go over: to repeat 重述。
2 to catch it: to suffer punishment 受罚。
3 to take courage: to become bold 胆子大起来了。
4 to blame: to be blamed; blamable 该骂。

笑,把我放在她膝上,开始慰我入睡;这是全部的经过,赫斯忒——这却都是真的;我的妈妈也知道这是真的,"她还是哭着说。我于是以为这孩子发烧了,假装相信她,当她重述她的故事——说了又说,总是一样的。后来多罗塞捧了洛沙萝德小姐的早餐上来打门;她对我说老太太们都在餐室里,她们要同我说话。她们前晚上都来夜间育婴房一下,但是洛沙萝德小姐已经入睡了;所以她们只瞧一下——没有问我什么话。

"我将挨骂了,"我自己想,当我走过北走廊。"然而,"我又想,胆子大起来了,"我是交给她们招呼的;这是她们的不是,不知不觉地让她偷跑出来。"所以我大胆地走进去,说出我所知道的经过。我把一切全告诉给斐妮发尔小姐,向她耳边大声嚷;但是当我提起雪中那个小姑娘,骗她,引诱她出去,用诡计带她到冬青树旁边堂皇美丽的贵妇人,斐妮发尔小姐忽然举起她的双臂——她那双衰老的,枯萎的手臂——大声喊道,"啊!天呀,赦宥罢!慈悲一些罢!"

Mrs. Stark took hold of her; roughly enough, I thought; but she was past Mrs. Stark's management, and spoke to me, in a kind of wild warning and authority.

"Hester! Keep her from that child! It will lure her to her death! That evil child! Tell her it is a wicked, naughty child." Then Mrs. Stark hurried me out of the room; where, indeed, I was glad enough to go; but Miss Furnivall kept shrieking out, "Oh! Have mercy! Wilt Thou never forgive! It is many a long year ago"—

I was very uneasy in my mind after that. I durst never leave Miss Rosamond, night or day, for fear lest she might slip off again, after some fancy or other; and all the more, because I thought I could make out that Miss Furnivall was crazy, from their odd ways about her; and I was afraid lest something of the same kind (which might be in the family, you know) hung over my darling. And the great frost never ceased all this time; and, whenever it was a more stormy night than usual, between the gusts, and through the wind, we heard the old lord playing on the great organ. But, old lord, or not, wherever Miss Rosamond went, there I followed; for my love for her, pretty helpless orphan, was stronger than my fear for the grand and terrible sound. Besides, it rested with me to keep her cheerful and merry, as beseemed her age. So we played together, and

斯塔克太太抓着她；很粗鲁地，我想；但是她是斯塔克太太管不住的，用一种狂热的警告和命令口吻向我说。

"赫斯忒！不要让那小孩近她！它会引她到死地！那个坏小孩子！告诉她它是个邪恶的，顽皮的小孩。"于是斯塔克太太推我出房外；我真是高兴地走出那里；但是斐妮发尔小姐还是嚷道，"啊！慈悲些罢！上帝，你不肯赦宥罢！那是许多年前的"——

此后我心里很不安。日夜我绝不敢离开洛沙萝德小姐，怕的是胡思乱想起来，她又偷跑掉了；尤其因为我想我能看出斐妮发尔小姐是疯的，从他们那种奇怪地待她；我怕的是有些相类的毛病（那也许是遗传的，你们要知道）将降临小姑娘身上。这些时候里我们老有严霜；每值比通常更风狂雨暴的晚上，一阵一阵狂风之中，有时杂在风声里，我们听到老爵爷弹那大风琴。但是不管有没有老爵爷，洛沙萝德小姐无论那里去，我总是跟在后面；因为我爱她，美丽的无依无靠的孤女，胜过我的怕那雄伟可怕的声音。并且，那也是我的责任，使她天天快乐活泼，她这样年龄是应该如是的。所以我们一道儿玩耍，一道

wandered together, here and there, and everywhere; for I never dared to lose sight of her again in that large and rambling house. And so it happened that one afternoon, not long before Christmas Day, we were playing together on the billiard-table in the great hall (not that we knew the right way of playing, but she liked to roll the smooth ivory balls with her pretty hands, and I liked to do whatever she did); and, by-and-by, without our noticing it, it grew dusk indoors, though it was still light in the open air, and I was thinking of taking her back into the nursery, when, all of a sudden[1], she cried out:

"Look, Hester! look! There is my poor little girl out in the snow!"

I turned towards the long narrow windows, and there, sure enough, I saw a little girl, less than my Miss Rosamond—dressed all unfit to be out-of-doors such a bitter night—crying, and beating against the window-panes, as if she wanted to be let in. She seemed to sob and wail, till Miss Rosamond could bear it no longer, and was flying to the door to open it, when, all of a sudden, and close upon us, the great organ pealed out so loud and thundering, it fairly made me tremble; and all the more, when I remenbered me that, even in the stillness of that dead-cold weather, I had heard no sound of little battering hands upon the window-glass, although the Phantom Child

---

1 all of a sudden: suddenly 突然间。

儿游荡，这儿，那儿，以及一切其它的地方，因为我绝不敢再看不见她，让她独自在这散漫的大屋里面了。一天下午，离圣诞日不远，我们刚好在大厅里台球桌旁玩（并不是我们知道打台球的规则，不过她喜欢用她那美丽的手推滚圆滑的象牙球，凡是她干的事情我都喜欢干）；渐渐，我们也不觉得，房里慢慢黑起来了，虽然在空旷处还是光亮的，我正想带她回育婴室里去，顿然间，她喊道：

"看，赫斯忒！看！外面雪中站着的就是我那可怜的小姑娘！"

我转过脸朝那狭长的窗子，那里我的确看见一位小姑娘，比我洛沙萝德年纪小些——穿的衣服完全不宜于这样天气在户外——哭着，打窗子上的玻璃，好像想进来。看起来，她啜泣哀啼着，一直到洛沙萝德小姐不能再忍了，飞跑到大门打算去开门，忽然间，刚在我们旁边，大风琴响得这么大声雷鸣地，使我浑身发抖；尤其是，当我记起，甚至于在死一般冷的空气的静寂里，我也没有听到小手敲玻璃窗的声音，虽然这"鬼孩

had seemed to put forth all its force[1]; and, although I had seen it wail and cry, no faintest touch of sound had fallen upon my ears. Whether I remembered all this at the very moment, I do not know; the great organ sound had so stunned me into terror; but this I know, I caught up Miss Rosamond before she got the hall-door opened, and clutched her, and carried her away, kicking and screaming, into the large bright kitchen, where Dorothy and Agnes were busy with their mince-pies.

"What is the matter with my sweet one?" Cried Dorothy, as I bore in Miss Rosamond, who was sobbing as if her heart would break.

"She won't let me open the door for my little girl to come in; and she'll die if she is out on the Fells all night. Cruel, naughty Hester," she said, slapping me; but she might have struck harder, for I had seen a look of ghastly terror on Dorothy's face, which made my very blood run cold.

"Shut the back-kitchen door fast, and bolt it well." Said she to Agnes. She said no more; she gave me raisins and almonds to quiet Miss Rosamond; but she sobbed about the little girl in the snow, and would not touch any of the good things. I was thankful when she cried herself to sleep in bed. Then I stole down to the kitchen, and

---

1 to put forth one's force: to exert one's strength 使出力气；努力。

子"好像用出了它所有的力气；虽然我看见它啜泣哀啼，连一些顶微弱的声音也没有落到我耳朵里。那时我有没有想起这许多，我现在是不知道的；大风琴的声音使我惊呆得只知道害怕；但是底下这件事是我所分明知道的，在洛沙萝德小姐把大厅门打开之前，我将她抓住，攫着，抱她去，她乱跳乱嚷，一直到明亮的大厨房里，多罗塞同阿格妮正忙着做她们的碎肉饼。

"我这可爱的人儿有什么事？"多罗塞说，当我抱洛沙萝德小姐进去时候，她哭到好像她的心将碎了。

"她不肯让我去开门给我的小姑娘进来；她会死，若使她整夜滞在外面山上。残忍的，顽皮的赫斯忒，"她说，打着我的脸；但是她可以再打重些，我也是不松手的，因为我看见多罗塞脸上现出惊恐到万分的神情，那使我身里的血都冷起来了。

"把后厨房的门关紧，好好地闩上，"她对阿格妮说。她不再说什么了；她拿葡萄干同杏仁给我去骗洛沙萝德小姐；但是她还是为着雪中的小姑娘呜咽；不肯沾这些好东西。我很感谢上帝，当她自己在床上哭睡着了。于是我偷偷地到厨房去，告诉多罗塞

told Dorothy I had made up my mind. I would carry my darling back to my father's house in Applethwaite; where, if we lived humbly, we lived at peace. I said I had been frightened enough with the old lord's organ-playing; but now, that I had seen for myself this little moaning child, all decked out as no child in the neighbourhood could be, beating and battering to get in, yet always without any sound or noise—with the dark wound on its right shoulder; and that Miss Rosamond had known it again for the phantom that had nearly lured her to her death (which Dorothy knew was ture); I would stand[1] it no longer.

I saw Dorothy change colour[2] once or twice. When I had done, she told me she did not think I could take Miss Rosamond with me, for that she was my lord's ward, and I had no right over her; and she asked me, would I leave the child that I was so fond of, just for sounds and sights that could do me no harm; and that they had all had to get used to[3] in their turns? I was all in a hot, trembling passion; and I said it was very well for her to talk, that knew what these sights and noises betokened, and that had, perhaps, had something to do with the Spectre-Child while it was alive. And I taunted her so, that she told me all she knew, at last; and then I wished I had never been told, for it only made me more afraid than ever.

---

1 to stand: to suffer; to abide 忍受。
2 to change color: to turn pale 脸色变为灰白。
3 to get used to: to become accustomed to 惯于。

我已经下个决心了。我将带我的乖乖回到阿普尔所威特地方我父亲家里；在那里，假使说我们过个低微的生活，总可以安静地过日子。我说老爵爷的弹风琴已经使我够害怕了；但是现在我亲眼看见这个哀泣着的小姑娘，穿得很讲究是邻近小孩子所办不到的，打着敲着窗子想进来，然而却一丝声音也没有——她的右肩膀上有个黑色的伤痕，洛沙萝德小姐又知道就是这个鬼孩子从前几乎把她引上死路（这件事多罗塞知道是真的）；我不能再忍受了。

我看见多罗塞为之色变了一两回。当我说完，她告诉我她以为我不能带她同走，因为她是受爵爷大人的保护，我没有权力可以带她走；她还问我，肯不肯离开我这么爱着的小孩，只为着一些与我无害的声音和幻形；他们一个个也都是渐渐惯了的？我那时整个人都在个热烈的，发抖的情感之下；我说她尽可以随便谈谈，因为她知道了这些幻形，这些声音含有什么意义，也许同那鬼孩子还有个什么关系，当它活着时候。我那样责备她，弄得她最后把所知道的全告诉我；那时我却希望从来没有人向我说这段故事，因为那使我比以前怕得更厉害了。

She said she had heard the tale from old neighbours, that were alive when she was first married; when folks used to come to the hall sometimes, before it had got such a bad name on the countryside; it might not be true, or it might, what she had been told.

The old lord was Miss Furnivall's father—Miss Grace, as Dorothy called her, for Miss Maude was the elder, and Miss Furnivall by rights. The old lord was eaten up[1] with pride. Such a proud man was never seen or heard of; and his daughters were like him. No one was good enough to wed them, although they had choice enough; for they were the great beauties of their day, as I had seen by their portraits, where they hung in the state drawing-room. But, as the old saying is, "Pride will have a fall"; and these two haughty beauties fell in love[2] with the same man, and he no better than a foreign musician, whom their father had down from London to play music with him at the Manor House. For, above all things next to his pride, the old lord loved music. He could play on nearly every instrument that ever was heard of; and it was a strange thing it did not soften him; but he was a fierce dour[3] old man, and had broken his poor wife's heart with his cruelty, they said. He was mad after music, and would

---

1 to be eaten up: to be consumed 缠着；被完全占住。

2 to fall in love: to have the affections deeply enlisted for one of the opposite sex 跟一个异性产生浓厚的爱情；堕入情海。

3 dour: hard; fierce; bold 凶狠。

她说这故事她是从邻近的老年人听来的,她们还活着,当她初出嫁时候;那时常有人们到大厅来,它在邻近还没有得到这么坏的一个名誉;她所听到的也许是真的,也许是假的。

老爵爷就是斐妮发尔小姐的父亲——或者可以说格累丝小姐,多罗塞是这样称呼她,因为摩德是顶大的,应该称做斐妮发尔小姐。老爵爷满心都是骄傲。这么一个骄傲的人是从来没有见过的,听过的;他的女孩也正同他一样。好像没有一个人配得上娶她们,虽然她们可以从许多人们里拣选一个;因为她们是当时的美人,这点我从挂在大厅里她们的画像已经瞧出了。但是,老话说得好,"骄傲的人们会摔一交";这两个睥睨的姑娘同时爱上一个男人了,他又只是一个外国音乐家,她们的父亲从伦敦找来,跟他在爵邸弹琴。因为,骄傲之外,他顶喜欢的就是音乐。凡是我们晓得的任一种乐器他几乎都能奏;这真奇怪,这种爱好并不会使他的性情变成温厚;他却是一个凶恶的,倔强的老人,他们说他的残酷使他的妻子心碎。他对于音乐具有狂热,无论出多少钱去学都是情愿的。所以他找这个外

pay any money for it. So he got this foreigner to come; who made such beautiful music, that they said the very birds on the trees stopped their singing to listen. And, by degrees, this foreign gentleman got such a hold over[1] the old lord, that nothing would serve him but that he must come every year; and it was he that had the great organ brought from Holland, and built up in the hall, where it stood now. He taught the old lord to play on it; but many and many a time, when Lord Furnivall was thinking of nothing but his fine organ, and his finer music, the dark foreigner was walking abroad in the woods with one of the young ladies; now Miss Maude, and then Miss Grace.

Miss Maude won the day[2] and carried off the prize, such as it was; and he and she were married, all unknown to any one; and before he made his next yearly visit, she had been confined[3] of a little girl at a farmhouse on the Moors, while her father and Miss Grace thought she was away at Doncaster Races. But though she was a wife and a mother, she was not a bit softened, but as haughty and as passionate as ever; and perhaps more so, for she was jealous of Miss Grace, to whom her foreign husband paid a deal of court[4] —by

---

1 to get a hold over: to have an influence 支配；迷住。
2 to win the day: to gain the victory 得胜。
3 to be confined: to be brought to bed of a child 分娩。
4 to pay court to: to court 求爱。

国人来；他弹出这么美的音乐，据说树上的鸟儿都停住不唱来细聆。这个外国人渐渐把那老爵士这样迷住了，他每年非找他来一下不行；也是这个外国人，从荷兰买来那架大风琴，镶在大厅里，现在还在那儿。他教老爵爷弹那风琴；但是许多回，当斐妮发尔爵士正在不想别的，专想他那美丽的风琴，和那更美丽的音乐，这位肤色棕黑的外国人却在森林中跟二个年青姑娘里的一个同散步；有时跟摩德小姐，有时跟格累丝小姐。

摩德小姐当时占优胜，把这么一个奖品得到手了；他同她结婚了，这件事谁也不知道；在他下一年再到这儿之前，她在摩尔斯地方一个农家里产下一个小姑娘，她父亲同格累丝小姐还以为她是去参与洞卡斯忒的赛马。但是她虽然是一个妻子，一个母亲了，她的心却一点儿也没有软下去，还是像一向那样骄傲，那么热情；也许更甚些，因为她妒忌格累丝小姐，她那外国的丈夫对于这位小姐也很献殷勤——他对他的妻子说，这只是为着要使她迷糊。然而格累丝小姐对于摩德小姐却现出得意神情，摩德小姐变得更凶了，对于她的丈夫，同对于她的妹

way of¹ blinding her—as he told his wife. But Miss Grace triumphed over Miss Maude, and Miss Maude grew fiercer and fiercer, both with her husband and with her sister; and the former—who could easily shake off what was disagreeable, and hide himself in foreign countries—went away a month before his usual time that summer, and half-threatened that he would never come back again. Meanwhile, the little girl was left at the farm-house, and her mother used to have her horse saddled and gallop wildly over the hills to see her once every week, at the very least—for where she loved, she loved; and where she hated, she hated. And the old lord went on² playing—playing on his organ; and the servants thought the sweet music he made had soothed down his awful temper, of which (Dorothy said) some terrible tales could be told. He grew infirm too, and had to walk with a crutch; and his son—that was the present Lord Furnivall's father—was with the army in America, and the other son at sea; so Miss Maude had it pretty much her own way³, and she and Miss Grace grew colder and bitterer to each other every day; till at last they hardly ever spoke, except when the old lord was by. The foreign musician came again the next summer, but it was for the last time; for they led him such a life⁴ with their jealousy and their passions,

---

1 by way of: for the purpose of 因为。
2 went on: advanced forward 依然进行。

妹；她的丈夫——他能够很容易地摆脱这些麻烦，隐在外国里面——那个夏天比往常早一月离开，还一半威吓道他绝不再来了。这些时间里，那小女孩就留在农家里，她的母亲常叫人把她的马装上马鞍，疯狂也似地飞跑过许多小山去看她，最少每星期一次——因为她一爱起来，就拼命地爱；一恨起来，就拼命地恨。老爵爷还是弹琴——弹他那大风琴；仆人们以为他所弹的悦耳音乐使他那可怕的癖〔脾〕气软化了，关于他的坏癖〔脾〕气（多罗塞说）可以说出几个可怕的故事。他也变衰弱了，走路要一个拐杖；他的大儿子——就是现在这位斐妮发尔爵士的父亲——跟军队一起在美洲，另一个儿子在海军里；所以摩德小姐许多事都能作主，她同格累丝小姐天天弄得越冷淡，恶感越深了；弄得最后，她们几乎不讲话，除非是老爵爷在旁边。外国音乐家下一个夏天又来，但是这是最后一次；因为她们以她们的妒忌同热情使他过个这么烦恼的生活，他厌倦了，

---

3 had her own way：由她作主。
4 such a life：a life as 这么一种生活。

that he grew weary, and went away, and never was heard of again. And Miss Maude, who had always meant to have her marriage acknowledged when her father should be dead, was left now a deserted wife—whom nobody knew to have been married—with a child that she dared not own, although she loved it to distraction; living with a father whom she feared, and a sister whom she hated. When the next summer passed over and the dark foreigner never came, both Miss Maude and Miss Grace grew gloomy and sad; they had a haggard look about them, though they looked handsome as ever. But by-and-by Miss Maude brightened; for her father grew more and more infirm, and more than ever carried away[1] by his music; and she and Miss Grace lived almost entirely apart, having separate rooms, the one on the west side, Miss Maude on the east—those very rooms which were now shut up. So she thought she might have her little girl with her, and no one need ever know except those who dared not speak about it, and were bound to believe that it was, as she said, a cottager's child she had taken a fancy to[2]. All this, Dorothy said, was pretty well known; but what came afterwards no one knew, except Miss Grace, and Mrs. Stark, who was even then her maid, and much more of a friend to her than ever her sister had been. But the

---

1 carried away：迷。
2 to take a fancy to：癖爱。

去了；人们再也听不到关于他的消息。摩德小姐，她一向想叫人们承认她的婚姻，当她父亲死去时候，现在留下来当个弃妇了——谁也不知道她曾经出嫁过——有一个她不敢认为自己生的孩子，虽然她爱他到如狂的地步；跟一个她所怕的父亲，一个她所恨的妹妹同住。当下一个夏天过去了，肤色棕黑的外国人还是没有来，摩德小姐同格累丝小姐都变愁闷；她们带了憔悴的形容，虽然她们还是漂亮得同从前一样。但是摩德小姐渐渐高兴起来了；因为她的父亲变得更衰弱，更被他的音乐迷住；她同格累丝小姐差不多完全离居，各有分开的房子，一个在西部，摩德小姐在东部——就是现在闭起来的那几间房子。所以她想她可以把她的小女孩弄来同她住一起，谁也用不着知道，除开那班人们，他们不敢谈这事，只好相信是，像她所说的，一个乡下人的小孩，她所爱的。这些事，多罗塞说，大家都知道；但是后来的事情没有人晓得，除开格累丝小姐和斯塔克太太，她那时还是她的女仆，可说是她的朋友，她的姐姐对她从来没有这么亲密过。但是仆人们从偶尔落下的话猜去，大概摩

servants supposed, from words that were dropped, that Miss Maude had triumphed over Miss Grace, and told her that all the time the dark foreigner had been mocking her with pretended love—he was her own husband; the colour left Miss Grace's cheek and lips that very day for ever[1], and she was heard to say many a time that sooner or later[2] she would have her revenge; and Mrs. Stark was for ever spying about the east rooms.

One fearful night, just after the New Year had come in, when the snow was lying thick and deep, and the flakes were still falling—fast enough to blind any one who might be out and abroad—there was a great and violent noise heard, and the old lord's voice above all, cursing and swearing awfully—and the cries of a little child—and the proud defiance of a fierce woman—and the sound of a blow—and a dead stillness—and moans and wailings dying away on the hill-side! Then the old lord summoned all his servants, and told them, with terrible oaths, and words more terrible, that his daughter had disgraced herself, and that he had turned her out of doors—her, and her child—and that if ever they gave her help—or food—or shelter—he prayed that they might never enter Heaven. And, all the while, Miss Grace stood by him, white and still as any stone; and

---

1 for ever: 永远。

2 sooner or later: in prophecies of what will happen for certain but at uncertain date 迟早总会发生的。

德小姐在格累丝小姐面前令胜,告诉她那些时光里肤色棕黑的外国人无非拿假装的爱情跟她开玩笑——他实在是她自己的丈夫;红润的颜色从那天起永远离开格累丝小姐的双颊和嘴唇了,人们有许多次听见她说迟早她总得报复一下;斯塔克太太就老在东部房子旁边侦探。

一个可怕的晚上,新年刚过去,雪深厚的铺在地面,雪花还是飘着——飘得这么快,使凡是在外面的人都看不见四旁——人们听到狂暴的大声喧哗,老爵爷的声音顶高,可怕地诅着,发誓着——一个小孩子的哭声——一个凶猛女人的骄傲的反抗——一下打击的声音——一种死一样的沉寂——哀啼怨哭的余音消灭在山旁!然后老爵爷召集他的全体仆役,用可怕的诅言同更可怕的话,告诉他们他的女孩自己干出下贱的事情,他把她赶出门外了——她和她的孩子——假使他们帮助她——给她食物——或者住宿地方——他祈祷上帝,愿他们永远不能进天堂。这些时候,格累丝小姐站在他身旁,惨白的,不动的,有如一块石头;当他说完,她叹一口气,等于说她的工作完成

when he had ended she heaved a great sigh, as much as to say her work was done, and her end was accomplished. But the old lord never touched his organ again and died within the year; and no wonder! For, on the morrow of that wild and fearful night, the shepherds, coming down the Fell side, found Miss Maude sitting, all crazy and smiling, under the holly-trees, nursing a dead child—with a terrible mark on its right shoulder, "But that was not what killed it," said Dorothy: "it was the frost and the cold; —every wild creature was in its hole, and every beast in its fold—while the child and its mother were turned out[1] to wander on the Fells! And now you know all! and I wonder if you are less frightened now?"

I was more frightened than ever; but I said I was not. I wished Miss Rosamond and myself well out of that dreadful house for ever; but I would not leave her, and I dared not take her away. But oh! how I watched her, and guarded her! We bolted the doors, and shut the window-shutters fast, an hour or more before dark, rather than leave them open five minutes too late. But my little lady still heard the weird child crying and mourning; and not all we could do or say could keep her from wanting to go to her, and let her in from the cruel wind and the snow. All this time, I kept away from Miss Furnivall and Mrs. Stark, as much as ever I could; for I feared them—I

---

1 to be turned out: to be driven away 被赶去。

了,她的目的也达到了。但是老爵爷再也不弹琴了,那年内就死去;这是不足奇!因为,那个狂暴可怕的夜的翌晨,从山边走下的牧羊人们看见摩德小姐坐在冬青树下,完全疯了,微笑着,怀里抱一个死孩子——孩子的右肩上有一个可怕的标记。"但是并不是这个创伤把它杀死,"多罗塞说;"却是风霜把它冻死;——那时个个野兽都在它的窟里,个个家畜都在栏里——这个小孩同它的母亲却被赶出到山上去飘荡!现在你全晓得了!我看你现在也未见得比从前少害怕些?"

我是比以前更怕得厉害了;不过我说我并没有。我希望洛沙萝德小姐同我永远离开那可怕的屋子;可是我不肯离她,又不敢带她走。但是,啊!我怎样注意她,保护她!我们把门闩好,把百叶窗闭紧,在天暗以前一个钟头,或者还要早些,不肯让它们开到太迟五分钟。然而我的小姑娘还听得到那鬼孩子悲啼的声音;用尽我们的手段和唇舌,总不能使她不想去找她,让她从冷酷的风和大雪里进来。这些时候里,我极力躲避斐妮发尔小姐和斯塔克太太;因为我怕她们——她们带着那种冷酷

knew no good could be about them, with their grey hard faces and their dreamy eyes, looking back into the ghastly years that were gone. But, even in my fear, I had a kind of pity—for Miss Furnivall, at least. Those gone down to the pit[1] can hardly have a more hopeless look than that which was ever on her face. At last I even got so sorry for her—who never said a word but what was quite forced from her—that I prayed for her; and I taught Miss Rosamond to pray for one who had done a deadly sin; but often when she came to those words, she would listen, and start up from her knees, and say, "I hear my little girl plaining and crying very sad—Oh! let her in, or she will die!"

One night—just after New Year's Day had come at last, and the long winter had taken a turn, as I hoped—I heard the west drawing-room bell ring three times, which was the signal for me. I would not leave Miss Rosamond alone, for all she was asleep—for the old lord had been playing wilder than ever—and I feared lest my darling should waken to hear the spectre child; see her I knew she could not. I had fastened the windows too well for that. So I took her out of her bed and wrapped her up in such outer clothes as were most handy, and carried her down to the drawing-room, where the old ladies sat

---

1 pit: hell 地狱。

的灰色脸孔，常在梦中般的眼睛，回顾那已经过去的可怖年时，我知道她们身边绝不会有善良的东西。但是，甚至于在我的恐惧里，我有一种怜悯——最少，对于斐妮发尔小姐。到地狱去的人们几乎还不能够有个更绝望的神气，比起她脸上常带有的。最后我简直这么可怜她——她除开被迫着非说不可的话外绝没有多讲一个字——我为她祈祷；我教洛沙萝德小姐为一个干了致命的罪恶的人祈祷；可是当她说到这几个字时，她常细聆着，从她跪的姿势跳起来，说，"我听到我的小姑娘很凄惨地诉苦着，哀啼着——啊！让她进来罢，否则她将死去！"

一天晚上——刚在新年最后也到了，悠长的冬天也有个转期了，像我所希望的，之后——我听见西部客厅的铃响了三回，那是叫我去的号令。我绝不肯让洛沙萝德小姐单独滞在房里，不管她睡得多么熟——因为老爵爷弹得比往常更狂野——我恐怕我的乖乖醒来会听见鬼小孩的哭声；至于看见她，我知道是不会的。因为我把窗子关得太紧了，绝不能见到。所以我把她从床上抱起，拿最方便的外面衣服将她包起，抱她到下面客厅去，老太太

at their tapestry work as usual. They looked up when I came in, and Mrs. Stark asked, quite astounded, "Why did I bring Miss Rosamond there, out of her warm bed?" I had begun to whisper, "Because I was afraid of her being tempted out while I was away, by the wild child in the snow," when she stopped me short[1] (with a glance at Miss Furnivall), and said Miss Furnivall wanted me to undo some work she had done wrong, and which neither of them could see to unpick. So I laid my pretty dear on the sofa, and sat down on a stool by them, and hardened my heart against them, as I heard the wind rising and howling.

Miss Rosamond slept on sound, for all the wind blew so; and Miss Furnivall said never a word, nor looked round when the gusts shook the windows. All at once she started up to her full height, and put up one hand, as if to bid us listen.

"I hear voices!" said she, "I hear terrible screams—I hear my father's voice!"

Just at that moment my darling wakened with a sudden start: "My little girl is crying, oh, how she is crying!" and she tried to get up and go to her, but she got her feet entangled in the blanket, and I caught her up; for my flesh had begun to creep at these noises,

---

1 to stop short: check 阻止。

们坐在那里照常做她们的编绣工作。当我走进来时,她们抬头望我,斯塔克太太很惊愕地问道:"为什么我〔你〕把洛沙萝德小姐从她温暖的床上抱到这儿来?"我才开始轻声说道,"因为我怕当我不在那儿时候,她又被雪中那疯孩子引出去了,"她就打断我的话(向斐妮发尔小姐偷看一下),说斐妮发尔小姐要我把她编错的,她们两人都看不见挑出的一部分弄清楚。我就将我那美丽的乖乖放在沙发上,坐在她们旁边的一个小凳子,我的心对于她们硬起来,当我听见大风在外面刮起,狂吼着。

无论狂风这么凶暴地吹着,洛沙萝德小姐还是好好地睡下去;斐妮发尔小姐一言不发,也不向旁边望,当一阵阵的风吹着窗子时候。忽然间她笔直地站起来,伸出一只手,好像叫我们仔细听着。

"我听到声音!"她说,"我听到可怕的叫喊——我听到我父亲的声音!"

刚在这个当儿,我的乖乖突然惊跳一下醒来:"我的小姑娘正哭着,啊,她哭得多么伤心呀!"她打算起来去找她,但是她的脚给毯绊住,我赶紧将她抱起;因为这些她们听得到,我们却

which they heard while we could catch no sound. In a minute or two the noises came, and gathered fast, and filled our ears; we, too, heard voices and screams, and no longer heard the winter's wind that raged abroad. Mrs. Stark looked at me, and I at her, but we dared not speak. Suddenly Miss Furnivall went towards the door, out into the ante-room, through the west lobby, and opened the door into the great hall. Mrs. Stark followed, and I durst not be left, though my heart almost stopped beating for fear. I wrapped my darling tight in my arms, and went out with them. In the hall the screams were louder than ever; they sounded to come from the east wing—nearer and nearer—close on the other side of the locked-up doors—close behind them. Then I noticed that the great bronze chandelier seemed all alight, though the hall was dim, and that a fire was blazing in the vast hearth-place, though it gave no heat; and I shuddered up with terror, and folded my darling closer to me. But as I did so, the east door shook, and she, suddenly struggling to get free from me, cried, "Hester! I must go! My little girl is there; I hear her; she is coming! Hester, I must go!"

I held her tight with all my strength; with a set will, I held her. If I had died, my hands would have grasped her still, I was so resolved in my mind. Miss Furnivall stood listening, and paid no regard to my darling, who had got down to the ground, and whom I, upon my knees now, was holding with both my arms clasped round

毫无所闻的声音使我怕得皮肤起栗。过一两分钟，那喧哗的声音来了，渐渐大声起来，充满我们的耳朵；我们也听到人们说话的声音同呐喊，不再单听到外面狂风的怒吼了。斯塔克太太望着我，我望着她，但是我们不敢说话。忽然间斐妮发尔小姐走向门去，走到前室，经过西穿堂，打开走进大厅的门。斯塔克太太跟着，我不敢独留在后面，虽然我的心差不多吓得停着不动了。在大厅里，那叫喊的声音比以前更大；它们仿佛是从东边来的——渐渐近了——到了锁着的门的那面了——紧靠在门外了。那时我看见青铜大烛台好像通亮了，虽然大厅还是朦胧的，大火炉上有火燃烧着，虽然那并没有产生热气；我怕得浑身发抖，更紧地抱我的乖乖。但是当我这样干时候，东边门动了，她突然挣扎要从我怀里逃去，喊道，"赫斯忒！我必定要去！我的小姑娘在那儿；我听到她的声音了；她来了！赫斯忒，我必定要去！"

我极力把她紧抱住；用一种坚决的意志，我抱着她。若使我死了，我的手还是抓着她，我的心是这么坚决的。斐妮发尔小姐站着听，不管我的乖乖，她现在已经到地上了，我现在双

her neck; she still striving and crying to get free.

All at once the east door gave way with a thundering crash, as if torn open in a violent passion, and there came into that broad and mysterious light, the figure of a tall old man, with grey hair and gleaming eyes. He drove before him, with many a relentless gesture of abhorrence, a stern and beautiful woman, with a little child clinging to her dress.

"O Hester! Hester!" cried Miss Rosamond. "It's the lady! The lady below the holly-trees; and my little girl is with her. Hester! Hester! Let me go to her; they are drawing me to them. I feel them—I feel them. I must go!"

Again she was almost convulsed by her efforts to get away; but I held her tighter and tighter, till I feared I should do her a hurt; but rather that than let her go towards those terrible phantoms. They passed along towards the great hall-door, where the winds howled and ravened for their prey; but before they reached that, the lady turned; and I could see that she defied the old man with a fierce and proud defiance; but then she quailed—and then she threw up her arms wildly and piteously to save her child—her little child—from a blow from his uplifted crutch.

膝贴地用我的双臂围住她的颈项；她还是哭着，用劲想跑开。

忽然间东边门打雷一样的响一声开起来，仿佛谁在盛怒之下把它冲开，从那里有一个须发灰白，眼光四射的高身量儿的老人走到这神秘明亮的光线里。他用许多残酷的厌恶态度，赶去一个严厉的美妇人，有一个小孩紧拉着她的衣裙。

"啊，赫斯忒！赫斯忒！"洛沙萝德小姐喊道。"这就是那位太太！坐在冬青树底下的那位太太；我的小姑娘也同她一起。赫斯忒！赫斯忒！让我去她那里罢；她们仿佛拉我到她们那里。我觉得她们拉着我——我觉得她们拉着我。我一定要去！"

她的努力挣脱几乎使她又抽搐起来；但是我更紧地，更紧地抱着她，等到我恐怕会把她弄伤；但是宁其伤她，却不愿让她去找这班可怕的鬼影。她们走向大厅的大门，那里狂风怒吼着，猛烈地抓住它们的俘掠品；但是在她们走到大门之前，那位太太回过头来；我能看见她用一种凶狠骄傲的反抗神情挑惹那老人；但是她退缩了——然后她疯狂地，怪可怜地举起她的双臂去救她的孩子——她的小孩子——使免受他举起来的拐杖的一击。

And Miss Rosamond was torn as by a power stronger than mine, and writhed in my arms, and sobbed (for by this time the poor darling was growing faint).

"They want me to go with them on to the Fells—they are drawing me to them. Oh, my little girl! I would come, but cruel, wicked Hester holds me very tight." But when she saw the uplifted crutch she swooned away, and I thanked God for it. Just at this moment—when the tall old man, his hair streaming[1] as in the blast of a furnace, was going to strike the little shrinking child—Miss Furnivall, the old woman by my side, cried out, "Oh, father! father! Spare the little innocent child!" But just then I saw—we all saw—another phantom shape itself, and grow clear out of the blue and misty light that filled the hall; we had not seen her till now, for it was another lady who stood by the old man, with a look of relentless hate and triumphant scorn. That figure was very beautiful to look upon, with a soft white hat drawn down over the proud brows, and a red and curling lip. It was dressed in an open robe of blue satin. I had seen that figure before. It was the likeness of Miss Furnivall in her youth; and the terrible phantoms moved on, regardless of old Miss Furnivall's wild

---

1 streaming: being blown out horizontally 横吹着。

洛沙萝德小姐好像被一个人过我的力量的力量抓住，在我怀里猛扭着，低声哭着（因为这时可怜的乖乖渐渐晕去了）。

"她们要我同她们到山上去——她们拉我到她们那里。啊，我的小姑娘呀！我极愿意去，但是残心〔忍〕的，坏恶的赫斯忒很紧地把我抱住。"但是当她看见那举起的拐杖时，她昏倒了，我那时感谢上帝。刚在这时候——当高身量儿的老人，他的头发飘着好像被镕铁炉的风吹着，正要打那退缩着的小孩时候——斐妮发尔小姐，我身旁那个老女人，喊道，"啊，爸爸！爸爸！不要害这个无辜的小孩子罢！"但是刚刚这时候我看见——我们大家都看见——另一个鬼影涌出来，从充满大厅的蓝色模糊的光线里渐渐轮廓分明了；我们在那时以前并没有看见她，她是另一个女人站在老人身旁，脸上带一种残酷的怨恨和得意的蔑视。那个人看起来很美丽，一项白色的软帽盖着骄傲的眉梢，有一个弯曲着的红嘴唇，穿一件胸前打开的蓝色长袍。我曾经看见过这个人。我看的是斐妮发尔小姐年青时候的肖像；这些可怕的鬼影继续走着，不管老斐妮发尔小姐疯狂般

entreaty—and the uplifted crutch fell on the right shoulder of the little child, and the younger sister looked on, stony and deadly serene. But at that moment, the dim lights, and the fire that gave no heat, went out of themselves, and Miss Furnivall lay at our feet stricken down by the palsy—death-stricken.

Yes! She was carried to her bed that night never to rise again. She lay with her face to the wall, muttering low but muttering alway: "Alas! Alas! What is done in youth can never be undone in age! What is done in youth can never be undone in age!"

的恳求——举高的拐杖打到小孩右肩上了,那个妹妹旁观着,石头一样,死一般的恬静。但是那时候,模糊的光线同不发热的火焰自己消灭了,斐妮发尔小姐受瘫痪病的打击躺在我们脚旁——致她的死命了。

是的!那晚上人们把她抬到床上去,再也不起来了。她脸朝着壁,低声喃喃道,却老是喃喃着:"嗳吓!嗳吓!年青时干的事情绝不能在年老时把它勾销了!年青时干的事情绝不能在年老时把它勾销了!"

In the Steppes

草 原 上

（英汉对照）

高尔基　著
梁遇春　译注

"英文小丛书"之一，上海北新书局，1931年5月付排，1931年6月初版

CONTENTS

目　次

Maxim Gorki（1868—　）

In the Steppes

草原上 ………………………………………………… 92

The Khan and His Son

可汗同他的儿子 …………………………………… 140

Maxim Gorki

（1868—   ）[1]

他的真名是 Alexey Maximovich Peshkov。他的父亲是一个家具商，他五岁时，父亲就去世了。母亲又嫁给别人，他寄养在外祖父家里。这位老头子是个染匠，生意却一年比一年坏。所以九岁时候他就出去混饭吃。他做了十五年各种的事情，有时当沿街喊卖的小贩，有时做轮船上厨子的助手，有时当书记，总之，尝尽人世的苦幸〔辛〕。但是同时他刻苦读书，于一八九二年开始写短篇小说，后来当一个小都会的新闻记者。过了五年，他出一本短篇小集，从此就享大名。

他的著作早年多半是短篇小说，中年写长篇小说同剧曲。一九一三年出版《儿时》（*Childhood*），一九一五年出版《在世界里》（*In the World*），一九二三年出版《大学时期》（*In University*），这三本长篇都是自传性质的，里面不单深刻地表现出他个人的性格，而且把当时社会各种性格都栩栩如生地画出。这三部书连同他的回忆录（*Recollections*）可算是他的杰作。

---

[1] 梁遇春翻译该作时作者高尔基尚健在，其确切生卒年为1868年至1936年。——编者注

In the Steppes

We left Perekop in the very worst of humours[1] —as hungry as wolves[2], and angry with the whole world. For more than twelve hours we had laboured[3] unsuccessfully, employing all our talents and efforts, to steal or earn something, and when at last we became convinced that we could not succeed one way or the other, we decided to move on[4]. Where? Anywhere—so long as we moved on.

We were ready to continue along precisely the same path of

---

1 in the very worst of humours: humour 本来作"汁液"解。中古生理学家相信人身具有四种汁液：blood, phlegm, choler, melancholy, 人的性情就是看他身体那种液汁多而定，比如 blood 多的人一定热情，phlegm 多的人大概是冷淡恬静，做事迟钝，choler 多的人易怒，melancholy 多的人总是怀个感伤的情调。因此 humour 这个字就解作心境，good humour 是高兴，ill humour 是不高兴了。

草　原　上

我们离开倍勒科普时候心里不高兴极了——饿得同狼一样，跟全世界上的人们生气。十二个钟头还要多些，用尽我们的本领同能力，设法去偷或者去挣一点东西，但是都失败了；最后我们相信这两条路都不能成功，就决定继续旅行。旅行到那里去呢？随便什么地方都可以——只要我们是望〔往〕前走着。

我们预备仍然完完全全过我们一向已经过得很久的那种生

---

2 as hungry as wolves：中国人说狼吞虎咽，觉得狼是最容易感到饥饿的，吃不饱的，外国人也以为狼是饿得最慌的动物，所以有这个比喻。

3 to labour：to endeavour 努力。

4 to move on：to proceed on one's way 继续走路。

life¹ we had long been following—this was silently decided by each of us and shone plainly in the surly glare of our hungry eyes.

We were three: we had all but² lately met, having knocked up against³ each other accidentally in a public-house in Kherson, on the banks of the Dnieper. One of us had been a soldier in a railway battalion, and afterwards, it appeared, foreman of a gang on one of the Vistula railways. He was a red-haired, muscular man with cold, grey eyes. He could speak German, and had a very intimate knowledge of prison life. Fellows of our class dislike talking much about their past, having always more or less⁴ well-founded reasons for silence; we therefore believed each other—at least outwardly we appeared to believe, for in his heart each of us had but⁵ little belief in himself.

When our second companion, a small, lean man with thin lips always sceptically pressed together, told us he had been a student of Moscow University, the soldier and I accepted it as a fact. Indeed, it was all the same to us if at any previous time he bad been student, detective, or thief—one thing only was important, that at the

---

    1 path of life: way of life 生活的路子；生活的方式。

    2 all but: almost 几乎。

    3 to knock up against: to meet with; to come across casually 偶然相逢。

    4 more or less: to a doubtful degree; there about 说不定到了什么程度，但是多少总有一些的。

活——这点我们各自默默地决定了,在我们饿眼的怒视里明白地现出。

我们一共三个人,差不多是最近才会面的,彼此在第聂珀尔河滨刻孙城里的一家店里偶然碰见。我们里面有一个从前在守护铁路的军队当过兵,后来好像做维斯杜拉铁路的一条干路上一班工人的监工。他是个红头发,有力气的人,有一双冷静的灰色眼睛。他能说德国话,对于监狱生活知道得很亲切。我们这个阶级的人们不爱多谈自己的过去,因为总有些应守缄默的实在理由。所以我们只得彼此互相信任——最少外表上我们好像是信任的,因为在我们各人自己心里,我们都不大相信自己。

当我们的第二个伴侣,一个短小清瘦的人,薄薄的嘴唇总是带着猜疑的神气紧锁着,告诉我们他曾经是莫斯科大学的一个学生,我们承认这句话是事实。由我们看起来,那的确都是一样的,假使他在从前什么时候当过学生,或者侦探,或者小窃——只有一件事情是重要的,那是在我们结识时候,他是我

---

5 but:only 只。

moment of our acquaintance he should be our equal: hungry, enjoying the special attention of the police in the towns and the suspicion of the muzhiks[1] in the villages; that he should hate both the one and the other with the hatred of a weak, hunted, hungry beast; that he should dream of universal revenge on all and everything; in a word[2], that both by his position among the monarchs of nature and the rulers of life, and by his own frame of mind[3] he shonld be a fruit of the same tree as ourselves.

The third was myself. Out of the modesty inherent in me from my earliest years, I will say not a word about my own qualities[4] but not wishing to appear naive to you I will be silent also about my defects; still, by way of[5] giving some clue to my characteristics, I will only add that I always thought myself better than others, and continue in the same opinion with undiminished success to this day.

Thus it was we left Perekop and went on farther, reckoning for the first day on[6] the shepherds, from whom one could always beg for bread and who seldom refused a passing stranger.

I walked in front with the soldier, the student followed us.

---

1 muzhik:（möozkik）a Russian peasant 俄国农夫。
2 in a word: briefly 总而言之。
3 frame of mind: state of mind 心情。
4 quality: general excellence 优美的性质。
5 by way of: for the purpose of 为……之故。

们同类的人：饿着，享受城里警察的特别注意同乡间农夫的猜疑；他应当以一个屠弱的，被迫害的，饥饿的走兽的怨恨来恨这两类人；他应当梦想一个普通的报复施之于一切的敌人；总而言之，从他在自然的皇帝们同生命的主宰们中间所处的地位，和他的本性这两方面来观察，他该是跟我们是同一棵树生出的叶子。

第三个就是我自己。我从最早的幼年我就具有一种谦逊，我现在决不说一个字，关于我自己的美德；但是不想让你们觉得我是天真纯朴，我对于我的缺点也守缄默；然而，为着给些认识我的性格的线索，我要说我一向总以为我比别人高明，一直到今天还是照从前一样成功地继续执着这个意见。

这样子我们离开倍勒科普，望〔往〕远处走去，打算第一天的粮食依靠着牧羊人，人们永远可以向他们讨面包，他们很少拒绝一个过路的生人。

我同兵士在前面走，学生跟着我们。他有一个似乎短衣的

---

6 to reckon on：to rely upon 依靠着。

Thrown over his shoulders he had something that resembled a jacket; the remains of a broad-brimined hat reposed on his sharp, angular, and closely cropped head. His thin legs were clad in tight-fitting trousers which had patches of many colours, and on the soles of his feet he had fastened with cords plaited out of strips torn from the lining of his jacket some object made of the upper of a high-boot he had found on the road. He called this contrivance "sandals[1]." He walked along in silence, kicking up a cloud of dust with his feet and blinking with his little greenish eyes. The soldier was dressed in a red cotton shirt, which he said he had acquired with his own hands in Kherson; over his shirt he wore a warm, wadded waistcoat; on his head was an old military cap of an undecided colour, which he wore according to the military regulations, well tilted on the right eyebrow; his legs were clad in wide flapping Cossack knickerbockers, his feet were bare.

  I too was clothed but bare-footed. Along we went, and around us on all sides stretched in noble luxuriance the undulating steppes, which as they lay there resembled a huge black dish covered over by the sultry, cloudless blue dome of the summer sky. The dusty, grey road cut through it like a broad band, and burned our feet. Some-

---

  1 sandals：希腊人所常穿的草鞋，学生要排他的学究架子，所以用这个古雅名字。

东西挂在背上；一顶宽边帽子的骸骨休息在他那尖的，有角的，剃得很光的头上。他那瘦腿穿着紧紧地附在身上的裤子，上面补缀有各种颜色的布片，他用从短衣的里子扯下的布条编成的绳子把他在大路上捡来的长靴的上半部制成的一个鞋底扎在足底上。他叫这个自己发明的东西做"草鞋"。他静默地走着，他的双脚踢起一阵尘埃，他那带绿色的小眼睛老是闪动着。兵士穿一件棉布的红色内衣，他说那是他在刻孙城里亲手得来的；内衣上面他盖有一件暖和的，填棉的背心；头上有一顶颜色模糊的旧军帽，他是按军队的规则戴着，右眉上歪得很厉害；他的腿穿着一条宽大的，飘动的哥萨克短裤，他的脚是不穿鞋子的。

我也穿着衣服，但是赤脚。我们望〔往〕前走去，四围高低起伏的草原开展于华丽的丰富里，这些草原躺在那里真像一个黑色大盆子，夏的天空的干燥无云的蓝色穹苍盖着。尘埃四起的灰色的路横断中间像一条宽带子，灼伤我们的脚。有时我们经过几块新割的，余蘖尚存的稻田，那和兵士的没

times we passed strips of stubbly and freshly reaped cornfield, which had a strange similarity to the soldier's long unshaven cheeks.

The soldier went along singing in a hoarse bass voice:

"Thy holy resurrection[1] we sing and praise."

During his time of service he had held a position in the church of the regiment not unlike that of precentor, and he knew an endless number of hymns, psalms, and chants, which knowledge he frequently misused[2] when our conversation flagged.

Before us on the horizon rose softly outlined forms, delicately coloured in tints from lilac to pale rose.

"Those are evidently the Crimean hills," said the student in a dry voice.

"Hills?" cried the soldier. "You see them rather soon, my friend. They are clouds, only clouds. Look at them—just like cranberry jelly with milk."

I remarked how pleasant it would be if the clouds were really made of jelly. This at once aroused our hunger—the curse of our days.

"Oh, the devil!" —the soldier swore and spat— "if we could only meet one living soul! There's nobody! We shall have to suck our paws as the bears do in winter."

---

1 holy resurrection：指耶稣复活。
2 misused：他拿赞美诗拿来随便应用于平常事情上，藉以解闷，所以说是误用了。

有刮脸的长面颊相似得出奇。

兵士走着时候用一种沙哑的低音唱道：

"我们歌颂你的神圣的复活。"

当他在军营时候，他在团部礼拜堂里居于似乎是领唱者的地位，他记得无数的赞美诗，诗篇，同音调和谐的祈祷文，这种知识他常常滥用，当我们谈话失掉趣味时候。

在我们前面，水平线上，涌现有轮廓轻柔的东西，精致地染上各种彩色，从淡紫色到淡红色。

"这些分明是克里米亚群山，"学生用一种干燥的声调说道。

"群山？"兵士喊道。"你看见它们太早一点儿罢，我的朋友。它们是云，只是云。看它们——正像蔓越橘的果冻加上牛乳。"

我说若使那些云真是果冻做的，那是多么快乐的事。这句话立刻勾起我们的饥饿——我们天天的灾殃。

"啊，魔鬼呀！"——兵士咒诅后又吐一下口水——"只求我们能够碰到一个生人！这里一个人都没有！我们将迫得吮啜自己的脚掌，像冬天里的熊那样。"

"I told you we ought to make for[1] more inhabited places, " said the student didactically.

"You told us! " answered the soldier irritably. "You're a scholar so you must talk. Where are the inhabited places here? The devil only knows where they are! "

The student remained silent and pressed his lips together. The sun was setting and the clouds on the horizon shone with many colours that words cannot describe. There was a smell of earth and salt.

This dry and scent taste only made our appetites sharper.

Our stomachs shrank together. It was a strange and unpleasant sensation; it appeared as though from all the muscles of our bodies the juices were gradually draining away, evaporating, and the muscles losing their vital suppleness. A feeling of prickly dryness filled our mouths and throats, our heads grew dizzy, and all the time black spots appeared and disappeared before our eyes. Sometimes they took the form of steaming pieces of meat, or loaves of bread; our memory gave these "visions of the past, dumb visions"[2], their characteristic smells, and then it was like a knife being turned about[3] in our entrails.

---

1 to make for: to go in the direction of 向某方走去。

2 "visions of the past, dumb visions": 在回忆里所看见的从前吃的东西。

"我早告诉你们了,我们应当向人烟更稠密的地方走去,"学生含着教训的神气说道。

"你早告诉我们了!"兵士生气地答道。"你是个学者,所以你非说话不可。在这里何处是人类稠密的地方?只有魔鬼知道那些地方是在何处罢!"

学生还是静默着,他的嘴唇上下紧锁。太阳下山了,水平线上的云发出许多彩色,是言语所不能形容的。空中有一种土气同盐味。

这个干燥的,适口的气味只是使我们食欲更强烈。

我们的胃收缩在一起。那是一种奇怪的不快之感;好像觉得我们身里一切筋肉的精液渐渐干涸了,蒸发着;筋肉也失掉它们具有生机的柔软自如了。一种如针刺的干燥感觉占着我们的嘴同咽喉,我们的头晕眩了,这些时间里黑点在我们眼前忽现忽隐。有时这些黑点形成几块冒着蒸气的肉,或者几块面包;我们的记忆使这些"过去的幻象,黯然的幻象"呈出它们特有的香味,那时真像一把刀在我们脏腑里打滚。

---

3 to turn about:to wheel about 转面另朝一个方向。

However, we went on describing our feelings to each other, and keeping a sharp eye[1] on every side, hoping to see somewhere a flock of sheep and listening to hear the shrill squeaking of a Tartar's cart, carrying fruit to an Armenian[2] bazaar.

But the steppes were empty and silent.

On the eve[3] of this hard day the three of us had eaten four pounds of rye bread and five water melons, and had walked about forty versts[4], —the outlay was not in proportion to the income[5], — and when we had fallen asleep in the market-place at Perekop we were awakened by hunger.

The student had very justly advised us not to lie down and sleep, but to occupy ourselves during the night[6]... in decent society, however, it is not the custom to talk aloud about plans for the violation of private property, so I hold my peace[7]. I only want to be truthful but it is not in my interest[8] to be rude. I know that people are growing every day more soft-hearted in our highly cultivated era, and even when they take their neighbour by the throat[9] with the evident intention of throttling him, they try to do so with the greatest

---

    1 to keep a sharp eye：to be vigilant 留神。

    2 Armenian：Armenia 的人。

    3 on the eve：on the evening before festival，etc. 宴会或其它事件发生的前一夜。

    4 verst：合中国二里。

可是，我继续互相描状我们的感觉，很注意地向各方望着，希望能够看见某处有一群羊，一面又静聆有没有鞑靼人车子的尖利的辗轧声音，那是运果子到一个亚美尼亚市场去。

但是草原是空旷的，寂寞的。

这个艰苦日子的前晚，我们三人吃了四磅裸麦面包同五只西瓜，却已走了将近四十个俄里的路，——这真入不敷出，——当我们在倍勒科普市场睡着时候，我们是被饥饿弄醒的。

学生很合乎道理地劝我们那晚不要躺下睡觉，夜里却要干些事情……但是在规矩人们的社会里，人们不常大声地谈到侵害私产的事情，所以现在我也不说这事了。我所求的只是真实的叙述，说出粗野的话于我是无益的。我知道在我们这深有修养的时代人们天天变得更心软了；甚至于当他们抓住他们邻人的咽喉，分明想闷死他时候，他们也是设法用最大的可能的慈

---

5 the outlay was not in proportion to the income：这里是做个比喻，就是吃的东西不足支持这么剧烈的走动。

6 to occupy ourselves during the night：指偷东西，拦路抢人这类事情。

7 to hold one's peace：to be silent 不说。

8 in one's interest：to one's advantage 与他有益的。

9 to take one by the throat：就是抓着一个人的头项的意思。比如说抓着一个人的臂，那么可以讲 take one by the arm，其余类推。

possible kindness, observing all the propriety suitable to the occasion. The experience of my own throat obliges me to mark this progress in morals, and I can affirm with a pleasant feeling of certainty that everything develops and improves in this world. In particular[1], this wonderful progress is weightily confirmed by the yearly increase in the number of prisons, public-houses, and maisons de tolérance[2].

Thus, feeling famished and trying by friendly talk to forget the pain in our stomachs, we went on through the waste and silent steppes, under the rays of the setting sun, in the faint hope of finding something. Before us the sun was quietly sinking into soft clouds, which were richly coloured by its rays, while behind us and on both sides a blue dimness seemed to rise from the steppes up to the sky and narrow the inhospitable horizon around us.

"Brothers, let us collect material for a fire, " said the soldier, picking up a small log of wood from the road. "We shall have to[3] pass the night in the steppes... there'll be a heavy dew. Dry cow dung, twigs—take everything."

We separated and began to collect whatever we could by the roadside: twigs, dry steppe grass, and anything that would burn. Every time we had to bend down, we were seized all through our bodies

---

1　in particular: especially 尤其。

2　maisons de tolérance: house of ill fame 名誉不佳的房子；妓院。

3　to have to: to be obliged to 不得不。

爱来行这件事，顾到这种机会应有的一切礼节。我自己咽喉的经验迫得我不能不看出这种道德上的进步，我能够快活地坚决说道在这个世界里一切东西都发展了，进步了。这个可惊的进步尤其得到很有力的证明，从监狱，酒店同妓院的数目的每年增大。

这样子，觉得饥饿，试用友谊的谈话去忘却我们胃里的苦痛，我们继续走过这些荒凉的，寂寞的草原，在落日的光线之下，怀个微弱的希望，想找到一些吃的东西。在我们面前，太阳静悄悄地沉到轻云里去，那些云被斜阳照成绚烂的彩色；我们的后面同两旁，一片蓝色的朦胧气象好像从草原升到天上，使我们四周残酷的边际更见狭小。

"兄弟们，让我们收集些燃料生火罢，"兵士说道，从路上捡起一小块木头。"我们免不了在草原里过夜……晚上会有浓厚的露。干牛屎，树枝——把一切东西都拿来罢。"

我们分散，开始去搜集我们在路旁所能找到的一切东西：树枝，草原上的干草，同凡是可以燃烧的材料。每次我不得不俯身时候，我整个躯体顿然有一个可怕的欲望，想拜伏地上，

with a terrible longing to fall down to the ground, to lie there immovable and eat of the earth, the black, fat earth, to eat much of it, to eat until we could eat no more, and then to fall asleep. To fall asleep perhaps for ever, only first to eat, to chew, to feel the warm, black porridge slowly going down from the mouth through the parched gullet into the craving, shrunken stomach, which was burning with desire to absorb anything.

"If we could only find some sort of roots, " sighed the soldier. "There are some edible roots..."

But in the black, ploughed earth there were no roots. The southern night came on quickly, and the last rays of the setting sun had not time to die away before the stars began to shine in the dark blue sky, and around us the black shadows blended together more closely and narrowed the endless flatness of the steppes that surrounded us.

"Brothers, " the student said in an undertone, "there—to the left—a man is lying."

"A man? " said the soldier doubtingly: "Why should he be lying there? "

"Go and ask him. He is sure to have bread, as he has settled down[1] in the steppe, " explained the student.

The soldier looked in the direction where the man was lying,

---

1 to settle down: to cease from wandering 不再游荡了；住下来了。

躺在那里不动,把地上的土吃进去,那些黑色的,肥沃的土,吃得许多,吃到我们不能再吃了,然后睡去。也许就长眠不醒了,只是先要吃,要嚼,要觉得那暖和的、黑色的粥慢慢地从嘴经过干燥的食道,达到渴望的,收缩了的胃,那正燃烧着一种欲望,想吞进任何东西。

"只求我们能够找到几种草,"兵士叹一口气说道。"有些草是可以吃的……"

但是在这黑色的,犁过的土地并没有草。南方的夜来得很快,落日最后的光线尚未完全消失,星儿已照在黑沉沉的蓝色天上了,我们四围的黑影更密地混合一起,把我们四面草原的无限平坦弄狭窄了。

"兄弟们,"学生低声说道,"那里——左边——一个人躺着。"

"一个人?"兵士带着怀疑口气说:"他为什么躺在那里呢?"

"去问他一下罢。他必定有些面包,因为他在草原里歇下,"学生解释道。

兵士向那个人躺的地方望着,坚决地吐一下口水,说道,

and spitting with determination said, "let us go to him."

Only the sharp green eyes of the student could have made out that the dark heap, some fifty sazhenes[1] to the left of the road, was a man. We went towards him, stepping quickly over the furrows of the ploughed field and sensible how the new-born hope of food sharpened our appetites. We were quite close to him. The man did not move.

"Perhaps it is not a man, " said the soldier gloomily, expressing the thought in all our minds.

But at that very moment[2] our doubts were dispelled, for the heap that was lying on the ground began to move and rise. We saw it was a real live man, kneeling down and stretching out his arms towards us.

He spoke to us in a dull, trembling voice: "Don't come near me; I shall shoot you."

A dry, sharp crack resounded in the dull air.

We stopped as if by command and were silent for a few seconds, stupefied by this unamiable reception.

"The villain! " mumbled the soldier expressively.

"Y-e-s—" the student said reflectively; "he goes about with a

---

1 fifty sazhenes: about 350 feet 将近三百五十尺。
2 that very moment: that identical moment 那个同一的时候。

"让我们到他那里去罢。"

只有学生的尖利的,绿色的眼睛才能够瞧出大路左旁,一两百丈远的那堆黑东西是一个人。我们向他那里走去,很快地踏过已耕的田的犁沟,心里觉得获食的新希望多么使我们的食欲亢强。我们走很近他的身旁。那个人并不动。

"也许那不是一个人,"兵士愁闷地说道,讲出我们大家心里共同的思想。

但是刚在那时候我们的怀疑被驱散了,因为躺在地上的那一团开始转动,要起来了。我们看见那是一个真的人,跪着,伸出他的双臂向我们。

他用一种沉闷的,战栗的声调对我们说道:"不要走近我;我将枪杀你们。"

一个干燥的,尖锐的爆裂声在沉闷的空气里回响着。

我们停步,好像听到了命令,有几分钟静默着,这是因为给这个卤莽的欢迎吓住了。

"这流氓!"兵士愤慨地喃喃着。

"是——的——"学生沉思地说道;"他带着手枪旅行——

revolver—it's clear he's a fish with roe[1]."

"Ho! " shouted the soldier; he had evidently decided on some plan.

The man did not change his position and remained silent.

"Ho, you there! We won't touch you, only give us some bread. I expect you've got some. Give us some, brother, for Christ's sake[2]. May you be cursed—damned! "

The last words the soldier mumbled in his beard. The man remained silent.

"Do you hear? " the soldier continued, trembling with rage and despair. "Give us some bread. We won't come near you. Throw it to us."

"All right! " said the man shortly.

He might have said to us, "My dear brethren, " and if he had poured into those three Christian words all the purest, holiest feelings, they would not have excited us as much, nor made us feel as human, as that dull, short "All right" did.

"Do not be afraid of us, good man, " said the soldier gently with a sweet smile on his face, though the man could not see his smile, as he was at a distance of at least twenty paces from us. "We are peaceful men going from Russia to Kuban—money

---

1 a fish with a roe：一条有卵的鱼。roe，the eggs of fish.
2 for Christ's sake：为着耶稣的缘故。耶稣一生行事以拯救他人为宗旨，现在请人们分面包，只好把他抬出来。

分明他身边有好东西。"

"听!"兵士喊道;他显然决定了一个计划。

那个人没有变更他的位置,仍然是无言。

"听,你躺在那里的这个东西!我们并不伤害你,只求你给我们几块面包。我预料你带有一些。给我们几块罢,兄弟,看着上帝的面上。你该受诅——受上帝的责罚!"

最后这几个字兵士藏在胡子后面轻声讲。那个人还是无言。

"你听见没有?"兵士继续说道,生气同失望得打颤。"给我们几块面包。我们不走近你。掷过来给我们罢。"

"好罢!"那个人简单地说道。

他很可以对我们说,"我亲爱的兄弟们",若使他拿最纯净的,最神圣的感情注进这几个字,这几个字的感动我们,同使我们觉得恢复人性,还不如那个沉闷的,简约的"好罢"。

"不要怕我们,好人儿,"兵士温和地说道,脸上还现出甜蜜的笑容,虽然那个人不能够看见他的笑容,因为他同我们最少也相隔二十步。"我们是安分的人们,从俄国到库班去——中

failed[1] us on the way—we have eaten up[2] all we had, and this is the second day we have been without food."

"Catch! " said our benefactor, waving his hand in the air, and something black flew past and fell in the ploughed field not far from us. The student hurried to pick it up.

"Catch again! Again! I have no more."

When the student had collected this strange gift, we found that we had about four pounds of dry wheaten bread. It was covered with earth and very dry. Dry bread is more satisfying than new bread, as there is less moisture in it.

"There, and there, and there, " said the soldier, carefully dividing the pieces. "Stop—they are not equal! —Now then you, professor[3], I must pinch a little bit from you, or he will have too little..."

The student submitted without question to the loss of a small piece of bread of about one-tenth of an ounce in weight. I received it and put it in my mouth.

I chewed it, chewed it slowly, with difficulty restraining the nervous action of my jaws, which were ready to crunch stones. The hurried, spasmodic movement of my gullet caused me great pleasure, and I satisfied it in small quantities. Morsel after morsel, warm,

---

1 to fail: to be insufficient for 缺乏；不够。
2 to eat up: to consume 吃尽。
3 professor: 因为他自认是大学生，人们调侃他，称他为"教授"。

途旅费用尽——我们把我们所有的全吃光了,这是我们绝食的第二天。"

"抓住!"我们的恩人说道,他的手向空中一挥,有些黑色的东西飞过来,降落在犁田里,离我们不远。学生跑去检〔捡〕起。

"再抓住!又一回!我也没有了。"

当学生把这个奇怪的礼物聚在一起,我们看出我们有将近四磅的干的麦制面包。上面有一层泥土盖住,非常干燥。干面包比新面包更可口。因为里面水分含得少些。

"这里一份,这里一份,这里一份,"兵士说道,细心地分配那几块面包。"等一下——分得不平均——现在,教授,我得从你的拧一小块下来,否则他得太少了……"

学生忍受损失一英两十分之一重的小块面包,并没有诘问。我接受那小块,放进口里。

我咀嚼它,慢慢地咀嚼它,很不容易制住我牙床强烈的动作,它们是石头都咬得碎的。我食道的迅速的,痉挛的运动给我很大的快乐,我故意分做小块慢慢去满足它。一口又一口,

incomprehensibly, indescribably tasty morsels, entered my burning stomach and seemed instantly to be transformed into blood and brains. Joy, such a strange, quiet, and vivifying joy warmed my heart, in proportion to the food that entered my stomach and my whole system seemed as in a doze. I forgot those accursed days of chronic hunger, I forgot my companions, being entirely immersed in the enjoyment of the feelings I was now experiencing.

But when I had thrown the last crumbs of bread from the palm of my hand into my mouth, I felt still a terrible desire to eat.

"He must still have some lard or meat, damn him, " grumbled the soldier, who was sitting on the ground near me rubbing his stomach.

"He must have, for the bread smelt of meat. He will have kept some bread too, " said the student, and added in an undertone, "if it were not for that revolver..."

"Who is he? Eh? "

"Evidently one of us Ishmaels[1]..."

"A dog! " decided the soldier.

We sat close together and cast sidelong glances at the place where our benefactor with the revolver was sitting. Neither sound nor sign of life reached us from there.

---

1 Ishmael: outcast, one at war with society 流氓；与社会冲突之人。见《圣经·创世记》第十六章。

暖和的，莫明其妙地，形容不出来地好吃的小块，走进我正燃烧着的胃，好像立刻化做血同脑。快乐，一种这么奇怪的，温柔的，使我有生气的快乐，使我的心温暖，那是同吃进我胃里的东西分量作正比例；我整个躯体好像在一顿微睡之中。我忘却了长久挨饿的灾难日子，我忘却了我的同伴，完全浸于我现在所经验的感觉的欣赏。

但是当我把最后几小块的面包从手掌掷到口里，我还是觉得一种可怕的食欲。

"他必定还有些猪油或猪肉，该死的人，"兵士不满意地说道，他坐在地上，靠近我，摸着他的肚子。

"他必定有，因为这些面包带了肉味。他也许还保留一些面包，"学生说道。他又低声说，"假使不是因为那把枪……"

"他是谁呀？"

"分明也是一个像我们这样被社会所摈弃的人……"

"一条狗！"兵士下个判词。

我们大家紧紧地坐在一起，斜着眼睛看我们恩人挟枪而坐的地方。没有声音，没有生命的象征从那里传到我们这儿。

The night drew its dark forces around us. The silence of death was in the steppes; we could hear each other's breathing. Now and then the melancholy whistle of a marmot could be heard. The stars—those live flowers of the sky—shone above us. We wanted to eat.

I say it with pride—on that strange night I was neither worse nor better than my chance companions. I proposed that we should get up and go for[1] that man, "We need not touch him, but we can eat all he has. He may shoot—let him! He can only hit one of the three, if he hits at all. And even if he does hit, a revolver shot is not likely to kill."

"Let's go, " said the soldier, jumping up.

The student got up more slowly than he did.

So we went almost running, the student keeping a little behind us.

"Comrade! " shouted the soldier reproachfully.

We were met by a low grumble and the sharp snap of the cock; there was a flash of light and the dry sound of a shot reached our ears.

"Missed! " cried the soldier joyfully, and in a single bound he reached the man. "Now, you devil, I'll give it you[2]..."

The student pounced on the knapsack. But the devil fell from

---

1 to go for: to attack 攻击。
2 to give it one: to punish one 责罚他。

夜安排它的黑暗势力在我们的四旁。死的静寂临到草原上；我们能够听到彼此呼吸声音。有时可以听到一只土拨鼠的悲吟。星空——天上的活色生香——在我们上面发光着。我们想吃东西。

我现在骄傲地说道——在那个奇怪的晚上，我既不比我偶然相逢的伴侣好，也不比他们坏。我提议我们可以起来，去攻击那个人。"我们用不着害他，可是我们可以把他所有的都吃个精光。他也许会开枪——让他罢！他也只能打中三人中的一个，假使他果然打中了。就说他打中了，手枪的打伤不一定是致命的。"

"我们去罢，"兵士跳起来说道。

学生站起来比较慢一点儿。

我们于是几乎是跑着，学生总居在稍微后面些。

"同伴！"兵士带着责备的口气喊道。

我们碰到低声的怨恨呻吟同枪机撩拨的尖利声音；火光一闪，一下开枪的干燥声音达到我们耳朵里。

"没有打中！"兵士欢喜地喊道，一跳他就到那个人面前了。"现在，你这魔鬼，我要报复一下……"

学生撄住背囊。但是那个魔鬼坐不住，躺下了，伸出他的

his knees on to his back, spread out his arms, and gasped.

"What the deuce is this? " said the soldier in a tone of surprise; he had already raised his foot to give the man a kick. "Can he have fired at himself ? You! You there! Eh? Have you shot yourself? "

"Here's meat, and cakes of some kind and bread; a lot, brothers! " shouted the student with delight.

"Then go to the devil! You may give up the ghost[1]! Let's eat, my boys! " cried the soldier. I took the revolver out of the man's hand, who had now ceased to gasp and was lying quite still. There was only one shot left in the revolver.

We ate again, ate in silence. The man lay there silent too, not moving a single limb. We took no notice of him.

A hoarse and trembling voice suddenly said: "Was this done only for bread, my dear brothers? "

We all startled. The student cleared his throat and bending to the earth began to cough.

The soldier finished chewing what he had in his mouth and uttered many oaths.

"You soul of a dog! May you burst like a dry trough! Do you think we wanted to skin you? What good would it be to us? A fool's

---

1 to give up the ghost: to die 死去; 让三魂七魄飞去。

四肢,喘气着。

"这弄什么鬼玩意儿?"兵士带着纳罕的声调说;他已经举起他的脚打算踢那个人。"难道他打中了自己?你!你这东西!呀?你打中了自己吗?"

"这儿有肉,某一种的饼,同面包;一大堆,兄弟们!"学生高兴得喊出来。

"那么你去找魔鬼罢!你可以死去!让我们来吃,我的孩子们!"兵士喊道。我从那个人手里把手枪拿去,他现在不喘气了,十分安详地躺着。枪里只剩有一粒子弹。

我们又吃,静默地吃东西。那个人也是静默地躺在那里,四肢丝毫不动。我们不理他。

一个战栗的沙声忽然说道:"你们干这事就为着这些面包吗,我亲爱的兄弟们?"

我们都吓了跳。学生清一清喉咙,弯下身来开始咳嗽。

兵士把他口里的东西咀嚼完,说出许多咒诅的话。

"你这像狗一样的灵魂!希望你能像干水管那样破裂!你以为我们想剥你的皮吗?那于我们有什么益处?一个傻子的猪一

snout, an unclean soul! A nice thing—arming himself and shooting at people! Damn you!"

He swore while he was eating, which took from his curses all their expressiveness and strength.

"Just wait—when we have eaten we will settle with[1] you," said the student ominously.

Then in the stillness of the night the sound of whimpering sobs frightened us.

"Brothers—as if I knew[2]! I fired because I was afraid. I am going from New Athos to the Smolensk Government. —Oh, good Lord! The fever seizes me—as soon as the sun sets. —It's my misfortune. —To escape the fever I left Athos. —Did joinery there. —I'm a joiner. —Have a wife at home—two girls—three years—nearly four —have not seen them—brothers! —Eat everything..."

"We shall eat everything, never fear[3]. You needn't ask us," said the student.

"Good God! Had I only known that you were peaceful, good people—would I have thought of firing? —It was the steppes, brothers—night[4]. —Forgive me! —Eh?"

---

1 to settle with: to adjust differences 结账。
2 as if I knew: 好像我是明知故犯。
3 never fear: don't be anxious 不用着急。
4 night: 因为是在夜里, 所以特别恐慌。

样的鼻孔，一个不干净的灵魂！一件好东西——武装保护自己，枪杀别人！愿上帝责罚你！"

他咒诅时正吃着东西，这使他的咒诅失掉了精彩同力气。

"等一会罢——我们吃完就来跟你结账，"学生不怀好意地说道。

然后在夜的寂静里呜咽饮泣的声音把我们吓一下。

"兄弟们——你们好像以为我早晓得你们是好人！我开枪因为我恐惧。我是从纽·亚托司到斯莫莲司克政府。——啊，仁慈的上帝呀！热病发作——到太阳下山的时候。——这是我的不幸。为着逃避那热病，我离开亚托司。——在那里做细木工。——我是一个细木匠。——家里有一个老婆——两个女孩——三年——差不多四年——没有见到她们了——兄弟们！——都吃完罢……"

"我们会吃个精光，你可以不用担心。你用不着请我们，"学生说道。

"仁慈的上帝！只要我知道了你们是和平的，安分的人们——我会想开枪吗？——那是因为草原，兄弟们——夜。——原谅我罢！——呀？"

He talked and cried, or rather gave out a trembling, frightened whimper.

"Snivel away, " said the soldier contemptuously.

"He must have money on him, " suggested the student.

The soldier half-closed his eyes, looked at him, and smiled.

"You're cute! Let's make up a fire and go to sleep."

"And he? " inquired the student.

"He may go to the devil! We can't roast him, can we? "

"We ought to[1], " and the student shook his sharp head.

We went for the stuff we had collected but dropped when the joiner had arrested us with his cry, brought it up, and were soon seated round a fire. It smouldered slowly in the windless night, and lighted up the small space where we were seated. We were getting sleepy, although we would gladly have supped again. "Brothers! " the joiner called to us. He was lying three paces from us, and at times it seemed to me that he was whispering something to himself.

"Yes, " answered the soldier.

"May I come to you—to the fire? I feel death approaching—all my bones ache.—Good Lord!—I see I shall never get

---

1 we ought to：学生说我们应当燔炙他，隐隐含有将他了结，把他的钱拿来的意思。

他说着，哭着，也可以说是发出一种战栗的，恐惧的呜咽。

"哭你的罢，"兵士鄙视地说道。

"他身上一定有钱，"学生向我们提醒。

兵士半闭他的眼睛，望着他，微笑。

"你真伶俐！我们弄一堆火，去睡觉罢。"

"他呢?"学生问道。

"他可以去找魔鬼！我们总不能燔炙他，我们能够吗?"

"我们却应当，"学生说时摇他的尖头。

我们去拿那些燃料，那是我们早已检〔捡〕好的，却扔下来，当细木匠喊声抓住我们的注意。我们这时候把它们聚在一起，不久就围火而坐。在这无风的夜里它慢慢冒烟，照亮我们坐的那小块地方。我们渐渐瞌睡了，虽然我们很想再吃一顿。

"兄弟们！"细木匠叫我们。他躺在离我们三步的地方，有时我好像觉得他对自己私语。

"是的，"兵士答道。

"我可以来到你们那里——到火旁吗？我觉得死的来临——我所有的骨头都疼痛着。——仁慈的上帝呀！——我看

home."

"Crawl here, " the student gave permission.

The joiner moved slowly along the ground towards the fire, just as if he were afraid to lose an arm or a leg. He was tall but terribly thin; every part of him shook strangely, and his dim eyes reflected the pain that was eating him up[1]. In the light of our fire his drawn and haggard face had a yellow, earthy, corpselike colour. He trembled all over, and aroused our contempt and pity. Stretching his long thin hands to the fire he rubbed his bony fingers, and their joints bent slowly, flabbily. At last it was repulsive to look at him.

"Why did you come in such a condition—and on foot too? Stingy, eh? " the soldier asked surlily.

"I was advised—don't go by water, they said—go through the Crimea—air[2], they said. And now I can't walk any more—I'm dying, brothers—I shall die alone in the steppes. —The birds will peck at me—nobody will know—my wife, the girls, will wait for me. —I wrote to them—and my bones will be washed by the rain in the steppes. —Good Lord! Good Lord! "

His whine was like the sad howl of a wounded wolf.

---

1 to eat one up: to wear out the life of a person 把一个人磨折死。
2 air: 草原上空气新鲜，与〔于〕病体有益。

出来永不能回家了。"

"爬到这里来罢,"学生允许他。

细木匠慢慢地靠着地面爬向火来,好似他害怕会失落一只臂或者一只腿。他身体很高,却瘦得可怕;他身上的各部分都奇怪地颤动,他那双蒙钝的眼睛映出蚕食他内身的苦痛。在我们的火光里,他瘦长憔悴的脸孔有一种黄色的,土一样的,死尸般的颜色。他浑身打颤,引起我们的蔑视同矜怜。伸出他那瘦长的手向着火,他摩擦他那只有骨头的手指,它们的关节慢慢地,软弱地弯下。最后我们觉得看见他令人难过。

"你为什么在这样情形之下旅行——而且是步行?舍不得花钱吗?"兵士怒气汹汹地问道。

"人们劝我——不要走水路,他们说——穿克里米亚走去——空气很好,他们说。现在我不能再走路了——我快死了,兄弟们——我将孤单单地死在草原里——鸟儿会来啄我——谁也不知道——我的妻子,女孩儿们,将等候我。——我从前写信告诉了她们。——我的骨头会被草原里的雨水洗着。——仁慈的上帝!仁慈的上帝!"

他的啼哭好像一个受伤的狼的哀号。

"Oh, the devil! " cried the enraged soldier, jumping up; "what are you whimpering for? Why can't you leave people in peace? Are you dying? Well then, die, but be quiet! Who wants you? Hold your tongue! "

"Give him a knock on the head, " suggested the student.

"Let's lie down and go to sleep," said I, "and you, if you want to be near the fire, don't howl, come now."

"Did you hear? " said the soldier sternly. "You just understand that. You think we are sorry for you and will look after[1] you, because you threw bread at us—and sent bullets after us? You're a sour devil! Others would have... Phew! "

The soldier said no more but stretched himself on the ground.

The student was already lying down. I lay down too. The frightened joiner came nearer and lay huddled together looking at the fire in silence. I was on his right and could hear his teeth chatter. The student lay curled up to his left and seemed to fall asleep at once. The soldier put his arms under his head and looked up at the sky.

"What a night! Eh? What numbers of stars! How warm! " he said to me a few minutes later. "What a sky! —A quilt, not a sky! I love this wandering life, good friend. It's cold and hungry, but very free. You have no chiefs over you—you're master of your own life.

---

1 to look after: to attend; to take charge of 照呼。

"啊，魔鬼！"生气的兵士跳起来喊道："你为什么呜咽？你为什么不能让别人享些安静？你快死吗？好罢，那么就死去，但是不要出声！谁要你这个人？带住你的舌头罢！"

"给他当头一拳罢，"学生提议说。

"让我们躺下睡去罢，"我说，"你，若使你想靠近火，那么不要乱喊，来罢。"

"你听见没有？"兵士声色俱厉地说道。"你该晓得这一点。你以为我们会可怜你，照顾你，因为你掷面包给我们——同对我们发子弹？你是一个脾气乖戾的魔鬼！别人一定会……呸！"

兵士不再说什么话了，却直挺地躺在地上。

学生已经躺下了。我也躺下。惊慌的细木匠更走近些，缩作一团，静默地望着火。我在他的右边，能够听到他的牙齿震颤作声。学生蜷伏在他左边，好似立刻睡着了。兵士枕臂面眠，眼望着天。

"多么好的夜！呀？多少星儿！多么温暖！"过几分钟他对我说道。"多么美丽的天空！——一床被褥，不是一个天空！我喜欢这种流浪的生活，好朋友。那是挨着饥寒，但是很自由。你没有什么上头人管着你——你是你自己生命的主人。你可以

You may eat your head off[1] —nobody dare say a word to you. It's fine! I've heen famished these days, and cross—and now I am lying here looking at the sky. The stars twinkle at me, as if to say 'Never mind, Lakutin, still go on in the world, and give in to[2] no man'. Yes, my heart is happy... And you—how are you? Eh, joiner, don't be cross with me, and don't be afraid of anything. It's nothing that we have eaten your bread—you had bread and we had none, so we ate yours. You're a ferocious man, to send bullets at us. Don't you understand bullets can harm a man? I was very cross with you just now[3], and if you had not fallen down, I would have thrashed you, brother, for your insolence. As for the bread, you will get as far as Perekop tomorrow and can buy some there—you have money I know. Is it long since you caught the fever?"

For a considerable time the bass voice of the soldier and the trembling voice of the sick joiner rang in my ears. The night—dark, almost black—sank always lower and lower on the earth, and fresh, sweet air poured into my breast.

The fire cast a steady light and a quickening heat around. My eyes closed.

"Get up, quick, come along[4]!"

---

1 to eat one's head off: to do anything 随便做什么事。
2 to give in to: to succumb 屈服于。
3 just now: a little moment ago 一会儿以前。

把你自己的头吃去——谁也不敢向你抗议一声。这真妙！我饿了三天，心里不高兴——现在我却躺在这儿望着天。星儿对我霎眼，好像说'不要担心，拉古丁，还是在世界上望〔往〕前进罢，对谁都不要让步。'是的，我的心是快乐的……你——你怎么样呢？唔，细木匠，不要跟我生气，不要害怕什么。那算不得什么，我们吃了你的面包——你有面包，我们没有，所以我们吃你的。你是一个凶猛的人，向我们开枪。你知道子弹能伤人吗？我刚才跟你很生气，假使你自己没有摔倒，我一定会打你，兄弟，报复你的无礼。至于面包，你明天会走到倍勒科普，在那里可以买一些——我知道你有钱。你得这热病已经很久吗？"

有许久时光兵士的低音同害病的细木匠的战栗声音在我耳朵里响着。夜——暗的，几乎是黑的——老是更低地更低地降到地面，新鲜的，甜蜜的空气灌到我胸里。

火射散出一个无变化的光同一个使我们有生命力的热气。我的眼睛闭了。

"起来，快些，赶快！"

----

4 come along：make haste 赶快！常用于命令口气。

I woke with a frightened start, opened my eyes, and jumped up quickly, the soldier helping me on my legs[1] and pulling me violently by the arm.

"Now, quick, step out[2]!"

His face was stern and alarmed. I looked round. The sun was rising and already a rose-coloured ray fell on the fixed grey face of the joiner. His mouth was open, his eyes stood out of their sockets and stared with a glazed look expressive of terror. The clothes were torn off his chest, and he lay in an unnatural, contorted position. The student was nowhere to be seen.

"Well, haven't you seen enough? Come along, I tell you, " insisted the soldier, trying to draw me away by pulling my arm.

"Is he dead? " I asked, shivering in the morning freshness.

"Of coures he is! If you were stifled you would be dead too, " the soldier explained.

"He? The student? " I cried.

"Well, and who else? Was it you? Or I perhaps? Yes. So much for the learned. He has finished with[3] the man cleverly and left his own comrades in the lurch[4]. If I had known I'd have killed that

---

1 to help one on one's legs: to help one stand up 扶一个人站起来。
2 to step out: to walk with long stride 大踏步走去。
3 to finish with: to bring to an end 结束。
4 to leave in the lurch: to desert in difficulty 困难中独自脱身而逃。

我吓了一跳地醒来,睁开我的眼睛,很快跳起来,兵士扶我站稳,卤莽地拉着我的臂。

"来,快些,大步走去!"

他的脸容是峻严的,恐慌的我向四面一望。太阳正在上升,已经有一线玫瑰色的光射到细木匠的呆板的灰色脸孔。他的嘴张开,他的眼睛露在眼眶之外,有种板滞的神气睁视着,表现出惊惶。他胸前的衣服扯破,他躺在一个不自然的,扭歪的位置里。学生是不知去向了。

"你已看够了没有?来,我告诉你,"兵士固执地说道,扯我的臂想把我拖开。

"他死了吗?"我问,在早晨的清露里震颤。

"他当然是死了!若使你被人窒闷,你也是死了,"兵士解释道。

"是他干的事吗?那个学生吗?"我喊。

"还有谁?是你吗?也许是我吗?是的。学者就是这样罢,他很聪明地结局那个人,让他的亲同伴处于不利的地位。假使我早知道他是这样的人,我昨天已将那学生杀死了,一拳把他

student yesterday, killed him with one blow. Bang with the fist in the temple—and there'd have been one less villain in the world. You understand what he's done? Now we must go on, so that[1] not a single human eye shall see us in the steppes. Understand? Because today the joiner will be found strangled and robbed. And they will search for the likes of us. 'Where do you come from? Where did you spend the night?' Well, and if they catch us? Even though you and I have nothing... and his revolver is in my breast pocket. That's the difficulty!"

"Throw it away," I advised the soldier.

"Throw it away?" said he reflecting. "It's a valuable thing. And perhaps they won't catch us just yet. No, I won't throw it away... Who knows that the joiner had arms on him? I won't throw it away. It's worth about three roubles. There's a bullet in it. Ah, me! What would I not give to fire this very bullet into our dear comrade's ear[2]. How much money has the dog carried off? Eh? Anathema!"

"So much for the joiner's daughters!" said I.

"Daughters? What daughters? Ah, his daughters. Well, they'll grow up; they won't marry us. There's no talk about them[3]. Let's be

---

1 so that：to the end that俾得；为的是。

2 what would I not give...：若使我能够……，要我出什么代价都可以。

3 there's no talk about them：we need not talk about them我们用不着谈她们。

了结。一拳打到额头——世上也少一个无赖汉了。你知道他干了什么吗？现在我们必得望〔往〕前走去，才不会有人看见我们在草原里。你懂得吗？因为今天人们会发现这个细木匠被人绞死同掠夺了。他们会去寻觅我们这类的人。他们会盘问：'你从那里来？你在那里过夜？'比如他们抓到了我们，要怎么办呢？就说你我并没有什么钱……而且他的手枪是在我的上衣袋里。这真是困难！"

"扔去罢，"我劝兵士。

"扔去？"他沉思着说道。"这是一件值钱的东西。也许他们现在还不会抓到我们。不，我不肯扔它去……谁知道细木匠身边带有武器？我不肯扔去。那差不多值得三卢布。里面还有一粒子弹。啊，天呀！我有什么东西舍不得，若使我能够把这粒子弹从我们亲爱同伴的耳朵打进去。那条狗拿去多少钱呢？呀？这个该咒的人！

"细木匠女儿们的款全被这东西拿去了！"我说。

"女儿？什么女儿？啊，他的女儿。她们自然会长大，她们又不会嫁给我们。不要谈她们罢。让我们跑开，兄弟，快

off[1], brother, quickly. —Which way are we to go?"

"I don't know, it's all the same."

"I don't know either, and I know it's all the same. Let's go to the right. The sea must be there."

We went to the right.

I looked back. Far away in the steppes rose a dark mound, and above it shone the sun.

"You're looking to see if he is risen. No fear[2], he won't get up and follow us. The student's a skillful lad, you see he's settled him thoroughly. What a comrade! He's done for[3] us well. Alas, brother, people get worse from year to year; they are always getting worse," said the soldier in a sad voice.

The steppes, silent and deserted, flooded with the morning sun, stretched all round us, melting on the horizon into the sky with such a clear, such a caressing, generous light, that every black and unjust deed appeared impossible in the midst of this immense simplicity, this open plain covered over by the blue dome of the sky.

"I could devour anything, brother," said my companion, making himself a cigarette[4].

---

1 to be off: to go away 离开。

2 no fear: not likely 大概不会。

3 to do for: to spoil the prospect of 损害某人的前途。

4 making himself a cigarette: 外国下等人常带着烟叶同纸，自己卷纸烟抽。

点。——我们望〔往〕那条路走去呢?"

"我不知道,都是一样的罢。"

"我也不知道,我只晓得都是一样的。我们向右边走罢。海一定是在那边。"

我们向右边走去。

我回头一望。在草原的远方涌起一座黑色的小山冈,太阳在上面照耀着。

"你是瞧着他会起来吗?大概不会,他不会站起,跟我们走。学生是一个伶俐的小孩,你看他彻底地把他了结了。这么一个同伴!他真害我们不浅。唉,兄弟,一年一年人们更坏了;他们总是愈变愈坏,"兵士用种悲哀的声音说道。

草原,静默无人的,充溢着清晨的阳光,布在我们的四旁,边际溶入天空时是带有这么清晰的,这么爱抚的,英俊的光线,一切黑暗的同不义的举动好像是不可能的,在这个庞大的单纯诚实之中,这个给蓝色的穹苍盖着的旷野。

"什么东西我都能够吃进去,兄弟,"我的伴侣说,一面自己卷一根纸烟。

"What shall we eat today? And where? And how?"

A puzzle.

At this point my neighbour in the hospital ward finished his tale, saying:

"That's all. I got very friendly with this soldier and we went together to the Kars district. He was kind and a man of experience, a typical bare-footed tramp. I respected him. We went on together to Asia Minor, and then we lost sight of each other."

"Do you remember the joiner sometimes?" asked I.

"As you see—or rather as you have heard."

"And—feel nothing?"

He laughed.

"What ought I to feel about it? I am not to blame[1] for what happened to him, as you are not to blame for what happened to me. And nobody is to blame for anything, for we are all alike—beasts."

---

1 to be to blame: to deserve censure 该受责备。

"今天我们吃什么呢？在那里吃呢？怎么吃呢？"

一个难题。

医院病房里我的邻人在这点结束他的故事了，说道：

"就是这些了。我同这个兵士很要好起来，我们一同到喀斯区。他是个仁爱的，有经验的人，一个十足的赤脚漂泊者。我敬重他。我们一同到小亚细亚，然后我们彼此分散了。"

"你有时还记起细木匠吗？"我问。

"记起来正同你所看见的——或者应当说正同你所听的。"

"不觉得——什么情感吗？"

他大笑了。

"我该觉得什么情感？他所碰到的事情与我无干，好像我所碰到的事情是与你无干的。无论什么事情发生，都不能把罪名搁在谁的身上，因为我们都是一样的——禽兽。"

The Khan and His Son

There lived once in the Crimea a Khan, Mosolayma-el-Asrab, and he had a son called Tolayk-Algalla.

With these words the blind Tartar beggar, seated with his back against the bright brown stem of an arbutus, began to relate one of those old legends of the peninsula, so rich in memories of the past. Round the story-teller a group of Tartars in bright-coloured khalats[1] and golden broidered caps were seated on fragments of stone that time had detached from the palace of some ancient Khan. It was evening, and the sun was slowly sinking into the sea; its red rays pierced the masses of dark green foliage surrounding the ruins and fell in bright spots on the moss-grown stones and the trails of

---

1 khalats：大概是衣服名字罢。

可汗同他的儿子

克里米亚从前有一个可汗,摩索雷马·厄尔·阿萨剌布,他有一个儿子,叫做托雷克·阿尔加拉。

用这些话,那个盲目的鞑靼叫花子,他的背靠在一棵杨梅的明媚棕色树干上,开始叙述这个半岛里一个旧传说,这半岛是很富于值得纪念的过去事情。围着这个说故事的人有一群鞑靼人,穿着颜色鲜明的衣服,戴着绣金的帽子,坐在残石上,那是古代某一位可汗的宫殿经过悠长的岁月分析出来的。这是黄昏时候,太阳慢慢地沉到海里去;它的红色光线穿透废墟四围的几丛暗绿色簇叶,射下鲜明的光点到苔侵的石上,同爬壁

clinging green ivy. The wind sang in the branches of the old planetrees and their leaves rustled as if invisible streams of water were flowing through the air. The blind beggar's voice was weak and shaky, and his stony face expressed nothing in its wrinkles but repose. The words he knew by heart[1] flowed one after the other and presented to his hearers a picture of the past days, rich in strength of feeling.

The Khan was old (said the blind man), but he had many women in his harem[2]. They loved the old man because he still had his meed of strength and fire and his caresses[3] were tender and burning, and women will always love him who can caress with strength, even if [4] he is grey, even if his face is wrinkled. Beauty lies in strength, and not in a soft skin and rosy cheeks.

They all loved the Khan, but he himself favoured a Cossack prisoner from the Dnieper steppes and always loved her more passionately than the other women of his harem, his large harem of three hundred women of all countries. Each was as beautiful as the spring flowers, and they all lived comfortably. The Khan ordered many sweet and tasty viands for them, and sufferd them to dance and play when they liked.

---

1 to know by heart: to have learnt by committing to memory 心中记忆着。
2 harem: 可汗的内院，里面藏有许多美女，好像中国的六宫。

的绿藤的尾端。风儿在筱悬木老树的枝里歌唱着,它们的叶子沙沙作响,好像有看不出的水流从空中流过去。盲目叫花子的声音是微弱的,振动的,他那硬得像石头的脸孔在它皱纹上没有现出别的,只是安详镇静。他心里熟记的话一字追着前一字流出,画在他的听众目前一幅过去事情的图画,富于强烈的情感的。

可汗是老了(瞎子说道),但是他有许多姬妾在他内院里。她们爱这个老头子,因为他还具有力气和火气这两个好处,他的拥抱是温柔而热烈得像火汤一样,女人始终会爱能够有力地拥抱的人,就说他的头发是花白了,就说他的脸孔满是皱纹。美是在乎力气,并不在于一片软弱的皮肤,一双玫瑰色的面靥。

她们都爱可汗,但是他特别喜一个从第聂珀尔草原来的哥萨克女囚,他爱她胜过他内院里的一切其他姬妾,他的大内院藏有三百个各国女子。个个都长得同春天的花一样的美丽,她们都过舒服的生活。可汗叫人们拿许多甜蜜可口的食物给她们,让她们随便跳舞嬉戏。

---

3 caress:拥抱。但是这个字隐含有其它意义,几乎包括尽一切性的行为。

4 even if: although 虽然。

He often called his Cossack girl to him in the tower, where you could see the sea, and where he had prepared for her all that a woman can need to make her life joyful: sweetmeats and all sorts of rich fabrics, gold and stones of many colours, music and rare birds from distant lands, and the burning caresses of the enamoured Khan. In this tower he amused himself with her for whole days, resting from the toil of his life in the knowledge[1] that his son Algalla would not lower the renown of the Khanate when like a wolf he raided the Russian steppes, whence he always returned with rich spoils, with new women, with new glory, leaving behind him terror and ashes, corpses and blood.

Once Algalla returned from a raid into Russia and great festivities were held in his honour. All the mirzas[2] of the peninsula came to them; there were games and feastings, and they shot arrows from their bows into the eyes of the prisoners, trying who had the greatest strength in the arm; and again they drank and extolled the bravery of Algalla, the terror of his enemies, the support of the Khanate. The old Khan was much pleased at his son's glory. It was good for him, an old man, to know that when he died, the Khanate would be in strong hands.

---

1 in the knowledge: knowing 知道。

2 mirza: the common title of honor for men in Persia, usually prefixed to the surname 波斯贵人的尊称,常放在姓氏前面。

他常召他的哥萨克女人到塔里同他住在一起，在那儿你们能够望见海，在那里他预备了一个女人所能需要的使她生活快乐的一切东西：糖渍果物，各种富丽的织物，金器，许多彩色的宝石，音乐，远处来的珍禽，同入迷的可汗火一般热的拥抱。在这个塔里，他整天同她闹着玩，从他一生的劳苦里休息下来，知道他的儿子阿尔加拉不会坠可汗领土的威名，当这个儿子像一只凶狼蹂躏俄国的草原，从那里回来时他总是带有丰富的掠夺品，新得的女人，新的光荣，剩下在他后面的是恐惧同劫灰，死尸同血。

有一次阿尔加拉到俄国大施侵掠一下回来，可汗领土里举行盛大的庆祝来恭维他。半岛里一切的皇族同大官都来参与大典，有游戏，有宴会，他们用他们的弓箭射到俘虏的眼睛里面，比一比谁的臂力顶强；他们又饮祝歌颂阿尔加拉的骁勇，那是他敌人的恐怖，可汗领土的支撑。老可汗看到他儿子的光荣心里很高兴。这对于他，一个老人，是件快意之事，知道当他死去之后，可汗领土是在一个英猛的人手里。

It was good for him to know this, and wishing to show his son the strength of his love, he spoke to him before all the mirzas and beks[1] who were there at the feast. Holding his goblet in his hand he said: "My own dear son, Algalla! Glory to Allah[2]! And glory be to the name of his prophet[3]."

They all sang in a chorus of powerful voices a hymn to the glory of the name of the prophet, and then the Khan said: "Allah is great! Even in my lifetime he has renewed my youth in my brave son; I see with my old eyes that when the sun will be shut off from them, and when the worms will gnaw at my heart, I shall live again in my son. Allah is great and Mahomet is his true prophet! I have a good son; his arm is strong, his heart is brave, his mind is clear. What do you wish your father's hands to give you, Algalla? Speak and I will give you all that you desire."

The old Khan's voice had hardly died away when Tolayk-Algalla rose with flashing eyes, black as the sea at night and burning as the eyes of a mountain eagle.

"O monarch and father, " he said, "give me the Russian prisoner[4]."

---

1 bek：大概是官名罢。
2 Allah：The Supreme Being 亚拉伯人和回教徒对于上帝的称呼。
3 his prophet：Mahomet 谟罕默德是上帝的预言者。
4 Russian prisoner：哥萨克是俄国的一部，所以这里所谓俄国女囚就他觉得高兴知道了这一点，想表示出给他儿子看他慈爱之情的强烈，他就当宴会上一切皇族高官面前向他儿子说话。他手里举起酒杯说道："我亲爱的亲儿子，阿尔加拉！饮祝上帝的光荣！赞扬他预言者的名字！"

他们用雄壮的声音合唱出一首赞扬他预言者的名字的诗篇，然后可汗说道："上帝是伟大的！甚至于当我在世之日，他在我勇敢儿子身上恢复了我的青春；我的老眼看出当我的双眼看不见阳光，蠕虫咬嚼我的心时候，我将重活在我儿子身上。上帝是伟大的，谟罕默德是他真正的预言者！我有一个好儿子，他的臂是有力气的，他的心是勇敢的，他的思想是清晰的。你要你父亲拿什么给你呢，阿尔加拉？你说罢，我就给你一切你所要的。"

老可汗的话几乎还没有讲完，托雷克·阿尔加拉目光炯炯地站起来，他的眼睛是同夜里的海一样地黑，像山鹰的利目那样燃烧着。

"啊，皇上，父亲，"他说，"给我那个俄国女囚犯。"

是指那个哥萨克女囚。

The Khan was silent, silent only as long as was necessary to quell the shudder in his heart, and after his silence he said in a loud, firm voice: "Take her! When the feast is over you may take her..."

The daring Algalla flushed with delight, his eagle eyes sparkled with great joy; he stood up to his full height, and said to the Khan his father: "I know what you give me, sovereign and father—I know it, I am your slave—your son. Take my blood, a drop each hour—twenty deaths will I die for you! "

"I want nothing, " said the Khan, and his grey head, crowned with the glory of long years and many great deeds, sank on his breast.

Soon the feast was over, and they both went out of the palace to the harem, walking side by side in silence.

The night was dark; neither the moon nor the stars could be seen, and clouds covered the sky like a thick curtain.

For a long time they went on in silence, and at last Khan-el-Asrab spoke:

"Day by day[1] my life is ebbing—my old heart beats ever slower and slower, there is always less fire in my breast. The light and warmth of my life were that Cossack girl's ardent caresses. Tell me, Tolayk, tell me—is she really necessary for you? Take a hundred of

---

1 day by day: as the days pass 天天过去。

可汗默然,只是在压下当下心里的战栗时默然,默然之后,他用一种洪亮的,坚决的声音说道:"带她去!当宴会散时,你可以带她去……"

精悍的阿尔加拉欢喜得满脸都是红光,他的鹰目也高兴得锋棱四射;他巍巍地直立起来,向他的父亲,可汗,说:"我晓得你给我的是什么,父王——我晓得。我是你的奴才——你的儿子。拿我的血去,每点钟一滴慢慢地磨折也可以——我肯为你尝二十次死的苦痛!"

"我是什么也不要的,"可汗说,他那已经斑白的头,戴有老年的同许多功绩的光荣,沉在胸前。

不久,宴会完了,他们两人默然从宫里望内院并肩走去。

夜是黑沉沉的;不能见到月亮同星群,云遮着天空像一幅挂幕。

有许多时候他们默然走着,最后厄尔·阿萨剌布可汗说:

"一天一天我的生命销沉了——我的心总是跳动得一天比一天慢,我胸里的火总是渐渐减少了。我生命现在的光和热是在于那个哥萨克女人热烈的拥抱。告诉我,托雷克,告诉我——她于你真是必须的吗?拿我一百个姬妾去——把她们都带走,

my wives —take them all, instead of her."

Tolayk-Algalla sighed and was silent.

"How many days have I left me? I have few days more on the earth. She is the last joy of my life—this Russian girl. She knows me, she loves me; who will love me when she is not there—me, an old man? Who? Not one of them all, not one, Algalla!"

Algalla was silent.

"How shall I live knowing that you are embracing her, that she is kissing you? For a woman we are not father and son, Tolayk; for a woman we are all men, my son! It were better if all the old wounds on my body had opened, Tolayk, that my blood had flowed out—it were better if I did not survive this night, my son!"

His son remained silent. They stopped at the door of the harem, and silently, their heads sunk on their breasts; they stood long before it. Darkness was around them, clouds chased across the sky, the wind shook the trees and seemed to be singing to them.

"Father, I have long loved her," said Algalla quietly.

"I know it, and I know that she does not love you," said the Khan.

"My heart is torn when I think of her!"

"What is my old heart full of now?"

And again they were silent. Algalla sighed.

却把她剩下罢。"

托雷克·阿尔加拉不言,只是叹息。

"我还剩有多少日子呢?我在世上没有多少日子了。她是我一生里最后的欣欢——这个俄国女子。她了解我,她爱我;谁会爱我,当她不在这儿时候——我,一个老头子?谁?她们里没有一个会爱我,没有一个,阿尔加拉!"

阿尔加拉默然。

"我怎么能够过活,当我知道你正拥抱她,她正在吻你?争一个女人时,我们不是父子,托雷克;争一个女人时,我们都不过是男人们,我的儿子!那到〔倒〕是还好些,若使我身上一切旧创伤都裂口了,托雷克,那么我的血可以流出——那还好些,若使我活不过今夜,我的儿子!"

他的儿子还是默然。他们停在内院门口,他们的头沉在他们胸前,他们默然地在门外站了许久。黑暗围着他们,云儿在天上追逐着,风儿吹摇树林,好像向他们歌唱。

"父亲,我久已爱上她了,"阿尔加拉安详地说。

"我知道,我也知道她不爱你,"可汗说。

"我的心是裂碎了,当我想起她!"

"我的老心现在是充满了什么呢?"

他们又默然。阿尔加拉微叹。

"I see what the wise mollah[1] told me is true. Woman is alway harmful to man. If she is beautiful she arouses in others the desire to possess her, and her husband is given over[2] to the pangs of jealousy. If she is ugly, her husband is envious of others, and suffers from envy. If she is neither pretty nor ugly, the man imagines she is beautiful, and understanding that he has made a mistake again suffers through her—through a woman."

"Wisdom is no medicine for[3] the pains of the heart, " said the Khan.

"Father, we must pity each other."

The Khan raised his head and looked sorrowfully at his son.

"Let us kill her, " said Tolayk.

The Khan thought a moment; then he quietly murmured: "You love yourself better than her and me."

"Yes, and you too."

Again they were silent.

"Yes, and I too, " said the Khan sadly. Grief had made him a child.

"Well, shall we kill her? "

"I cannot give her to you, I cannot! " said the Khan.

---

1 mollah: 师，土耳其的尊称语。

2 to be given over: to addict one's self to 专务。

3 to be no medicine for: cannot cure 不能医。

"我看出智慧的先生告诉我的话是对的。女人对于男子总是有害的。若使她长得美丽,她引起别人想占有她,她丈夫就得受猜忌的苦痛了。若使她是丑的,她丈夫是嫉妒别人的妻子,沉溺于嫉妒的苦痛。若使她既不美,也不丑,那么男人起先以为她是美的,知道了他错了、又因为她而受苦——因为一个女人。"

"智慧不能医心的剧痛,"可汗说。

"父亲,我们应当互相矜怜。"

可汗抬起他的头,悲哀地望着他的儿子。

"让我们把她杀死,"托雷克说。

可汗想一会儿;然后他温和地低声说,"你爱自己胜过爱她同爱我"。

"是的,你也是这样。"

他们又默然。

"是的,我也是一样的,"可汗悲哀地说道。悲哀使他变成一个小孩了。

"呀,我们把她杀死吗?"

"我不能把她让给你,我不能!"可汗说。

"And I can suffer no longer; tear out my heart, or give her to me."

The Khan was silent.

"Or let us throw her into the sea from the cliffs."

"Let us throw her into the sea from the cliffs, " the Khan repeated the words like an echo of his son's voice.

Then they went into the harem, where already she was asleep on the floor on her sumptuous carpet. They stopped before her and looked—they looked long at her. Tears flowed from the old Khan's eyes and ran down his silver beard, where they shone like pearls, and his son stood there with flashing eyes, grinding his teeth to suppress his passion as he aroused the Cossack girl. She awoke: from her face, rosy and delicate as the dawn, her eyes opened out like cornflowers. She did not see Algalla, and stretched out her red lips to the Khan.

"Kiss me, my eagle! "

"Get up—you must come with us, " the Khan said gently.

Then she saw Algalla, and the tears in her eagle's eyes; she was quick to perceive[1], and so understood all.

"I will come, " she said, "I will come. Neither for the one nor for the other? —Is that how you have decided? Strong hearts had to

---

1 quick to perceive: quick to discern 易领悟；悟性好。

"我不能再受苦了；把我的心扯出罢，否则将她让给我。"

可汗默然。

"让我们从悬岩把她掷到海里，好不好。"

"让我们从悬岩把她掷到海里，"可汗也说一遍这句话，好像是他儿子声音的回响。

然后他们走进内院，她已经睡在地板上她那富丽地毡之上了。他们站在她面前，望着——他们对着她望了许久。眼泪从老可汗眼睛涌出，流下他银白的胡须，在那里它们发光像明珠，他儿子站在那里，目光闪烁，咬牙按下他的热情，当他弄醒那哥萨克女子。她醒来：从她的脸孔，玫瑰色的同细嫩的像朝阳，她眼睛睁开好像矢车菊。她没有瞧见阿尔加拉，向可汗伸出她的一双红嘴唇。

"吻我，我的鹰鸟！"

"起来——你非跟我们同走不可，"可汗温和地说。

她就看见阿尔加拉了，和她鹰鸟眼中的泪珠；她是聪明颖悟的，所以立刻了解全部的情形。

"我一定跟你们同走，"她说，"我一定走。既不让这个占住，也不让那个占住？——你们是这样决定吗？气魄雄壮的人

decide thus! I will come."

Then all three went towards the sea in silence. They went by narrow paths, and the wind howled loudly.

The girl was frail, and soon became tired, but she was proud and did not want to tell them.

When the Khan's son noticed that she was staying behind them, he said to her, "Are you afraid?"

Her eyes sparkled at him and she showed him her bleeding feet.

"Let me carry you," said Algalla, holding out his arms to her. But she put her arms round the neck of her old eagle. The Khan lifted her up like a feather and carried her, while she resting in his arms, bent the branches away from his face for fear[1] they might hurt his eyes. Long they walked on, and at last they heard the sound of the sea in the distance. Then Tolayk, who was following them along the footpath, said to his father, "Let me go in front, or I shall desire to stab you in the neck with my dagger."

"Pass on. Allah will fulfil your desire or forgive it—His will be done. I, your father, forgive you. I know what it is to love."

At last the sea lay before them. There, far below them was space, black and boundless. Dully the waves sang at the foot of the rocks; it was dark down there, and cold, and terrible.

---

1 for fear: lest 恐。

们应该这样决定！我一定走。"

于是三个人默然望〔往〕海走去。他们顺着窄路走，狂风怒吼着。

那个女子身体孱弱，很快就累了，但是她很骄矜，不想告诉他们。

当可汗的儿子看见她滞在他们后面，他向她说，"你害怕吗？"

她的眼睛向他闪烁，她指她流血的脚给他看。

"让我抱你走，"阿尔加拉说，向她伸出他的双臂。但是她将双臂围住她老鹰鸟的颈项。可汗把她举起，像一根羽毛，抱着她走，她就躺他怀里，把树枝从他面前拨开，怕的是它们会伤他的眼睛。他们走了许久，最后他们听到远处海里波涛的声音。托雷克本来是跟他们缘着小路走，那时对他父亲说道，"让我在前面走，否则我会想用我的短剑刺进你的颈项"。

"走过去罢。上帝会满足你的欲望，或者赦宥你这罪恶——愿上帝的旨意可以实现。我，你的父亲，赦宥你。我知道恋爱是使人不顾一切。"

最后，大海躺在他们面前。在那里，远在他们下面，是一片黑暗的同无边的空旷，波浪在悬岩脚旁单调地唱着；下面是黑暗的，冰冷的，可怕的。

"Farewell, " said the Khan, kissing the girl.

"Farewell, " said Algalla, bowing to her.

She looked down where the waves were singing and shrank back pressing her hands to her breast.

"Throw me down! " she said to them.

Algalla stretched out his arms to her and groaned, but the Khan took her in his arms, pressed her tightly to his breast, and kissed her; then, lifting her above his head, he threw her over the cliff.

Below the waves dashed and sang; so loud were they that neither of them heard when she reached the water, not a cry nor a sound did they hear. The Khan sank on the rocks and silently looked down into the darkness and distance, where the sea was merged in the clouds, whence swept the dull sound of the splashing waves and the wind came flying past and blew about his grey beard. Tolayk stood by him, hiding his face in his hands, motionless and speechless as a stone. Time passed and the clouds sped over the sky one after another, chased by the wind. Dark and heavy they were, like the thoughts of the old Khan who lay above the sea at the top of the high cliffs.

"Father, let us go, " said Tolayk.

"Wait, " whispered the Khan, as if listening. Again time sped by, the waves splashed below, and the wind flew over the rocks and howled in the trees.

"别矣，"叮汁说，吻着那女子。

"别矣，"阿尔加拉说，向她鞠躬着。

她俯视波涛歌唱的地方，向后退缩；她两手压住她的胸部。

"把我扔下罢！"她对他们说道。

阿尔加拉向她伸出他的双臂，发出呻吟，但是可汗双臂抱着她，紧紧地搂着她在他胸前，吻她；然后，将她提到头上，他从悬岩把她扔下去。

下面波涛泼溅歌唱；它们的声音是这么响，他们都没有听到她落进海里的声音，他们没有听到一声呼喊，或者一些别的声音。可汗气馁地坐在石上，默然地向黑暗同远处望，在那里大海跟天边的云溶在一起了，波浪单调的泼溅声也是从那里来，风儿吹过，吹着他斑白的胡子。托雷克站在他身旁，他的脸掩在他手里，默然不动，像一块石头。时间消逝去了，云儿被狂风吹得在天上接连着疾飞。这些云是黑暗的，沉重的，像老可汗心里的思想，他躺在削壁的顶端，高临海面。

"父亲，我们回去罢，"托雷克说。

"等一下，"可汗低声说，好像正细聆着。时间又消逝了，浪花在下面泼溅，风儿在悬岩之上飞驰，树林里怒吼。

"Father, let us go."

"Wait a little longer."

Many times did Tolayk-Algalla say: "Father, let us go." But the Khan would not move from the place where he had lost the joy of his remaining days.

But everything has an end! At last he rose, vigorous and proud; he rose, frowned, and said in a hollow voice, "Let us go."

They went, but soon the Khan stopped.

"But why am I going, Tolayk, and where? " he asked his son. "Why should I live now, when all my life was in her? I am old, no one will love me again, and if nobody loves you it is senseless to live in the world."

"You have glory and riches, father."

"Give me one of her kisses, and you may have all those as a reward. They are dead, it is only the love of woman that lives. If he has not that love, man has not life—he is a beggar and his days are pitiable. Farewell, my son; may Allah's blessing rest on your head, and remain with you for all the days and nights of your life! " And the Khan turned his face to the sea.

"Father, " cried Tolayk, "father! " —And he could say no

"父亲，我们回去罢。"

"再等一会儿。"

托雷克说了许多次："父亲，我们回去罢。"但是可汗不肯离开他失丢他余年的欣欢的地方。

但是一切事总有个结束！最后他站起来，有精力的同骄傲的；他站起来，皱一下眉头，用一种渺茫的声音说道，"我们回去罢。"

他们走了，但是很快可汗停步不前。

"我为什么走着，托雷克，到那里去呢？"他问他的儿子。"我现在为什么活着，我一切的生命既然都在她身上？我老了，谁也不会再爱我了，若使没有人爱你，活在世上真是无意义呀。"

"你有光荣同财富，父亲。"

"给我她的一吻，这许多都可以送给你做报酬。这些东西是死的，只有女人的爱是活的。若使他没有那个爱，他是没有生命——他是个叫花子，他的生活是可怜悯的。别矣，我的儿子；希望上帝的祝福降临你头上，老同你在一起，当你活在人世时候！"可汗转过脸来望着海。

"父亲，"托雷克喊道，"父亲！"——他不能再说什么了，

more, for you can say nothing to man on whom death smiles[1], you can say nothing which would restore the love of life to his soul.

"Let me go..."

"Allah..."

"He knows..."

With rapid steps the Khan went to the edge of the cliff and threw himself down. His son did not prevent him—he could not, for there was not time. Again nothing was heard from the sea, not a cry, not the noise of the Khan's fall. Only the waves splashed below and the wind droned wild songs.

Long did Tolayk-Algalla look down the cliff; at last he said aloud: "Give me too such a strong heart, O Allah!"

Then he went into the darkness of night...

Thus perished Khan Mosolayma-el-Asrab, and Khan Tolayk-Algalla reigned in the Crimea.

---

1 on whom death smiles: 当一个人厌倦于无聊的生活,想解脱烦恼,投到永寂的怀中时,我们可以说死神向他现出笑脸,因为他觉得死是可乐的。

因为你对于一个人不能说什么,当死神向他微笑,你不能说出什么话,能够使他的灵魂又具有对于生命的留恋。

"让我去罢……"

"上帝……"

"他晓得……"

可汗快步走到削壁的边端,投身下去。他儿子没有阻止他——他不能够,因为来不及了。又是从海里听不到什么别的声音,听不到一声呼喊,听不到可汗掉下的声音。只是波涛在下面泼溅着,风儿单调地发出狂歌。

托雷克从悬岩俯视了许久,最后他大声说道:"也给我一个这么英猛的心罢,啊,上帝!"

于是他走进夜的黑暗里去……

这样子摩索雷马·厄尔·阿萨剌布可汗死了,托雷克·阿尔加拉可汗开始统治克里米亚了。

Youth
青　春
（英汉对照）

Joseph Conrad　著

梁遇春　译注

"世界文学名著"之一，上海北新书局，1931年6月付印，1931年7月出版

Joseph Conrad

（1857—1924）

　　他的名字正式写起来是 Teodor Josef Konrad Korzeniowski。他的父亲是波兰的地主，非常爱国，总想使波兰能够恢复独立的地位。一八六三年革命失败，被流徙到 Vologda 去。他的母亲自愿也到这荒凉的地方去做苦工，跟她丈夫作伴，可是身体太弱，不久就过世了。他父亲后来虽然放回来，可惜没有多久也死了。于是我们这位二十年沧海寄身的文豪十二岁时就成为一个孤儿。

　　他幼年时候对于海就有极强的趣味，成人后决心当个舟子，不管戚友种种劝诱，终于扬帆跟孤舟去相依为命。他的父亲曾将莎士比亚，嚣俄译成荷文，他很早就博览文学作品，深有文学情调。海上无事时随便写下一本长篇小说，有时间断，有时接续下去，一共写了五年，脱稿后还搁置了许久。后来偶然碰到一位搭客，读他的稿子，劝他出版，这算做他文学生涯的开始，这位上帝派来的搭客就是现在英国最伟大的小说家 John Galsworthy。

　　他的著作都是以海洋做题材，但是他不像普通海洋作家那样只会肤浅地描写海上的风浪；他是能抓到海上的一种情调，写出满纸的波涛，使人们有一个整个的神秘感觉。他对于船仿佛看做是一个人，他书里的每只船都有特别的性格，简直跟别个小说家书里的英雄一样。然而，他自己最注重的却是船里面个个海员性格的刻划。他的人物不是代表那一类人的，每人有他绝对显明的个性，你念过后永不会忘却，但是写得一点不勉强，一点不夸张，这真是像从作者的灵魂开出的朵朵鲜花。这几个妙处凑起来使他的小说愈读，回甘的意味愈永。

他的著作有二十余册，最有名的是 *Lord Jim*，*The Nigger of the Narcissus*，*Nostromo* 等长篇小说，*Youth*，*Typhon*，*The Heart of Darkness* 等短篇小说，还有几本散文 *A Personal Record*，*The Mirror of the Sea*，*Notes on Life and Letters*，里面尤以《海镜》极能道出海的无限神秘。

这篇是他最有名的短篇小说，里面的事实却是真的，那是他在一八八一年第一次来东方去的冒险故事。亲身经历过的事情因为对于自己太有趣味了，写出来常常平凡得可怜。自己觉得有意思，就以为别人一定也会喜欢，这是许多自传式小说家的毛病。一篇自述的东西能够写得这么好像完全出于幻想的，玲珑得似非人世间的事实，从这一点也可以看出这位老舟子的艺术手腕同成就了。

Youth

This could have occurred nowhere but in England, where men and sea interpenetrate, so to speak[1] —the sea entering into the life of most men, and the men knowing something or everything about the sea, in the way of[2] amusement, of travel, or of bread-winning.

We were sitting round a mahogany table that reflected the bottle, the claret-glasses, and our faces as we leaned on our elbows. There was a director of companies, an accountant, a lawyer, Marlow, and myself. The director had been a Conway boy, the accountant had served four years at sea, the lawyer—a fine crusted[3] Tory, High

---

1 so to speak: if I may say thus 若使我可以这样说。
2 in the way of: as regards 关于。
3 crusted: inveterate 根深蒂固的；顽梗的。

青　春

这件事只能发生于英国，别的地方都不行，因为在英国，人同海可以说是互相贯穿——海走进许多人的生活里面去，人们也都知道一些，也许完全晓得，海上的娱乐，海上的旅行，或者海上挣面包的生涯。

我们围着一个乌木桌子，它反映出酒瓶，红葡萄酒酒杯，同我们的脸孔，当我们倚肘而坐。一个是公司经理，一个是会计员，一个是律师，一个叫做马罗，还有一个是我。公司经理从前是昆威船上的水手，会计员在海上服务过四年，律师——一个值得敬爱的根深蒂固的保守党，高派教会信徒，是一个极

Churchman[1], the best of old fellows, the soul of honour—had been chief officer in the P. & O. service in the good old days when mail-boats were square-rigged at least on two masts, and used to come down the China Sea before a fair monsoon with stun'sails[2] set alow and aloft. We all began life in the merchant service. Between the five of us there was the strong bond of the sea, and also the fellowship of the craft, which no amount of enthusiasm for yachting, cruising, and so on[3] can give, since one is only the amusement of life and the other is life itself.

Marlow (at least I think that is how he spelt his name)[4] told the story, or rather the chronicle, of a voyage: —

"Yes, I have seen a little of the Eastern seas; but what I remember best is my first voyage there, You fellows know there are those voyages that seem ordered for the illustration of life, that might stand for[5] a symbol of existence. You fight, work, sweat, nearly kill yourself, sometimes do kill yourself, trying to accomplish something —and you can't. Not from any fault of yours. You simply can do

---

1 High Church: party attaching much importance to ceremonies and symbols 英国注重仪式派的教会。

2 stun'sails: studding sail; light sail set at the side of a principal square sail in free wind 补助帆。

3 and so on: and more of the similar kind 和其它同类的事情。

4 Marlow: 这个字本来应当拼做 Marlowe, 后面这个 e 字却没有音, 粗人拼这个字时常把它省略了, 所以这里这样说。

好的老头子，一位知耻的君子——曾经当俾·奥公司船上的大副，在从前好日子时候，那时邮船最少有两只桅装了横帆，常乘一阵合式的时令风走下中国海，低处高处都安有许多补助帆。我们大家起始都是靠着商船谋生。所以在我们五个人里面，有海这个坚固的关系，还有同行的友谊，这种亲切之感是对于游艇，航行取乐和其它海上玩意儿的任何热心都不能给的，因为一个只是人生的游戏，而那个却是人生本身的事情。

马罗（最少我相信他自己是这样子拼他的名字）说出某一次航行的故事，或者还是说某一次航行史比较妥当些：——

"是的，我也见过一些东半球的海；但是我记得最清楚的是我第一次到那里去的航行。你们诸位知道有些航行好像是上天安排好来做人生的解释，它简直可以说是人生的象征。你奋斗，你工作，你出汗，你几乎把自己杀死，有时的确把你自己杀死，只是为着要干一件事情——而结果你不能成功。并不是因为你有什么错处。你无非什么也做不好，无论大小的事情——简直

---

5 to stand for: to be the representative of 代表。

nothing, neither great not little—not a thing in the world—not even marry an old maid, or get a wretched 600-ton cargo of coal to its port of destination.

"It was altogether a memorable affair. It was my first voyage to the East, and my first voyage as second mate; it was also my skipper's[1] first command. You'll admit it was time[2]. He was sixty if a day[3], a little man, with a broad, not very straight back, with bowed shoulders and one leg more bandy than the other, he had that queer twisted-about[4] appearance you see so often in men who work in the fields. He had a nutcracker face—chin and nose trying to come together over a sunken mouth—and it was framed in iron-gray fluffy hair, that looked like a chin-strap of cotten-wool sprinkled with coal-dust. And he had blue eyes in that old face of his, which were amazingly like a boy's, with that candid expression some quite common men preserve to the end of their days by a rare internal gift of simplicity of heart and rectitude of soul. What induced him to accept me was a wonder. I had come out of a crack[5] Australian clipper[6], where I

---

1 skipper: captain of ship, especially of small trading ship 船主，特别指小商船的船主。

2 time: a period of time as favorable for something 宜于某件事的时期；适当的时候。

3 He was sixty, if a day: 假使我们承认他活过一天，我们就得承认他是六十岁了。这无非是一种加重语气。

4 twisted-about: distorted; warped 扭歪的。

世界上没有一件事你能够做——甚至于连娶一个老处女，或者把无聊的六百吨煤运到原定地的港口都办不到。

"那次航行从头到尾是个值得纪念的事情。那是我第一次到东方去的航行，又是我第一次当二副的航行，又是我船主第一次带船。你们会承认这是个极有意思的时候。他最少也有六十岁了；一个身材矮小的人，背宽大，却不很直，肩膀弯着，一只腿比那只腿更望〔往〕外曲，他有那种绞扭的形态，在田地上工作的人们所常俱有的。他有一副像破坚果的家伙的脸孔——下巴同鼻子想相遇，把陷进去的嘴遮住——脸的四围有绒毛一样的铁灰色须发，那好像洒有煤灰的棉织围巾。他这副古老脸孔里有一双蓝色的眼睛，出奇地活像一个小孩的眼睛，俱有一种坦白的神情；有些很普通的人们靠着天生难得的纯洁心地同正直胸怀能够一直到死都保存有这种情调。什么使他肯雇我当船员，的确是件奇怪的事。我刚从一条走奥斯大利亚洲的

---

5 crack：of superior excellence；having qualities to be boasted 优美的；值得夸口的。

6 clipper：a kind of fast-sailing vessel, with a sharp bow 船首尖小的轻快船。

175

had been third officer, and he seemed to have a prejudice against crack clippers as aristocratic and high-toned[1]. He said to me, 'You know, in this ship you will have to work.' I said I had to work in every ship I had ever been in. 'Ah, but this is different, and you gentlemen out of them big ships; ... but there! I dare say you will do[2]. Join tomorrow.'

"I joined tomorrow. It was twenty-two years ago; and I was just twenty; How time passes! It was one of the happiest days of my life. Fancy! Second mate for the first time—a really responsible officer! I wouldn't have thrown up my new billet for a fortune. The mate looked me over carefully. He was also an old chap. but of another stamp. He had a Roman nose[3], a snow-white, long beard, and his name was Mahon, but he insisted that it should be pronounced Mann. He was well connected; yet there was something wrong with his luck, and he had never got on[4].

"As to the captain, he had been for years in coasters, then in the Mediterranean, and last in the West Indian trade. He has never been round the Capes. He could just write a kind of sketchy[5] hand, and didn't care for writing at all. Both were thorough good seamen of

---

1 high-toned: elevated; fashionable 尊荣的；时髦的。
2 to do: to serve the purpose 合用。
3 Roman nose: 罗马人鼻梁特别高，高到连高鼻子的西洋人都觉它太高了。
4 to get on: to succeed; prosper 成功；诸事顺利。

上等快帆船出来,我在那里当三副,他对于上等快帆船好像有个偏见,认为是贵族的,时髦的。他对我说,'你知道,在这条船里,你得工作。'我说我一向到无论那一条船都得工作。'啊,可是这里的工作跟你所说的不同,而且你们这班从大船出来的先生们……好罢!我敢说你干得下。明天来加入罢。'

"我第二天去加入。这是二十二年前的事情;那时我才二十岁。时间过得多么快呀!那是我一生里最快乐日子里的一个。请想一想!第一次当二副——一个真真有责任的职务!我不肯把我这个新任命状拿去换百万家产。大副仔细地把我打量一下。他也是个老头子,但是另外一个派头。他有罗马人的高鼻子,雪白的长胡子,他的名字是马洪,但是他坚持这个字该念做冒纳。他的亲友很有权势;然而他的命运总不好,他老没有成功。

"至于船主,他有许多年头都在海岸上来往的小船里,后来到地中海去,最后进走西印度群岛的商船。他从来没有绕过好望角。他只能写出麻糊〔马虎〕的字,根本就不大注意写字。这两位当

---

5 sketchy:lacking detail or finish 缺乏精细。

course, and between those two old chaps I felt like a small boy between two grandfathers.

"The ship also was old. Her name was the Judea. Queer name, isn't it? She belonged to a man Wilmer, Wilcox—some name like that; but he has been bankrupt and dead these twenty years or more, and his name don't matter. She had been laid up in Shadwell basin for ever so long. You may imagine her state. She was all rust, dust, grime—soot aloft, dirt on deck. To me it was like coming out of a palace into a ruined cottage. She was about 400 tons, had a primitive windlass, wooden latches to the doors, not a bit of brass about her, and a big square stern. There was on it, below her name in big letters, a lot of scrollwork, with the gilt off, and some sort of[1] a coat of arms, with the motto 'Do or Die' underneath. I remember it took my fancy[2] immensely. There was a touch[3] of romance in it, something that made me love the old thing—something that appealed to my youth!

"We left London in ballast—sand ballast—to load a cargo of coal in a northerm port for Bankok. Bankok! I thrilled. I had been

---

1 some sort of: something like to 颇像……的东西。
2 to take one's fancy: to please one 称他的心；使他悦意。
3 touch: tinge; trace 色泽；痕迹。

然都是极好的海员，夹在这两个老汉之中，我觉得像一个小孩子跟两个当祖父的人们一起。

"船也是古老的。它的名字是犹太。这是一个奇怪的名字吗？它属于一个叫做维尔麦的，也许是叫做维尔可克斯——大概总是这类的名字罢；但是他破产了，死了，已经有二十年了，或者还要多些，他的名字也是无关紧要的。这只船起先在沙德卫尔小池塘里搁了不少时候。你们可以想像出它的情形。它满身都是铁锈，尘埃，垢腻——上面有烟泥，船面有污秽东西。对于我，这好像从一座皇宫出来，走进一所颓废的茅屋。它是四百吨左右的船，有一个简陋的绞盘车，门闩都是木做的，整个船没有一点铜，有一个四方形的大船尾。船尾上用大字写出它的名字，下面有许多云形装饰，泥金已经脱落了，还画有某种徽章，底下有一句铭语，'工作，否则灭亡。'我记得我非常喜欢这句话。这里面含有浪漫的情绪，有一种色彩使我爱这个老东西——有一种色彩感动了我少年的心境。

"我们离开伦敦时船上带个镇船重物——沙包——去北方一个海港装上煤运到盘谷去。盘谷！我高兴极了。我在海上已经

six years at sea, but had only seen Melbourne and Sydney, very good places, charming places in their way[1]—but Bankok!

"We worked[2] out of the Thames under canvas, with a North Sea pilot on board. His name was Jermyn, and he dodged all day long about the galley drying his handkerchief before the stove. Apparently he never slept. He was a dismal man, with a perpetual tear sparking at the end of his nose, who either had been in trouble, or was in trouble, or expected to be in trouble—couldn't be happy unless something went wrong. He mistrusted my youth, my common-sense, and my seamanship, and made a point of[3] showing it in a hundred little ways. I dare say he was right. It seems to me I knew very little then, and I know not much more now; but I cherish a hate for that Jermyn to this day.

"We were a week working up as far as Yarmouth Roads, and then we got into a gale—the famous October gale of twenty-two years ago. It was wind, lightning, sleet, snow, and a terrific sea. We were flying light, and you may imagine how bad it was when I tell you we had smashed bulwarks and a flooded deck, On the second night she shifted her ballast into the lee bow, and by that time we

---

1 in their way: in their special manner 各有其（好处）。
2 to work: to move or progress laboriously 费劲地前进。
3 to make a point of: to be particular about 非常留心；坚持。

有六年了。但是只见到墨尔本同悉德尼，很好的地方，也各有它的妙处——但是怎么能比得上盘谷呢！

"我们扬帆乘着顺风驶出泰晤士河，有一个北海的引港者在我们船上。它的名字是泽明，他整天躲在船上厨房里面，向着炉火烘干他的手巾。他分明没有睡觉。他是一个悲愁的人，总有一粒眼泪挂在他鼻子尖端发光着，他也许曾经遇到灾难，或者正在灾难之中，或者预料将有灾难来临——不会高兴，除非有什么乱子出来。他瞧不起我的年青，我的常识，同我的驶船本领，一定要用几十个态度来表示他的不信任。我敢说他的意见是对的。我现在觉得那时我知道得很少，现在也没有多知道了许多；但是我一直到如今还怀恨这个泽明。

"我们驶了一星期才走到雅穆斯码头，然后我们遇到狂风——二十二年前有名的十月狂风。那是风，电，冰片，雪花合在一起，海里波涛涌得可怕。我们的船因为太轻就飞飘着，你们可以猜想那是多么不妙，当我告诉你们我们上层甲板的船舷打成碎片，船面同洪水一样。第二晚，它把沙包移到下风边，

had been blown off somewhere on the Dogger Bank. There was nothing for it but¹ go below with shovels and try to right her, and there we were in that vast hold, gloomy like a cavern, the tallow dips² stuck and flickering on the beams, the gale howling above, the ship tossing about like mad on her side³; there we all were, Jermyn, the captain, every one, hardly able to keep our feet, engaged on that gravedigger's work, and trying to toss shovelfuls of wet sand up to wind-ward. At every tumble of the ship you could see vaguely in the dim light men falling down with a great flourish of shovels. One of the ship's boys (we had two), impressed by the weirdness of the scene, wept as if his heart would break. We could hear him blubbering somewhere in the shadows.

"On the third day the gale died out, and by-and-by a north-country tug picked us up. We took sixteen days in all to get from London to the Tyne! When we got into dock we had lost our turn for loading, and they hauled us off to a tier where we remained for a month. Mrs. Beard (the captain's name was Beard) came from Colchester to see the old man. She lived on board. The crew of runners⁴ had left, and there remained only the officers, one boy and the stew-

---

1 nothing for it but: no way of meeting the case but 没有其它对付法子，只好……。

2 dip: candle 洋烛。

3 side: the outer surface of a ship on either side above the water line 船舷水线的两侧。

那时我们已被吹到多革海岸了。没有办法,我们只好拿着铲下去,试把船身弄平,我们就在那广大的船底里,阴森森像一个洞穴,油脂做的烛插在横梁上,闪烁发光,暴风在上面怒号,船斜倾着发狂似地颠簸;我们都在那里,泽明,船主,以及个个人,几乎站不住脚,干这掘墓的勾当,努力把满铲的湿沙掷到上风边。船每翻动一下,你能够在朦胧的光线里模糊见到人们摔交同乱挥铲子。船里一个男仆(我们有两个)感于这个情境的怪异,哭得好似他的心要碎了。我们能够听到他在阴影里某处痛哭着。

"第三天暴风停住了,不久一只北方的拖船把他们检〔捡〕起。我们从伦敦到泰因一共花了十六天!当我们走到船坞,我们装货的时机已经过去了,他们拖我们到一个码头,在那里我们滞了一个月。卑尔太太(船主的名字是卑尔)从科尔拆斯忒来看这个老头子。她就住在船上。野鸡水手都走了,只剩下船员,一个男仆,同一个管事,他是黑人同白人生下的杂种,他叫做亚

---

4 runner:runaway 偷逃的。

ard, a mulatto who answered to the name of Abraham. Mrs. Beard was an old woman, with a face all wrinkled and ruddy like a winter apple, and the figure of a young girl. She caught sight of me once, sewing on a button, and insisted on having my shirts to repair. This was something different from the captains' wives I had known on board crack clippers. When I brought her the shirts, she said: 'And the socks? They want mending, I am sure, and John's—Captain Beard's—things are all in order now. I would be glad of something to do.' Bless the old woman. She over-hauled my outfit for me, and meantime I read for the first time Sartor Resartus[1] and Burnaby's Ride to Khiva[2]. I didn't understand much of the first then; but I remember I preferred the soldier to the philosopher at the time; a preference which life has only confirmed. One was a man, and the other was either more—or less. However, they are both dead and Mrs. Beard is dead, and youth, strength, genius, thoughts, achievements, simple hearts—all dies... No matter.

"They loaded us at last. We shipped a crew. Eight able seamen and two boys. We hauled off [3] one evening to the buoys at the dockgates, ready to go out, and with a fair prospect of beginning the voy-

---

1 Sartor Resartus：英国大思想家 Thomas Carlyle 的杰作，用古怪的文笔说出他那宇宙间万物无非上帝的衣服的哲学思想。
2 Burnaby's Ride to Khiva：大概是一个军人著的书。
3 to haul off: to change the course 驶船离开。

伯拉罕。卑尔太太是个老妇人，满脸皱纹，而且是通红的，像冬天的苹果，她的身材却像个少女。她有一次瞧见我正在缝上一粒钮扣，她坚持要把我的一切汗衫修补好。这跟我所知道的住在上等快帆船上的船主太太的确有些不同。当我把许多汗衫拿去给她修补，她说：'袜子呢，我敢说，它们也需要补缀，约翰的——船主卑尔的——东西现在都料理好了。我很想干些事情。'愿上帝祝福这个老妇人。她把我的行装替我详细检查缝缮过，那时候我第一次读《衣裳哲学》同柏那比的《基发骑行记》。前一本书我不大懂得；但是我记得我喜欢兵士过于哲学家；我后来对于人生的体验更证实了这个偏爱。一个是个俱有人性的人，那一个是超过人性的——或者低于人性的。然而，他们两位都死了，卑尔太太也死了，青春，体力，天才，思想，成功，单纯的心——这一切都死了……不要紧。

"他们最后把我们这只船也装上货了。我们雇了一队水手。八个能干的水手同两个男仆。一天晚上，我们驶开到船坞门口的浮标旁边，预备出去，有个很好的希望，明天可以开始航行。

age next day. Mrs. Beard was to start for home by a late train. When the ship was fast we went to tea. We sat rather silent through the meal—Mahon, the old couple, and I. I finished first, and slipped away for a smoke, my cabin being in a deck-house just against the poop. It was high water, blowing fresh with a drizzle; the double dock-gates were opened, and the steam-colliers were going in and out in the darkness with their lights burning bright, a great plashing of propllers, rattling of winches, and a lot of hailing on the pier-heads. I watched the procession of head-lights gliding high and of green lights gliding low in the night, when suddenly a red gleam flashed at me, vanished, came into view again, and remained. The fore-end of a steamer loomed up close. I shouted down the cabin, 'Come up, quick! ' and then heard a startled voice saying afar in the dark, 'Stop her, sir. ' A bell jingled. Another voice cried warningly, 'We are going right[1] into that barque, sir. ' The answer to this was a gruff 'All right, ' and the next thing was a heavy crash as the steamer struck a glancing[2] blow with the bluff of her bow about our fore-rigging. There was a moment of confusion, yelling, and running about. Steam roared. Then somebody was heard saying. 'All clear sir. '... 'Are you all right?' asked the gruff voice. I had jumped

---

1 right: directly 一直。
2 glancing: striking obliquely 斜击。

卑尔太太将搭晚车动身回家。当船泊好时候,我们去用茶点。吃的时候我们都不大说话——马洪,老夫妇,同我。我先吃完,溜出去抽烟,我的卧室是在甲板室里,刚靠着船尾楼。正是满潮时候,新鲜的海风夹些微雨飞来;船坞的双重门开着,运煤的汽船在黑暗中来来往往,它们的灯明亮地照着,螺旋推进机溅水发出大声,绞车也戛戛作响,码头上有许多呼唤的声音。我注视夜间在高处寂然滑过的一排头灯同在低处寂然滑过的一排绿灯,那时忽然间一线红光向我闪映,立刻隐没了,又看得见,就老滞在那儿。一只汽船的前头涌现在近旁。我向下面船员寝室喊道,'上来,赶快!'然后听到有个惊愕的声音在远处暗中说,'把它停住,先生。'一阵铃响。又一个声音警告地喊道,'我们将一直穿到那只帆船里去了,先生。'这句的回答是个粗暴的,'好了,'过一下子就是个沉重的撞击,当这个汽船的船头峭壁跟我们的齿轮擦过去地碰一下。接着就是暂时的纷乱,呼号同奔跑。蒸气〔汽〕咆哮起来。然后听到一个人说,'全离开了,先生'……'你没有碰坏吗?'那个粗暴的声音问道。我跳

forward to see the damage, and hailed back, 'I think so.' 'Easy astern,' said the gruff voice. A bell jingled. 'What steamer is that?' screamed Mahon. By that time she was no more to us than a bulky shadow maneuvering a little way off. They shouted at us some name— a woman's name, Miranda or Melissa—or some such thing. 'This means another month in this beastly hole,' said Mahon to me, as we peered with lamps about the spintered bulwarks and broken braces. 'But where's the captain?'

"We had not heard or seen anything of him all that time. We went aft to look. A doleful voice arose hailing somewhere in the middle of the dock, 'Judea ahoy!'[1] ... How the devil did he there?... 'Hallo?' we shouted. 'I am adrift in our boat without oars,' he cried. A belated[2] water-man offered his services, and Mahon struck a bargain with him for half-a-crown to tow our skipper alongside; but it was Mrs. Beard that camp up the ladder first. They had been floating about the dock in that mizzly cold rain for nearly an hour. I was never so surprised in my life.

"It appears that when he heard my shout 'Come up' he understood at once what was the matter, caught up his wife, ran on deck, and across, and down into our boat, which was fast to the ladder. Not

---

1 ahoy: used in hailing (nautical term) 海上呼喊时用的话。
2 belated: overtaken by darkness 黑夜追到，来不及回家的。

到前面去瞧一下所受伤害，向他喊道'我想大概没有。''慢慢向后退，'那个粗暴声音又说道。一阵铃响。'那是什么汽船？'马洪尖声问道。这时候它对于我们不过是一个庞大的影子设法驶走一些路了。他们向我们喊出一个名字——一个女人的名字，米兰大或者麦力萨——或者这类其它的名字。'这么一来，在这个兽窟一样的洞里还得滞一个月，'马洪对我说，当我提着灯细看破碎的上层甲板船舷同冲断的舵轴。'但是船主在那儿呢？'

"我们这些时候一点也没有听见他同看到他。我们到船尾去看。一个悲哀的高呼从船坞中间某处出来，'犹太来呀！'……他怎么会鬼混到那里去呢？'唔？'我们叫喊。'我在我们的小船里飘流，没有桨了，'他说。一个在外面滞到太迟了来不及回家的船夫愿意帮忙，马洪同他商好给他半块银币把我们船主拖过来；但是先走上梯子的却是卑尔太太。他们于这轻寒的零雨之下在船坞里差不多飘荡了一个钟头。我一生里没有这么惊愕过。

"事情的经过是如此：当他听到我喊'上来，'他立刻知道是什么事，抓起他的妻子，跑上甲板，跑过去，走到我们的小船，那是

bad for a sixty-year-old. Just imagine that old fellow saving heroically in his arms that old woman—the woman of his life. He set her down on a thwart, and was ready to climb back on board when the painter came adrift somehow, and away they went together. Of course in the confusion we did not hear him shouting. He looked abashed. She said cheerfully, 'I suppose it does not matter my losing the train now?' 'No, Jenny—you go below and get warm, ' he growled. Then to us: 'A sailor has no business with[1] a wife—I say. There I was, out of the ship. Well, no harm done this time. Let's go and look at what that fool of a steamer smashed. '

"It wasn't much, but it belayed us three week. At the end of that time, the captain being engaged with his agents, I carried Mrs. Beard's bag to the railway-station and put her all comfy[2] into a third-class carriage. She lowered the window to say, 'You are a good young man. If you see John—Captain Beard—without his muffler at night, just remind him from me to keep his throat well wrapped up. ' 'Certainly, Mrs. Reard. ' I said. 'You are a good young man; I noticed how attentive you are to John—to Captain— ' The train pulled out suddenly; I took my cap off to the old woman; I never saw her again. ... Pass the bottle.

---

1 to have no business with: to have nothing to do with 没有关系不该有胶葛。

2 comfy: comfortably 舒适地。

缚在梯边。六十老翁能够这么灵活也算难得了。请你们想一想这个老汉英雄地双手救起这个老妇人——他一生里最宝贵的女人。他把她放在坐板上，正预备跑回到船上去，船头系船的绳索却落下，他们就一同漂去了。当然在纷乱之中我们没有听到他的叫喊。他现出赧然的神气。她高兴地说，'我想现在我赶不上火车也不要紧了？''不，真妮——你到下面去，那里暖和些，'他含怨说道。然后向我们说：'一个海员不该有个妻子——我说。你看我却到船外去了。好罢，这次没有什么大损伤。让我们去看这条傻汽船打坏了什么。'

"那并不是大损坏，但是使我们又迟留了三星期。这时期终止时候，船主跟他的经理们接洽事情，我拿卑尔太太的旅行囊到火车站，将她很舒服地安顿在三等车中。她把窗门扯下向我说，'你是个好青年。若使你看见约翰——卑尔船主——夜里没有用围巾，请你向他提一声，说我吩咐他脖子要好好包起。''一定的，卑尔太太，'我说。'你是个好青年；我看出你多么留心照呼约翰——船主……'火车忽然开走了；我对这个老妇人脱帽；我再也没有看见她了……请把酒瓶递过来。

"We went to sea next day. When we made that start for Bankok me had been already three months out of London. We had expected to be a fortnight or so—at the outside[1].

"It was January, and the weather was beautiful—the beautiful sunny winter weather that has more charm than in the summer-time, because it is unexpected, and crisp, and you know it won't, it can't, last long. It's like a windfall, like a godsend, like an unexpected piece of luck.

"It lasted all down the North Sea, all down Channel; and it lasted till we were three hundred miles or so to the westward of the Lizards: then the wind went round to the sou'west and began to pipe up[2]. In two days it blew a gale. The Judea, hove to, wallowed on the Atlantic like an old candle-box. It blew day after day: it blew with spite, without interval, without mercy, without rest. The world was nothing but an immensity of great foaming waves rushing at us, under a sky low enough to touch with the hand and dirty like a smoked ceiling. In the stormy space surrounding us there was as much flying spray as air. Day after day and night after night there was nothing round the ship but the howl of the wind, the tumult of the sea, the noise of water pouring over her deck. There was no rest

---

1 at the outside: at most 充其量；顶多不过。
2 to pipe up: to blow fiercely 大刮起来。

"我们第二天驶进海里去。当我们这下开始向盘谷航行,我们离伦敦已有三个月了。我们起先以为顶多不过两星期左右的时光。

"那是正月,天气佳美——那种和煦有阳光的冬天日子,比夏天的更妙得多,因为那是出乎意料之外,轻脆的,你又知道那不会,那不能继续很久。那好像是一笔横财,好像上帝赏赐的好东西,好像是一下意外的幸运。

"这种天气一直维持到北海,到海峡,一直维持到我们在利查底西面三百哩左右的地方;然后转个风势,刮起东南风了。两天内成为暴风。犹太随波浮沉,在大西洋中打滚像一只旧洋烛箱子。天天有暴风;含着憎恶地,不停地,毫无慈悲地,一下子也不歇息地刮着。世界无非是一大片打出白沫的大浪向我们冲来,上面的天低得伸手可触,龌龊得像个烟熏的天花板。我们四周的狂风雨里飞舞的浪花同空气一样的多。天天夜夜船的四旁没有别的,只是风的啸号,海的骚动,水倾泻到船面时的嘈声。船是没有一刻的休息,我们也没有一刻的休息。它颠

for her and no rest for us. She tossed, she pitched, she stood on her head, she sat on her tail, she rolled, she groaned, and we had to hold on while on deck and cling to our bunks when below, in a constant effort of body and worry of mind.

"One night Mahon spoke through the small window of my berth. It opened right into my very bed, and I was lying there sleepless, in my boots, feeling as though I had not slept for years, and could not if I tried. He said excitedly—

" 'You got the sounding-rod in here, Marlow? I can't get the pumps to suck. By God! It's no child's play. '

"I give him the sounding-rod and lay down again, trying to think of various things—but I thought only of the pumps. When I came on deck they were still at it[1], and my watch relieved at the pumps. By the light of the lantern brought on deck to examine the sounding-rod I caught a glimpse of their weary, serious faces. We pumped all the four hours. We pumped all night, all day, all the week—watch and watch. She was working herself loose[2], and leaked badly—not enough to down us at once, but enough to kill us with the work at the pumps. And while we pumped the ship was going from us piecemeal: the bulwarks went, the stanchions were torn out, the

---

1 at it: hard at work 勤作，奋斗。
2 to work loose: to become loose 变松散了。

簸,它竖起,它倒栽,它坐在尾巴上,它滚动,它呻吟,我们在船面时就得抓住东西,在底下时就得依着寝棚,身体总是用力,心里总是焦虑。

"一天晚上马洪从我卧室的小窗子对我说话。那正朝着我睡的床铺,我躺在那里睡不着,穿着长靴,觉得我好像有许多年没有睡过,若使去试睡,也办不到。他兴奋地说道:

'你这里有测水尺吗,马罗?我无法使抽水机吸水。天呀!这绝不是儿戏。'

"〈我〉拿一把测水尺给他,又躺下来,打算去想些其它事情——但是我老想着那抽水机。当我走上船面,他们还在抽水机旁边努力工作,我当值时间到了,就同他们调班。靠着带到船面来看测水尺的灯笼的光线,我瞥见他们疲倦严重的脸孔。我们抽了整整四个钟头。整〈夜〉,整天,整个星期,我们轮班接连抽着。它自己渐渐松散了,漏水很多——没有多到会立刻将我们沕死,却足以把抽水工作累死我们。当我们抽水时候,船是一块一块地离散了,上层甲板的船舷去了,直杆也给风吹跑了,

ventilators smashed, the cabin-door burst in. There was not a dry spot in the ship. She was being gutted[1] bit by bit. The long-boat changed, as if by magic, into matchwood where she stood in her gripes. I had lashed her myself, and was rather proud of my handiwork, which had withstood so long the malice of the sea. And we pumped. And there was no break in the weather. The sea was white like a sheet of foam, like a caldron of boiling milk; there was not a break in the clouds, no—not the size of a man's hand—no, not for so much as ten seconds. There was for us no sky, there were for us no stars, no sun, no universe—nothing but angry clouds and an infuriated sea. We pumped watch and watch, for dear life; aud it seemed to last for months, for years, for all eternity, as though we had been dead and gone to a hell for sailors. We forgot the day of the week, the name of the month, what year it was, and whether we had ever been ashore. The sails blew away, she lay broadside on under a weathercloth, the ocean poured over her, and we did not care. We turned those handles, and had the eyes of idiots. As soon as we had crawled on deck I used to take a round turn with a rope about the men, the pumps, and the mainmast, and we turned, we turned incessantly, with the water to our waists, to our necks, over our heads. It

---

1 to be gutted: to be disembowel 挖出肚肠。

通气筒打成粉碎，房门也冲开了。船里没有一块干燥的地方。它的肠脏是一块一块地被取出。一只长方形的船好像受了魔力变成为木片，它就站在上面受绞肠的苦痛。我自己也曾鞭挞过它，我都还喜欢我的手艺，那能够这么久阻挡海的恶意。我们老是抽水。天气一些也没有改变。海是白得像一片白沫，像一锅煮滚的牛乳；密云没有一些破晴，不——连一手掌大的晴空都没有——不，连十秒钟的好天气都没有。对于我们可以说没有天，没有星，没有太阳，没有宇宙——什么都没有，除开盛怒的云同疯狂的海。我们轮班抽水，为着要救我们这可爱的生命；这个工作仿佛继续了好几个月，好几年，永久继续着的，好像我们死过去，到地狱当水手了。我们忘却当下是星期几，我们忘却月名，我们忘却是何年，我们也不知道我们曾经住过岸上没有。帆吹掉了，它斜躺着，盖着油布，海倾泻到它上面，我们也不去理。我们只是转动抽水机的柄，眼神同傻子的一样。我们一爬到船面，我常用一根绳把人，抽水机，同主桅圈在一起，我们转动，不停地转动，水到我们腰间，到我们颈部，过

was all one¹. We had forgotten how it felt to be dry.

"And there was somewhere in me the thought: By Jove!² This is the deuce of³ an adventure—something you read about; and it is my first voyage as second mate—and I am only twenty—and here I am lasting it out as well as any of these men, and keeping my chaps up to the mark⁴. I was pleased. I would not have given up the experience for worlds⁵. I had moments of exultation. Whenever the old dismantled craft pitched heavily with her counter high in the air, she seemed to me to throw up, like an appeal, like a defiance, like a cry to the clouds without mercy, the words written on her stern: 'Judea, London. Do or Die.'

"O youth! The strength of it, the faith of it, the imagaination of it! To me she was not an old rattletrap carting about the world a lot of coal for a freight—to me she was the endeavour, the test, trial of life. I think of her with pleasure, with affection, with regret—as you would think of someone dead you have loved. I shall never forget her... Pass the bottle.

---

1 all one：just the same 一样的。
2 By Jove：Jove是罗马人所崇奉的天帝的名字，就是希腊的Jupiter或Zeus。据说生下来时命里带这个星宿的人是心境快乐的，jovial，joviality这几个字也都是从这个字变化出来的。所以by Jove是高兴所发的感叹词。
3 the deuce of：a notable 一个奇异的；一个值得纪念的。
4 to keep up to the mark：to keep as usual 使照常。
5 for worlds：for any consideration 无论如何。

我们的头了。这于我们还是一样的。我们早已忘却干的感觉是怎么样了。

"我心中隐隐想着：哈哈！这真是个怪有意思的冒险——活像你在书里所念的；这又是我第一次当二副的航行——我才二十二岁——此刻我也能挨着，不下于任何人，而且也使这班水手们照常工作。我感到愉快。我绝不肯抛弃这个经验，就说拿整个世界来给我换。我有狂欢的时候，每次这只裸露的小船使劲地竖起来，它的后尾艕高举在空中，由我看来，它好像把它船尾上所写的字：'犹太，伦敦。工作，否则灭亡，'扔上去，当做个恳求，当做个挑衅，当做个向毫无慈悲的云团的叫喊。

"呵，青春！它的力气，它的信仰，它的想像力！对于我，它并不是个发出戛戛声音的破旧东西，为着运费载一大堆煤在世界上跑来跑去——对于我，它是人生的努力，人生的试验，人生的磨练。我现在想起它时，还带有欣欢，带有感情，带有惋惜——正好似你想起一个你曾爱过的已死的人。我绝不会忘记它……请把酒瓶递过来。

"One night when tied to the mast, as I explained, we were pumping on, deafened with the wind, and without spirit enough in us to wish ourselves dead, a heavy sea[1] crashed aboard and swept clean over us. As soon as I got my breath I shouted, as in duty bound, 'keep on[2], boys!' When suddenly I felt something hard floating on deck strike the calf of my leg. I made a grab[3] at it and missed. It was so dark we could not see each other's faces within a foot—you understand.

"After that thump the ship kept quiet for a while and the thing, whatever it was, stuck my leg again. This time I caught it—and it was a saucepan. A first, being stupid with fatigue and thinking of nothing but the pumps, I did not understand what I had in my hand. Suddenly it dawned upon[4] me, and I shouted, 'Boys, the house on deck is gone. Leave this, and let's look for the cook.'

"There was a deck-house forward, which contained the galley, the cook's berth, and the quarters of the crew. As we had expected for days to see it swept away, the hands[5] had been ordered to sleep in the cabin—the only safe place in the ship. The steward, Abraham, however, persisted in clinging to his berth, stupidly, like a mule—

---

1 heavy sea: stormy sea 狂风暴浪的海。
2 to keep on: to continue 继续；坚持下去。
3 grab: sudden clutch 忽然间抓一抓。
4 to dawn upon: to begin to be understood by 开始明白。

"一天晚上，像我前面所说的，缚在主桅旁边，我们在正抽水，给风声弄聋了，没有精神到无力去希望自己是个死人，一阵波涛砰磕而来，冲到船面，把我们洗一遍。我一有力气呼吸，就按着我的责任喊道，'坚持到底，孩子们！'那时我忽然觉得一件浮在船面的硬东西打我的小腿。我去攫取，却没有抓到手。你们知道——四面是黑得一尺之内我们不能看清彼此的脸孔。

"这下砰击之后，船安稳了一会儿，那个东西，不管它是什么东西，又打我的小腿。这一回给我拿住了——那是一只汤锅。起先，因为我疲累得傻了，心里又只想那抽水机，我不知道我手里拿的是什么。忽然间，我明白了，我喊道，'孩子们，甲板室去了。离开这个工作罢，让我们去看厨子怎么样。'

"船的前头有一所甲板室，包含厨房，厨子的寝棚，同水手的住所。因为我们已经有好几天就预料出会看见它被水冲去，所以叫水手们到下面房间去睡——那是船里惟一安全的地方。我们的管事亚伯拉罕却偏要依恋他的寝棚，愚蠢地，像一只驴子——

---

5 hands：workers 工人；水手。

from sheer fright I believe, like an animal that won't leave a stable falling in an earthquake. So we went to look for him. It was chancing death, since once out of our lashings we were as exposed as if on a raft. But we went. The house was shattered as if a shell had exploded inside. Most of it had gone overboard—stove, men's quarters, and their property, all was gone; but two posts, holding a portion of the bulkhead to which Abraham's bunk was attached, remained as if by a miracle. We groped in the ruins and came upon this, and there he was, sitting in his bunk, surrounded by foam and wreckage, jabbering cheerfully to himself. He was out of his mind; completely and for ever mad, with this sudden shock coming upon the fag-end[1] of his endurance. We snatched him up, lugged him aft, and pitched him head-first down the cabin companion. You understand there was no time to carry him down with infinite precautions and wait to see how he got on. Those below would pick him up at the bottom of the stairs all right. We were in a hurry to go back to the pumps. That business could not wait. A bad leak is an inhuman thing.

"One would think that the sole purpose of that fiendish gale had been to make a lunatic of that poor devil of a mulatto. It eased before morning, and next day the sky cleared, and as the sea went

---

1 fag-eng: the end of a web of cloth, of a rope, etc 网子，绳子等的末端。

我相信完全出于恐惧，像一只牲口地震时不肯离开快坍下的兽栏。我们于是去看他。这是拿生命去冒险，因为一离开我们的捆绑，我们毫无掩护，正同在筏子上面一样。可是我们去了。那间屋子成为粉碎，好像一粒炸弹在里面爆发了。一大半东西都掉海里去了——炉子，人们的宿所，他们的财产，全掉海里去；但是扶着一部分船舱的间壁却留有两根柱子。大有神迹的意味，亚伯拉罕的床架就钉在上面。我们在遗迹之中摸索，碰到这个，他就在那里，坐床架上，四围是白沫同残物，高兴地向自己喃喃。他是神经错乱了；完全而且永久疯了，因为这个突然的惊骇刚乘着他忍奈〔耐〕到无可再忍的时候。我们把他检〔捡〕起，强曳他到船尾，将他倒栽地扔给在下面房子里的人们。你们知道我们没有时间去非常小心抬他下去，再等候着看他的情形有何变化。在下面的人们当然会在楼梯底将他拖起，一点儿也不错。我们〔是〕赶快跑回抽水机那里去工作。那件事是不能等候我们的。一个坏漏是个不近人情的东西。

"人们会以为这回魔鬼般的狂风的惟一目的是要把这可怜的杂种鬼弄疯。还不到天亮，风势就已平下了，第二天，天也晴

down the leak took up¹. When it came to bending a fresh set of sails the crew demanded to put back—and really there was nothing else to do. Boats gone, decks swept clean, cabin gutted, men without a stitch but what they stood in, stores spoiled, ship strained. We put her head for home, and—would you believe it? The wind came east right in our teeth². It blew fresh, it blew continuously. We had to beat up³ every inch of the way, but she did not leak so badly, the water weeping comparatively smooth. Two hours' pumping in every four is no joke—but it kept her afloat as far as Falmouth.

"The good people there live on casualties of the sea, and no doubt were glad to see us. A hungry crowd of shipwrights sharpened their chisels at the sight of that carcass of a ship. And, by Jove! they had pretty pickings off us before they were done. I fancy the owner was already in a tight place. There were delays. Then it was decided to take part of the cargo out and caulk her topsides. This was done, the repairs finished, cargo reshipped; a new crew came on board, and we went out—for Bankok. At the end of a week we were back again. The crew said they weren't going to Bankok—a hundred and

---

1 to take up: to close spontaneously 自己塞住。
2 in our teeth: in direct opposition to us 同我们正相对。
3 to beat up: to tack against an adverse wind 逆风用劲行驶。

朗起来，海既然平静下去，漏口也自己塞住了。当我们安上一套新的帆，水手们要求驶回去——的确没有别的办法。小艇都吹掉了。船面给水洗得空无一物，下面的房子内部也破坏得不堪，人们除开身上穿的之外没有一丝的衣服，粮食损失了，船身也过劳了。我们转过船头，向家乡驶去，——你们会相信吗？现在却刮起东风，正是我们的对头风。它重新刮起来，而且是不停地。每走一吋的路程，我们都得很费劲，但是它没有漏那么厉害了，水的呜咽也比较和平些。四个钟头中间得抽水二个钟头，这真不是开玩笑的事情——但是这样子它居然在水面挣扎到法尔马司。

"那里的善良住民在靠海上的灾难为生，看见我们一定是很高兴的。一群饥饿的造船匠瞧到这只死尸般的破船，赶紧磨利他们的凿子。天呀，在他们工作完了之前，的确骗了我们不少的钱。我想船的所有者已经很窘迫了。种种的停搁使它多滞了许久。然后决定把一部分的货运出，将它的干舷重新钉铁。这做完了，一切修理都已竣工，货也再运上去；一班新雇的水手上船，我们又扬帆到——盘谷。过了一星期，我们又回来。水手说他们不肯到盘谷——那有

fifty days' passage—in a something hooker that wanted pumping eight hours out of the twenty-four; and the nautical papers inserted again the little paragraph: 'Judea, Barque. Tyne to Bankok; coals; put back to Falmouth leaky and with crew refusing duty.'

"There were more delays—more tinkering. The owner came down for a day, and said she was as right as a little fiddle. Poor old Captain Beard looked like the ghost of a Geordie[1] skipper—through the worry and humiliation of it. Remember he was sixty, and it was his first command. Mahon said it was a foolish business, and would end badly. I loved the ship more than ever, and wanted awfully to get to Bankok. To Bankok! Magic name, blessed name. Mesopotamia wasn't patch on[2] it. Remember I was twenty, and it was my first second-mate's billet, and the East was waiting for me.

"We went out and anchored in the outer roads with a fresh crew—the third. She leaked worse than ever. It was as if those confounded shipwrights had actually made a hole in her. This time we did not even go outside. The crew simply refused to man[3] the windlass.

"They towed us back to the inner harbour, and we became a fixture, a feature, an institution of the place. People pointed us out to visitors as 'That 'ere barque that's going to Bankok—has been here

---

1 Geordie: collier 煤矿夫；运煤的人。
2 not a patch on: much inferior 相差得多。
3 to man: to supply with the necessary men 配置必需的人。

一百五十大的路程——在一只二十四钟头里要抽水八个钟头的像两桅船的破船里;航海日报又登上这一小段新闻:'犹太。三桅船。自泰因到盘谷;煤;回到法尔马司,因为漏水同水手不肯服务。'

"又耽搁了许多——又修补一番。船的所有者来住一天,说它一点毛病也没有,简直像一架小提琴。可怜的卑尔老船主憔悴不堪,活像一只煤船船主的鬼——因为经过了这些忧虑同耻辱。请你们记住他已六十岁了,这是他第一次带船。马洪说这是一回无聊的事情,准会有个不好的结果。我比从前更喜欢这条船,非常想到盘谷去。到盘谷去!神秘的名字,幸福的名字。美索不达米绝对比不上它。请记住我才二十岁,这是我第一次得到二副的任命状,东方正在等候着我。

"我们驶出去,泊在外面码头,有一班新雇的水手——第三班的。它漏水比从前更厉害。真好像这班该死的造船匠的确在它上面打一个洞。这一次我们简直没有驶出海口。水手根本就不肯去料理绞盘。

"他们又把我们拖到内港里去,我们变为那地方的一个固定物,一个景色,一个名胜了。人们指出给游客看,说道,'这就是

six months—put back three times.' On holidays the small boys pulling about in boats would hail. 'Judea, ahoy!' and if a head showed above the rail shouted. 'Where you bound to? —Bankok?' and jeered. We were only three on board. The poor old skipper mooned[1] in the cabin. Mahon undertook the cooking, and unexpectedly developed all a Frenchman's genius for preparing nice little messes. I looked languidly after the rigging. We became citizens of Falmouth. Every shopkeeper knew us. At the barber's or tobacconist's they asked familiarly, 'Do you think you will ever get to Bankok?' Meantime the ower, the underwriters, and the charterers squabbled amongst themselves in London, and our pay went on... Pass the bottle.

"It was horrid. Morally it was worse than pumping for life. It seemed as though we had been forgotten by the world, belonged to nobody, would get nowhere; it seemed that, as if bewitched, we would have to live for ever and ever in that inner harbour, a derision and a byword to generations of long-shore loafers and dishonest boatmen. I obtained three months' pay and a five days' leave, and made a rush for London. It took me a day to get there and pretty well another to come bcak—but three months' pay went all the same. I don't know what I did with it. I went to a music-hall, I believe,

---

1 to moon: to go listlessly about 无精打采〔彩〕地走着。

到盘谷去的那只三桅船——在这里已经六个月了——回来三次.'放假的日子,小孩子摇着小船,会喊道,'犹太,唔!'若使有一个人在栏杆上露出头来,他们会喊道,'你们到那里去[里]?——盘谷吗?'嘲笑了一番。我们只有三个人在船上。可怜的老船主在下面房间徘徊踯躅。马洪去当厨子,出乎意表地现出法国人做精美小菜的一切天才。我无聊赖地照料船缆。我们变为法尔马司的市民。个个开店铺的人们都认得我们。在理发店或者烟铺里,他们亲密地问道,'你想你真会到盘谷吗?'当时,船的所有者,保险商,雇船者在伦敦彼此争吵着,我们的薪水继续下去……请把酒瓶递过来。

"这真是可怕。在精神方面,这比为着要救自己生命而抽水还坏。仿佛我们被世界忘却了,不属于谁的,也不会驶到任何地方;好像,给魔力所迷,我们不得不永久住在这个内港里,做一代一代长海岸上游手好闲的人们同不老实的船夫的嘲弄材料和笑柄。我支三个月薪水,告了五天假,跑到伦敦去。去的路程费了一天,回来的路程差不多也费了一天——可是三个月的薪水仍然是用光了。我不知道怎样花去。我相信,我到游戏

lunched, dined, and supped in a swell[1] place in Regent Street, and was back to time, with nothing but a complete set of Byron's works and a new railway rug to show for three months' work. The boatman who pulled me off to the ship said: 'Hallo! I thought you had left the old thing. She will never get to Bankok.' 'That's all you know about it,' I said, scornfully—but I didn't like that prophecy at all.

"Suddenly a man, some kind of agent to somebody, appeared with full powers. He had grog-blossoms all over his face, an indomitable energy, and was a jolly soul. We leaped into life again. A hulk came alongside, took our cargo, and then we went into dry dock to get our copper stripped. No wonder she leaked. The poor thing, strained beyond endurance by the gale, had, as if in disgust, spat out all the oakum of her lower seams. She was recaulked, new coppered, and made as tight as a bottle. We went back to the bulk and re-shipped our cargo.

"Then, on a fine moonlight night, all the rats left the ship.

"We had been infested with them. They had destroyed our sails, consumed more stores than the crew, affably shared our beds and our dangers, and now, when the ship was made seaworthy, concluded to clear out. I called Mahon to enjoy the spectacle. Rat after

---

1 swell: of distinction; smart 特别的；漂亮的。

场去,在里真街上一家华美的馆子里用小吃,用大餐,用午餐,刚好赶回来,没有带了别的,只有一套拜仑全集同一副新旅行囊,算做我三个月工作的成绩。渡我到大船去的船夫说:'唔!我起先还以为你离开那家伙了。它绝不会驶到盘谷。''你只知道这些,'我轻蔑地说道——但是我心里在非常不高兴这个预言。

"忽然间有一个人,某人的某一种代表。带了全权而来。他满脸都是酒龇,有个不屈不挠的魄力,是个嘻嘻哈哈的人。我们又生气勃勃起来。一只旧船来到船旁,搬去我们的货,然后我们到干船坞,将我们船的铜皮剥下。它会漏水真是不足奇的。这个可怜东西,给暴风摧残到忍无可忍了,好像不胜厌恶,把它夹板缝里的填塞物都吐出来。它重新钉过铁,新包上一层铜皮,弄得坚固像一只瓶子。我们回到旧船,把货又搬回来。

"然后,一个良好的月夜,所有耗子都离开这只船了。

"我们一向受他们的骚扰,他们咬坏我们的帆布,吃我们的粮食比水手还厉害,殷勤地与我们同床,患难相共,现在当这只船可以航海了,却决定离开。我叫马洪来赏玩这个奇观。耗

rat appeared on our rail, took a last look over his shoulder, and leaped with a hollow thud into the empty hulk. We tried to count them, but soon lost the tale. Mahon said: 'Well, well! Don't talk to me about the intelligence of rats. They ought to have left before, when we had that narrow squeak from foundering. There you have the proof how silly is the superstition about them.[1] They leave a good ship for an old rotten hulk, where there is nothing to eat, too, the fools! ... I don't believe they know what is safe or what is good for them, any more than you or I. '

"And after some more talk we agreed that the wisdom of rats had been grossly overrated, being in fact no greater than that of men.

"The story of the ship was known, by this, all up the Channel from Land's End to the Forelands, and we could get no crew on the south coast. They sent us one all complete from Liverpool, and we left once more—for Bankok.

"We had fair breezes, smooth water right into the tropics, and the old Judea lumbered along in the sunshine. When she went eight knots everything cracked aloft, and we tied our caps to our heads; but mostly she strolled on at the rate of three miles an hour. What could you expect? She was tired—that old ship. Her youth was

---

1 航海的人们有一种迷信,以为耗子离开的船一定会倒霉,他们却很欢迎耗子来同居。

子跟着耗子现在我们栏干〔杆〕上，从肩上回头作最后的一顾，空洞地砰的一声掉到破旧的空船里。我们想去数他们，但是一会儿就数乱了。马洪说：'好罢！别同我说耗子是多么聪明。他们从前该离开，当我们万分危险，几乎沉没了。现在你有个证明，可以看出关于他们的迷信是多么无谓。他们离一只好船，到一个老朽的旧船，那里什么吃的都没有，这是傻瓜！……我不相〈信〉他们比你我更知道什么是他们的安全，和什么事于他们有好处。'

"又谈论了一下子，我们公认耗子的智慧是太称赞得过分了，其实并不比人们的高明多少。

"这只船的遭遇这样子从兰斯恩德一直到福耳兰这条海峡的人们都知道了，我们从南海岸无法雇到水手。他们从利物浦送一全班水手来，我们又出发——到盘谷去。

"我们风平浪静，一直驶到热带，这条老船犹太就在阳光之下行步艰难地望前进。当它每小时走八哩时，上面的一切东西都响起来，好像将折断了，我们把小帽紧缚在头上；但是它常是每小时走三哩，慢慢溜着。你们怎能期望它不是这样呢？它是疲倦

where mine is—where yours is—you fellows who listen to this yarn; and what friend would throw your years and your weariness in your face[1]? We didn't grumble at her. To us aft, at least, it seemed as though we had been born in her, reared in her, had lived in her for ages, had never known any other ship. I would just as soon have abused the old village church at home for not being a cathedral.

"And for me there was also my youth to make me patient. There was all the East before me, and all life, and the thought that I had been tried in that ship and had come out pretty well. And I thought of men of old who, centuries ago, went that road in ships that sailed no better, to the land of palms, and spices, and yellow sands, and of brown nations ruled by kings more cruel than Nero the Roman[2], and more splendid than Solomon the Jew[3]. The old bark lumbered on, heavy with her age and the burden of her cargo, while I lived the life of youth in ignorance and hope. She lumbered on through an interminable procession of days, and the fresh gilding flashed back at the setting sun, seemed to cry out over the darkening sea the words painted on her stern, 'Judea, London. Do or Die.'

---

1 to throw in one's face: to use as a taunt or challenge 拿来做辱骂的材料。
2 Nero the Roman: 公元37—68〈年〉罗马的一个暴君, 杀死他的母亲, 杀死他的妻子, 最后兵败杀死自己。
3 Solomon the Jew: 希伯来王, 纪元前九六〇年, 喜挥霍, 建筑极庄丽的宫殿。

了——这只老船。它的青春正同我的青春一样，是已过去了——也正同你们的青春一样，你们诸位听这个故事的先生们。有那位朋友肯当面说你们年纪太大，或者太疲劳了呢？我们并不责备它。最少，在我们住在船尾的官员眼里，好像我们是生于斯，长于斯，在这里面住了许多年头了，仿佛绝没有知道过别只船。我的不打算骂它，正如我不会因为家乡的老礼拜堂不是个大教堂，就去说它的坏话。

"至于我，我的青春也使我更有耐心。在我的前途有整个的东方同一切的生活，想到在这只船我遇到磨折，居然对付得很不错，我更觉得高兴。我就想起古代的人们，他们几世纪以前坐在并不更高明的船，也走这条航路，到棕树、香料同黄沙的国土，那里有棕色种的人民，他们的皇帝比罗马的尼罗王更残酷，比犹太的所罗门更奢华。老船还是步履蹒跚地望〔往〕前走，因为上了年纪同载了货物变得很沉重了，我却是在无知识同热烈希望里渡青春的生活。它步履蹒跚地望前走，一天又一天，好像永无止期；在落照之下反映出的新涂泥金好像向这将暝的大海喊出画在它船尾的几个字：'犹太，伦敦，工作否则灭亡。'

"Then we entered the Indian Ocean and steered northernly for Java Head. The winds were light. Weeks slipped by. She crawled on, do or die, and people at home began to think of posting us as overdue.

"One Saturday evening, I being off duty, the men asked me to give them an extra bucket of water or so—for washing clothes. As I did not wish to screw on the fresh-water pump so late, I went forward whistling, and with a key in my hand to unlock the forepeak scuttle, intending to serve the water out of a spare tank we kept there.

"The smell down below was as unexpected as it was frightful. One would have thought hundreds of paraffin lamps had been flaring and smoking in that hole for days. I was glad to get out. The man with me coughed and said, 'Funny smell, sir.' I answered negligently, 'It's good for the health they say,' and walked aft.

"The first thing I did was to put my head down the square of the midship ventilator. As I lifted the did a visible breath, something like a thin fog, a puff of faint haze, rose from the opening. The ascending air was hot, and had a heavy, sooty, paraffiny smell. I gave one sniff, and put down the lid gently. It was no use choking myself. The cargo was on fire.

"然后，我们驶进印度洋，望〔往〕北朝着爪哇·赫德走去。海上只有微风。一星期一星期过去了。它还是慢爬着，努力否则灭亡，家乡的人们开始打算出布告，说我们过期未到。

"一天星期六黄昏时候，我正在休息，水手们请我给他们另外一桶左右的水——为着洗衣服用。我不愿意这么迟还去扭上淡水唧筒，就吹着哨子望〔往〕前走，手里拿一把钥匙去打开船头舱的舱口，想从我们放在里面的一个多余的水柜取水。

"下面的臭味真是出乎意料之外的，真的可怕。闻到这臭味，人们会以为有一百枝白蜡灯在那个洞里吐焰薰烟了许多日子。我走出来，如释重负。跟我同去的人咳嗽说道，'怪味，先生。'我不留心地答道，'据说这于身体有益，'走向船尾去了。

"我第一件干的事情是低下头，伸进船中间气筒的方口。当我揭开那盖子，一些看得见的气，有点像薄雾，一阵细微的烟雾，从口里出来。上升的气是热的，有一种浓厚的，烟煤的，白蜡的臭味。我只闻一下，就轻轻地把盖子关上。把我自己弄得窒息是没有用的。下面的货物分明是燃烧起来了。

"Next day she began to smoke in earnest. You see it was to be expected, for though the coal was of a safe kind, that cargo had been so handled, so broken up with handling, that it looked more like smithy coal than anything else. Then it had been wetted—more than once. It rained all the time we were taking it back from the hulk, and now with this long passage it got heated, and there was another case of spontaneous combustion[1].

"The captain called us into the cabin. He had a chart spread on the table, and looked unhappy. He said, 'The coast of West Australia is near, but I mean to proceed to our destination. It is the hurricane month, too; but we will just keep her head for Bankok, and fight the fire. No more putting back anywhere, if[2] we all get roasted. We will try first to stifle this 'ere[3] damned combustion by want of air.'

"We tried. We battened down everything, and still she smoked. The smoke kept coming out through imperceptible crevices; it forced itself through bulkheads and covers; it oozed here and there and everywhere in slender threads, in an invisible film, in an incomprehensible manner. It made its way into the cabin, into the forecastle; it poisoned the sheltered places on the deck, it could be sniffed as high as the mainyard. It was clear that if the smoke came

---

1 spontaneous combustion: 指没有外物来点着，内部自己燃烧起来。
2 if: even if 就说；纵令。
3 'ere: here

"第二天，它真真冒出烟来。你们看这是在意料之内的，虽然所运的煤是属于安全那一种的，可是这些货搬来搬去，搬的时候又弄得这么碎，看起来，它不像别的，简直像铁匠铺的煤块。后来又浸了水——还不止一次。当我们把它从破旧的空船取回，天老是下雨，现在走了这么长的路程，它发热了，这又是自然燃烧的一个例子。

"船主叫我们到他的房间。他有一张地图铺在桌面，现在忧愁的神气。他说：'西奥大利亚海岸离这儿不远，但是我想向我们的目的地走去。这又是暴风的月令；但是我们决定使船头朝着盘谷，跟火奋斗。绝不再回转去停泊在任何地方了，就说我们都烤焦了。我们要先用缺乏空气来熄灭这个倒霉的燃烧。'

"我们尝试一下。我们拿一切东西去喂它，它仍然冒烟。烟老是从看不见的裂缝出来；它由船舱的间壁同船面的盖布冲透出来；它一丝丝地这里，那里，到处泄漏出来，一片薄雾，怎么能够跑出真是不可思议。它走进房间里面，走到船头甲板；它使船面有遮盖的地方也染上毒气，甚至于大帆顶上也闻得出

out the air came in. This was disheartening. This combustion refused to be stifled.

"We resolved to try water, and took the hatches off. Enormous volumes of smoke, whitish, yellowish, thick, greasy, misty, choking, ascended as high as the trucks. All hands cleared out aft. Then the poisonous cloud blew away, and we went back to work in a smoke that was no thicker now than that of an ordinary factory chimney.

"We rigged the force-pump, got the hose along, and by-and-by it burst. Well, it was as old as the ship—a prehistoric hose, and past repair. Then we pumped with the feeble head-pump, drew water with buckets, and in this way managed in time[1] to pour lots of Indian Ocean into the main hatch. The bright stream flashed in sunshine, fell into a layer of white crawling smoke, and vanished on the black surface of coal. Steam ascended mingling with the smoke. We poured salt water as into a barrel without a bottom. It was our fate to pump in that ship, to pump out of her, to pump into her; and after keeping water out of her to save ourselves from being drowned, we frantically poured water into her to save ourselves from being burnt.

"And she crawled on, do or die, in the serene weather. The sky

---

1 in time: sufficiently early 还来得及。

它烟味。若使烟能走出,那么空气分明能够进去。这叫我们寒心。这个燃烧不肯息灭。

"我们决定用水来试一试,将货舱口打开。一阵一阵大卷的烟,白色的,黄色的,浓厚的,油腻的,雾一般的,使人不能通气的,上升一直到桅顶的木球。一切人们都躲到船尾去。然后,这阵毒云吹走了,我们回去工作,四围的烟现在只有普通烟囱的烟那么浓厚了。

"我们装好压水唧筒,接上水龙软管,可是软管渐渐破裂了。唉,那是跟这只船同样老——一个前史时的水龙软管,已是无法修补了。我们于是就用微弱的抽水筒,拿桶子来盛水,这样子设法及时将好些印度洋的水灌到货舱大舱口。明亮的海水在太阳光中发光,倾泻到一层慢爬着的白烟里去,就消失于煤块的黑色表面上了。蒸气混着烟一同上来。我们好像将盐水灌注一个无底的大桶。这是我们的命运,在这只船里抽水,把水从船里抽出,又从外面抽水到船里去;从前使船里没有水,免得我们沕死,我们现在却疯狂地灌水进去,救我们自己,免得烧死。

"它却迟缓地望〔往〕前爬,努力否则灭亡,在恬静的天气

was a miracle[1] of purity, a miracle of azure. The sea was polished, was blue, was pellucid, was sparkling like a precious stone, extending on all sides, all round to the horizon—as if the whole terrestrial globe had been one jewel, one colossal sapphire, a single gem fashioned into a planet. And on the lustre of the great calm waters the Judea glided imperceptibly, enveloped in languid and unclean vapours, in a lazy cloud that drifted to leeward, light and slow; a pestiferous cloud defiling the splendour of sea and sky.

"All this time of course we saw no fire. The cargo smouldered at the bottom somewhere. Once Mahon, as we were working side by side, said to me with a queer smile: 'Now, if she only would spring a tidy leak—like that time when we first left the Channel—it would put a stopper[2] on this fire. Wouldn't it?' I remarked irrelevanty, 'do you remember the rats?'

"We fought the fire and sailed the ship too as carefully as though nothing had been the matter. The steward cooked and attended on us. Of the other twelve men, eight worked while four rested. Everyone took his turn, captain included. There was equality, and if not exactly fraternity, then a deal of good feeling. Sometime a man, as he dashed a bucketful of water down the hatchway, would

---

1 miracle: event due to supernatural agency 神迹。这里是说天色澄蓝得出乎意料之外，好像不是自然的现象，而是天神弄出来的。
2 stopper: one that which stops 制止者；塞阻的东西。

里。天是洁净得出奇，蔚蓝得出奇。海是光滑的，澄蓝的，透明的，发光像一粒宝石，向四面伸长，一直到天边——仿佛地球是一粒钻石，一粒大碧玉，一粒宝石造成的行星。在这没有风波的大海里，犹太偷偷地溜走，有沉闷不洁的烟雾包着，藏在徐行的云里，那向下风处飘去，轻轻的，慢慢的；这是一阵含有毒质的云，把海天的光荣弄脏。

"这些时候里我们自然没有看见火。货在底下某处冒烟着。有一回，马洪，当我们站在一排工作时候，现出一种古怪的笑容，向我说道：'吓，若使它此刻会生一个刚合式的漏口——像我们第一次离开海峡时候那样——就可以把这阵火止着了。你看会不会？'我所答非所问地说道：'你记得耗子吗？'

"我们跟火奋斗，小心地驶船，仿佛并没有什么意外事情发生。管事在厨房里煮菜，伺候我们。其余十二人，八个工作，四个休息。个个人轮班，船主也在内。真是平等，虽然不能严格地说有友爱，可是彼此都很怀有好感。有时一个人，当他倒满桶的水到舱口里去，会喊道，'哈哈，到盘谷去！'其它人们

yell out, 'Hurrah for Bankok!' and the rest laughed. But generally we were taciturn and serious—and thirsty. Oh! how thirsty! And we had to be careful with the water. Strict allowance¹. The ship smoked, the sun blazed... Pass the bottle.

"We tried everything. We even made an attempt to dig down to the fire. No good, of course. No man could remain more than a minute below. Mahon, who went first, fainted there, and the man who went to fetch him out did likewise. We lugged them out on deck. Then I leaped down to show how easily it could be done. They had learned wisdom by that time, and contented themselves by fishing for me with a chainhook tied to a broom-handle, I believe. I did not ofter to go and fetch up my shovel, which was left down below.

"Things began to look bad. We put the longboat into the water. The second boat was ready to swing out. We had also another, a 14-foot thing, on davits aft, where it was quite safe.

"Then, behold, the smoke suddenly decreased. We redoubled our efforts to flood the bottom of the ship. In two days there was no smoke at all. Everybody was on the broad grin. This was on a Friday. On Saturday no work, but sailing the ship, of course, was done.

---

1 strict allowance：海水太咸不能吃，所以船上都带有陆地里面的水。若使把这种水饮罄，那里虽然四面是一片汪洋，还可以叫你渴死，这真是"自然"的嘲讽。这只船一再遇灾难，饮料有限，所以"严格限制"。

就大笑起来。但是通常我们是静默同严重——而且口渴。啊，多么渴呀！我们又不敢随便用水。严格的限制。船冒烟着，太阳是灼热的……把酒瓶递过来罢。

"我们试尽了一切法子。我们甚至于想掘到发火的地方。这当然是办不到的。没有一个人能够在底下滞过一分钟。马洪第一个下去，晕倒在那里，去救他出来的人也晕倒了。我们把他们强曳出来，放在船面上。然后，我跳下去，为的是给他们看这是多么容易办到的。他们现在学乖了，只有链钩缚在，我相信是，寻柄上把我钩起来。我也不愿意再下去检〔捡〕起我的铲子，那就滞在下面。

"情形有些不妙了。我们将长艇放在水里去了。第二条艇我们也预备让它去随潮旋转。我们还有一只，十四英呎长的小艇，挂在船尾吊艇架上，那是很安全的。

"然后，你们看，烟忽然间减少了。我们加倍我们的力量去灌船底。两天后，一缕烟也没有了。个个人都笑逐颜开。这是星期五的事情。星期六不做什么工作，船当然还是照常驶着。

The men washed their clothes and their faces for the first time in a fortnight, and had a special dinner given them. They spoke of spontaneous combustion with contempt, and implied they were the boys to put out[1] combustions. Somehow we all felt as though we each had inherited a large fortune. But a beastly smell of burning hung about the ship. Captain Beard had hollow eyes and sunken cheeks. I had never noticed so much before how twisted and bowed he was. He and Mahon prowled soberly about hatches and ventilators, sniffing. It struck me suddenly poor Mahon was a very, very old chap. As to me, I was as pleased and proud as though I had helped to win a great naval battle. O! Youth!

"The night was fine. In the morning a homeward bound ship passed us hull down[2]—the first we had seen for months; but we were nearing the land at last, Java Head being about 190 miles off, and nearly due north.

"Next day it was my watch on deck from eight to twelve. At breakfast the captain observed, 'It's wonderful how that smell hangs about the cabin.' About ten, the mate being on the poop, I stepped down on the maindeck for a moment. The carpenter's bench stood about the mainmast. I leaned against it sucking at my pipe, and the carpenter, a young chap, came to talk to me. He remarked, 'I think

---

1 to put out: to extinguish 熄灭。

2 hull down: at such distance that masts are visible and hull is not visible 远到看过去只见桅樯，不见船身。

人们两星期来第一次洗净他们的衣服同脸孔,享受一顿特别丰富的大餐。他们谈到天然燃烧时现出蔑视,隐含着他们是扑灭天然燃烧的好汉这个意思。我们都觉得仿佛承受了一笔大财产。但是有一种可厌的焦味回绕船中。卑尔船主双目凹下,脸颊陷进去。我从前绝没有注意到他的身体是这么扭歪弯曲。他同马洪严重地在舱口同通气筒旁边暗中考察,伸着鼻子闻。我忽然觉得可怜的马洪是个非常,非常老的汉子。至于我自己,我是骄傲高兴,好像我出力打胜一仗大海战。呵!青春!

"夜是佳美的。早上,在一只回国的船从我们道上经过,船身隐于水平线下,只看得见帆樯——这是好几月来我们第一次遇见的船;但是我们终于走近目的地了。跟爪哇·赫德只隔一百九十哩,差不多一直望〔往〕着北方走。

"第二天从八时至十二时是我在船面轮班的时候。早餐时候,船主说:'真奇怪,那种味老缠在船上房间里面。'十点时候,大副在船尾甲板上,我走下到中甲板滞一会儿。木匠的长凳站在中桅旁边;我靠着它,一面抽我的烟斗,木匠,一个年

we have done very well, haven't we?' and then I perceived with annoyance the fool was trying to tilt the bench. I said curtly 'Don't, Chips[1],' and immediately became aware of a queer sensation, of an absurd delusion, —I seemed somehow to be in the air. I heard all round me like a pent-up[2] breath released—as if a thousand giants simultaneously had said Phoo! —and felt a dull concussion which made my ribs ache suddenly. No doubt about it—I was in the air, and my body was describing a short parabola. But short as it was, I had the time to think several thoughts in, as far as I can remember, the following order: 'This can't be the carpenter—What is it? — Some accident—Submarine volcano?—Coals, gas! —By Jove! we are being blown up—Everybody's dead—I am falling into the after-hatch—I see fire in it.'

"The coal-dust suspended in the air of the hold had glowed dull-red at the moment of the explosion. In the twinkling of an eye, in an infinitesimal fraction of a second since the first tilt of the bench, I was sprawling full length[3] on the cargo. I picked myself up and scrambled out. It was quick like a rebound. The deck was a wilderness of smashed timber, lying crosswise like trees in a wood after a hurricane; an immense curtain of solid rags waved gently before

---

1 Chips：a carpenter 木匠。
2 pent-up：inclosed 被关闭的。
3 full length：with the body lying extended 身体伸直躺着。

青的人，来同我闲谈。他说，'我想我们干得不坏，是不是？'然后我心里有些不痛快，看到这个傻家伙想把这长凳踢走。我不客气地说道：'不要这样，木匠，'立刻有一个奇怪的感觉，一个荒谬的幻觉，——我好像到空中去了。我听见四周仿佛有一个闭住的气息松吐出来——好像一千位巨人同时喊一声'孚！'——感到一个沉闷的打击，那使我的肋骨忽然痛起来。这是无可疑的——我是在空中，我的身体正画一条短抛物线。但是虽然很短，我还有时间想几个念头，就我记忆所及，大概是底下这样一个次序：'这不是木匠捣乱——是什么呢？一些意外的事变——海底火山吗？——煤，煤气！——哈哈！我们的船爆发了——个个人都死了——我掉到后货舱舱口——我看见里面的火。'

"货舱空中浮动的煤屑当爆发时候呈出暗红色的光辉。一霎眼间，从长凳的被踢后一秒钟几千万万分之一的时间之内，我已全身爬〔趴〕在货上面了。我自己站起，赶紧跑出来。那是快得有如反响。船面是一片碎木的矿〔旷〕野，交叉躺着，像狂风后的森林；一块非常大的坚固烂幕布在我们面前飘荡——那是扯

me—it was the mainsail blown to strips. I thought, the masts will be toppling over directly; and to get out of the way bolted on all-fours[1] towards the poop-ladder. The first person I saw was Mahon, with eyes like saucers, his mouth open, and the long white hair standing straight on end round his head like a silver halo. He was just about to go down when the sight of the maindeck stirring, heaving up, and changing into splinters before his eyes, petrified him on the top step. I stared at him in unbelief, and he stared at me with a queer kind of shocked curiosity. I did not know that I had no hair, no eyebrows, no eyelashes, that my young moustache was hurnt off, that my face was black, one cheek laid open, my nose cut, and my chin bleeding. I had lost my cap, one of my slippers, and my shirt was torn to rags. Of all this I was not awere. I was amazed to see the ship still afloat, the poop-deck whole—and, most of all, to see anybody alive. Also the peace of the sky and the serenity of the sea were distinetly surprising. I suppose I expected to see them convulsed with horror... Pass the bottle.

"There was a voice hailing the ship from somewhere—in the air, in the sky—I couldn't tell. Presently I saw the captain—and he was mad. He asked me eagerly. 'Where's the cabin-table?' and to hear such a question was a frightful shock. I had just been blown up,

---

1 on all-fours: on hands and knees 双手双膝爬着。

成碎条的大帆。我想，樯桅立刻会倒下；为着免受伤，我突然双手双脚爬到船尾甲板的楼梯旁。我第一个看见的人是马洪，眼睛同碟子一样大，嘴张开着，长的白发一根一根直着站在他头上，像银色的灵光。他正要走下来，看见中甲板蠢动，掀起，在他眼前变成碎片，却把他吓住了，木鸡般站在楼梯最高那一格上。我不相信地瞧着他，他也带个古怪的惊骇的好奇钉〔盯〕着我。我自己不知道我没有头发，没有眉毛，没有睫毛，我年青的髭须烧掉了，我的脸孔是墨黑的，一边脸颊破了，我的下巴流血。我遗失了我的帽子，一只拖鞋，我的汗衫也扯成碎布了。这许多情形我都不晓得。我很惊奇，看到船还是浮着，船尾甲板还是整个——尤其看到还有人活着。海天的恬静也是很骇异的。我想我预料会看见它们吓得抽筋……请把酒瓶递过来。

"有一个声音，喊我们船名，从某处发出——从空中呢，从天上呢——我说不清。我立刻看见船主——他是疯了。他热烈地问我，'房里的桌子到那里去？'听见人家问这样一句话，真叫我恐慌无所措。你们知道，我刚被掷到空中去，神经还为着

you understand, and vibrated with that experience, —I wasn't quite sure whether I was alive. Mahon began to stamp with both feet and yelled at him, 'Good God! don't you see the deck's blown out of her?' I found my voice, and stammered out as if conscious of some gross neglect of duty, 'I don't know where the cabin-table is.' It was like an absurd dream.

"Do you know what he wanted next? Well, he wanted to trim the yards[1]. Very placidly and as if lost in thought, he insisted on having the foreyard squared[2]. 'I don't know if there's anybody alive,' said Mahon, almost tearfully. 'Surely,' he said, gently, 'there will be enough left to square the foreyard.'

"The old chap, it seems, was in his own berth winding up the chronometers, when the shock sent him spinning. Immediately it occurred to him—as he said afterwards—that the ship had struck something and ran out into the cabin. There, he saw, the cabin-table had vanished somewhere. The deck being blown up, it had fallen down into the lazarette of course. Where we had our breakfast that morning he saw only a great hole in the floor. This appeared to him so awfully mysterious, and impressed him so immensely, that what he saw and heard after he got on deck were mere trifles in comparison. And, mark, he noticed directly the wheel deserted and his

---

1 to trim the yards: to brace the yards so that the wind will strike the sails at the proper angle 张帆桁使于适当之角度受风。

2 to square the foreyard: to bring the foreyard to a right angle with the mast 使帆桁与桅成为直角。

这个经验而颤动,——我还没有十分把握,我自己是否活着。马洪顿起双脚来,向他喊道:'天呀!你还不知道船面冲掉了吗?'我能发出声音了,结巴地说道,好像觉得自己有很大的失职,'我不晓得房里桌子跑那里去。'这活像一场荒谬的狂梦。

"你们猜得出他接着要干什么吗?他要我们调整帆桁。很沉静地,好像浸在默想里面,他坚持把帆桁跟桅樯〈调〉成为直角。'我不知道船上还有人活着没有,'马洪说,差不多是含泪地。'可是,'他温和地答道,'剩下的人们总够调整帆桁。'

"这个老头子好像正在他床铺上开时计,这个打击使他颠旋房里。他立刻想到——他后来说——船碰到什么东西了,就跑到外面房间去。那里他看见房间的桌子消失得不知去向。船面既然炸飞,这当然也流落到船尾积物室里去了。那天我们用早餐的地方,他现在只看见地板上一个大空窟。这件事他觉得这么神秘可怕,这样深刻地感动了他,他到船面后的所见所闻跟这个一比较,都成为无关紧要的细事了。你们看,他立刻注意到舵轮没有人管,他的船离开它的航路了——他惟一的观念是

barque off her course—and his only thought was to get that miserable, stripped, undecked, smouldering shell of a ship back again with her head pointing at her port of destination. Bankok! That's what he was after[1]. I tell you this quiet, bowed, bandy-legged, almost deformed little man was immense in the singleness of his idea and in his placid ignorance of our agitation. He motioned us forward with a commanding gesture, and went to take the wheel himself.

"Yes; that was the first thing we did—trim the yards of that wreck! No one was killed, or even disabled, but everyone was more or less hurt. You should have seen them! Some were in rags, with black faces, like coalheavers, like sweeps, and had bullet heads[2] that seemed closely cropped, but were in fact singed to skin. Others, of the watch below[3], awakened by being shot out from their collapsing bunks, shivered incessantly, and kept on groaning even as we went about[4] our work. But they all worked. That crew of Liverpool hard cases had in them the right stuff. It's my experience they always have. It is the sea that gives it—the vastness, the loneliness surround-

---

1 to be after: to be in pursuit of 追求。
2 bullet heads: small heads.

使这个可怜的，裸体的，无甲板的，冒烟的船壳还是朝着它的目的地走去。向盘谷开驶！这是他所想办的。我告诉你们这个恬静驼背，腿向外弯，差不多可以算做残缺的矮小老头子，他观念的古怪同他毫不慌张地不了解我们的震惊真是有些过度。他用一种命令的姿势指挥我们望〔往〕前工作，他自己去管舵轮。

"是的；这是我们所干的第一件事情——调整这个破船的帆桁！一个人也没有死，甚至于没有一个人成为残废，但是每人多少受些损伤。你们真该瞧见我们当时的情形！有些穿着破烂的衣服，脸孔黑得同运煤夫的一样，简直像扫烟囱的人，头小得有如弹丸，那好像剃光了，其实是烧到头皮。其他在下面的船员因为寝棚塌了，被扔出来而惊醒，不断地颤抖，甚至于我们工作时候，还在那儿呻吟。但是他们都做工。这班利物浦的硬汉身里到〔倒〕有真正的好气质。这是我的经验，他们总是如此。海——他们蒙昧灵魂四围的空旷同寂寞，赋他们以这个

---

3 watch：that part of the officers and crew who attend to the working of a vessel during the same watch 同时轮班船员的总名。

4 to go about：to endeavor to do 努力工作。

ing their dark stold souls. Ah! Well, we stumbled, we crept, we fell, we barked our skins on the wreckage, we hauled. The masts stood, but we did not know how much they might be charred down below. It was nearly calm, but a long swell ran from the west and made her roll. They might go[1] at any moment. We looked at them with apprehension. One could not foresee which way they would fall.

"Then we retreated aft and looked about us. The deck was a tangle of planks on edge, of planks on end, of splinters, of ruined woodwork. The masts rose from that chaos like big trees above a matted[2] undergrowth. The interstices of that mass of wreckage were full of something whitish, sluggish, stirring—of something that was like a greasy fog. The smoke of the invisible fire was coming up again, was trailing, like a poisonous thick mist in some valley choked with dead wood. Already lazy wisps were beginning to curl upwards amongst the mass of splinters. Here and there a piece of timber, stuck upright resembled a post. Half of a fife-rail had been shot through the foresail, and the sky made a patch of glorious blue in the ignobly soiled canvas. A portion of several boards holding together had fallen across the rail, and one end protruded overboard, like a gangway leading upon nothing, like a gangway leading over

---

1 to go: to topple down 倒下。

性质。吓！我们摔交，我们爬动，我们的胫骨触着破碎木头擦去踵皮，我们拖扯东西。桅樯站着，但是我们不知道它们底下烧焦了多少。天气差不多是恬静的，但是一阵浪涌从西方来，使它转动。那些桅樯随时可以颠覆。我们恐惧地望着它们。人们无法预料它们会向那面倒下。

"然后我们退到船尾去，看一看四面的情境。船面是破板，零段，碎片同毁坏的木头家伙的堆积所。桅樯从这混乱的杂物里抽出，好像大树从密生的矮林里伸出。这堆破烂物的空隙满是一种白色蠕动的东西——同油腻的雾差不多。看不见的火的烟又上升了，回绕着，有如充塞于朽木的山谷里浓密的毒雾。已经有些慢飘的鬼火开始从这杂碎里望〔往〕上蜿蜒。这儿那儿有些木头壁直插着，像一根柱子。围桅的栏杆一半穿到前樯的纵帆里去，天空在这沾污得难看的帆布破处现出一块光荣的蓝色。几块架在一起的木板有一部分横在栏杆外面，一头突出船外，像一个到虚空去的舷门，像一个到深海去的舷门，引我

---

2 matted: twined together like a mat 缠在一起像席那样。

the deep sea, leading to death—as if inviting us to walk the plank[1] at once and be done with[2] our ridiculous troubles. And still the air, the sky—a ghost, something invisible was hailing the ship.

"Someone had the sense to look over, and there was the helmsman, who had impulsively jumped overboard anxious to come back. He yelled and swam lustily like a merman, keeping up with[3] the ship. We threw him a rope, and presently he stood amongst us streaming with water and very crestfallen. The captain had surrendered the wheel, and apart, elbow on rail and chin in hand, gazed at the sea wisfully. We asked ourselves, what next? I thought, now, this is something like. This is great. I wonder what will happen. O youth!

"Suddenly Mahon sighted a steamer far astern. Captain Beard said, 'We may do something with her yet.' We hoisted two flags, which said in the international language of the sea, [4] 'On fire. Want immediate assistance.' The steamer grew bigger rapidly, and by-and-by spoke with two flags on her foremast, 'I am coming to your assistance.'

"In half an hour she was abreast, to windwards, within hail,

---

1 to walk the plank—to walk blindfold into sea on plank laid over ship's side 眼睛用布盖着，走上一块一边放在船外的跳板。这是海贼杀人的办法。
2 to be done with—to have no further concern with 不再有关系了。
3 to keep up with—not to be left behind 并进。
4 海上的旗语各国都是一样的，所以叫做海上的世界语。

们走上死路——好像请我们立刻去走跳板,将我们这可笑的麻烦结束。在空中,在天上——仿佛有个精灵,一个看不见的东西叫我们的船名。

"有人倒晓得向船外望一下,看见我们的舵工,他起先一时冲动跳到海里去,焦急地想回来。他大声喊叫,很带劲地浮水,像一条人鱼,总在船旁边,不敢落后。我们抛一条绳子给他,他立刻站在我们中间,水同江河一样从他身上流下,很垂头丧气样子。船主也不理那舵轮了,独自在一处,肘倚着栏杆,手支着颐,默然凝视着海。我们问自己道,'再会有什么事情呢?'我想,这才像冒险,这真是伟大。我纳罕着会有什么事情发生。啊,青春!

"忽然间马洪瞧见一条汽船远在船后。卑尔船主说,'我们还可以向它去设法。'我们挂起两面旗,那用海洋上的世界语说,'着火。需急救。'汽船很快就变大了,渐渐也在前桅上挂两面旗,旗语的意思是,'我正来救你。'

"半点钟内,它同我们居在同一行列上,在上风那一边,彼

and rolling slightly, with her engines stopped. We lost our composure, and yelled all together with excitement, 'We've been blown up.' A man in a white helmet, on the bridge, cried 'Yes! All right! all right! ' and he nodded his head, and smiled and made soothing motions with his hand as though at a lot of frightened children. One of the boats dropped in the water, and walked towards us upon the sea with her long oars. Four Calashes[1] pulled a swinging stroke. This was my first sight of Malay seamen. I've known them since; but what struck me then was their unconcern: they came alongside, and even the bowman standing up and holding to our main-chains with the boat-hook did not deign to life his head for a glance. I thought people who had been blown up deserved more attention.

"A little man, dry like a chip and agile like a monkey, clambered up. It was the mate of the steamer. He gave one look, and cried, 'O boys—you had better quit. '

"We are silent. He talked apart with the captain for a time, — seemed to argue with him. Then they went away together to the steamer.

"When our skipper came back we learned that the steamer was the Somerville, Captain Nash, from West Australia to Singapore via Batavia with mails, and that the agreement was she should tow us to

---

1 Calashes：大概是马来群岛的一种人。

此相喊听得见，微微颠簸着，它的机器停住。我们失掉了镇静，齐声激昂地喊道，'我们被火冲飞了。'一个戴白色窄边拿坡仑式帽子的人站在舰桥上喊，'是的！不要紧！不要紧！'他点头微笑，用手做安慰的姿势，好像对着一群吓了的小孩子。一只小船下水，荡它的长桨向我们走来。四个加拿士人轻快地划来。这是我第一次见到马来水手。此后我很知道他们，那时使我觉得奇怪的是他们的不关心：他们来到旁边，甚至于站起，拿船钩搭在我们的大铁链上面的划头桨的人也不肯赏脸抬头望我们一眼。我心里想，被火冲到天上去的人们总值得受更大的注意。

"一个矮小汉子，干枯像根木屑，活泼像只猴子，爬上来。这是汽船的大副。他看了一眼，就说道，'呵，孩子们——你们还是离开这只船好些罢。'

"我们都默然。他独自跟船主谈一会儿，——仿佛是跟他辩论。然后他们一同上汽船去。

"当我们船主回来，我们听他说这只汽船叫做散麦维尔，船主是那士，从西奥大利亚到新加坡去，路遇巴塔菲亚，带有邮

Anjer or Batavia, if possible, where we could extinguish the fire by scuttling[1], and then proceed on our voyage—to Bankok! The old man seemed excited. 'We will do it yet,' he said to Mahon, fiercely. He shook his fist at the sky. Nobody else said a word.

"At noon the steamer began to tow. She went ahead slim and high, and what was left of the Judea followed at the end of seventy fathom of tow-rope, —followed her swiftly like a cloud of smoke with mast-heads protruding above. We went aloft to furl the sails. We coughed on the yards, and were careful about the bunts. Do you see the lot of us there, putting a next furl on the sails of that ship doomed to arrive nowhere? There was not a man who didn't think that at any moment masts would topple over. From aloft we could not see the ship for smoke, and they worked carefully, passing the gaskets with even turns. 'Harbour furl—aloft there!' cried Mahon from below.

"You understand this? I don't think one of those chaps expected to get down in the usual way. When we did I heard them saying to each other, 'Well, I thought we would come down overboard, in a lump—sticks and all—blame me if I didn't.' 'That's what I was

---

1 scuttling: making hole in ship 船底打个洞。

件，我们订的合同是它拖我们到盘革，假使可能，就到巴塔菲亚，在那里我们可以在船侧打一个孔把火弄灭，然后继续我们的航程——到盘谷去！老头子好像兴奋起来。'我们还要干下去，'他凶猛地向马洪说。他握拳向天。别人不则一声。

"中午时候汽船开始拖我们。它苗条高高地在前面走，犹太这个残破的船在七十呎船缆的末端跟着——轻快地跟它，像一团黑烟，桅杆的顶露在上面。我们爬到帆索的高处去卷船帆。到帆桁时我们咳嗽，到帆腹时非常小心。你们看见我们这班人吗，仔细地卷起那命定了永不会抵任何地方的船的帆？个个人都认为随时桅樯会倾覆下来。从上面，我们只见烟，看不见船，他们小心地工作，好好地接连着传递束帆索。'向港口卷去——你们这班在上面的人们！'马洪从底下喊道。

"你们懂得这一点吗？我不相信这几个汉子里面有一个预料会照通常的样子下来。当我们平安着地了，我听见他们彼此说道，'呀，我起先想我们将从船上掉到海中，一大堆的——木头和我们一起——你可以骂我，假使我不是这样想。''这正是我

thinking to myself, ' would answer wearily another battered and bandaged scarecrow. And, mind, these were men without the drilled-in[1] habit of obedience. To an onlooker they would be a lot of profane scallywags[2] without a redeeming point. What made them do it—what made them obey me when I, thinking consciously how fine it was, made them drop the bunt of the foresail twice to try and do it better? What? They had no professional reputation—no examples, no praise. It wasn't sense of duty; they all knew well enough how to shirk, and laze, and dodge—when they had a mind to[3] it—and mostly they had. Was it the two pounds ten[4] a month that sent them there? They didn't think their pay half good enough. No; it was something in them, something inborn and subtle and everlasting. I don't say positively that the crew of a French or German merchantman wouldn't have done it, but I doubt whether it would have been done in the same way. There was a completeness in it, something solid like a principle, and masterful like an instinct—a disclosure of something secret—of that hidden something, that gift of good or evil that makes racial difference, that shapes the fate of nations.

"It was that night at ten that, for the first time since we had

---

1 drilled-in：well-trained 训练得很好的。
2 scallywags：a good-for-nothing wastrel 没有用的人。
3 to have a mind to：to be inclined to 倾向于；喜欢。
4 two pounds ten：two pounds and ten shillings 二镑十先令。

对自己想的,'另一个受伤了,缚了绷带的憔悴的人疲倦地答道。请你们注意,这班人并没有受过训练,养成服从习惯。在一个旁观人眼里,他们是一群毫无虔信心境的流氓,绝没有什么好处。什么使他们工作——什么使他们服从我,当我自觉地想到这是多么有意思,叫他们一再放下前帆的帆腹,为的是要弄得更牢靠些?什么呢?他们并没有职业上的荣誉——没有什么例子,也得不到赞美。这也不是出于他们的责任心;他们都很知道怎样躲懒偷闲——当他们想这样干的时候——他们多半都有这种念头。是不是因为叫他们来的这个每月二镑十先令的薪金呢?他们觉得他们该受一倍多的报酬,不;这是他们身里的性质,一些天生的,微妙的,永久的气分〔氛〕。我并没有积极地说一只法国或者德国商船上的水手不能干这些事,但是,我怀疑他们会不会这样干。这里面有一种完善的态度,坚固得有如主义,能够驾驭一切有如本能——露出一些秘密的性质——一些隐晦的气分〔氛〕,一种先天的善恶之分,那做成种族的差别,那铸定国家的命运。

"这是在那晚上十点钟,我们第一次看见火,自从我们跟它

been fighting it, we saw the fire. The speed of that towing had fanned the smouldering destruction. A blue gleam appeared forward, shining below the wreck of the deck. It wavered in patches, it seemed to stir and creep like the light of a glowworm. I saw it first, and told Mahon. 'Then the game's up[1],' he said. 'We had better stop this towing, or[2] she will burst out suddenly fore and aft before we can clear out.' We set up[3] a yell; rang bells to attract their attention; they towed on. At last Mahon and I had to crawl forward and cut the rope with an axe. There was no time to cast off the lashings. Red tongues could be seen licking the wilderness of splinters under our feet as we made our way back to the poop.

"Of course they very soon found out in the steamer that the rope was gone. She gave a loud blast of her whistle, her lights were seen sweeping in a wide circle, she came up ranging close alongside, and stopped. We were all in a tight group on the poor looking at her. Every man had saved a little bundle or a bag. Sunddenly a conical flame with a twisted top shot up forward and threw upon the black sea a circle of light, with the two vessels side by side and heaving gently in its centre. Captain Beard had been sitting on the gratings still and mute for hours, but now he rose slowly and advanced in front of us, to the mizzed-shrouds. Captain Nash hailed: 'Come

---

1 up: hopeless 绝望了。
2 or: otherwise 否则。
3 to set up: to begin uttering 开始喊。

奋斗以来。拉纤的速度扇动了冒烟的烈火。一线绿光现于前面,照亮底下甲板上的残破情形。它变成小块火球摇动着,蠕动慢爬,像一只流萤的光。我先瞧见,告诉马洪。'那么失败了,'他说。'我们还是停止这个拉纤好罢,否则它会前后爆裂,在我们能够走开之前。'我们狂叫起来;摇铃引他们的注意;他们还是向前拖。末了,迫得马洪同我爬到前面,用一把斧头把绳子砍断。因为来不及去解绳索了。在我回到船尾的途中,我们看得见红火舌舐我们脚下的一片木屑的旷野。

"他们在汽轮上当然很快就发觉绳子断了,它的汽笛大叫一声,我们看船上的灯光飞快地兜个大圈子,它走来排在我们船旁,停住了。我们紧紧地挤成一圈站在船尾甲板上,望着它。每个人手里都保留有一捆或者一包的东西。忽然一个带螺旋形顶的圆锥形火焰冲上天去,投一个光圈到黑海上面,这两只船并排在这个圈的中心轻轻起落着。卑尔船主坐在铁格上发呆有好几个钟头了,但是现在他慢慢站起来,走到我们前面,一直走到尾桅桅索上。那士船主喊道:'快些!当心点。我船上有邮

along[1]! Look sharp[2]. I have mail-bags on board. I will take you and your boats to Singapore.'

"'Thank you! No!' said our skipper. 'We must see the last of the ship.'

"'I can't stand by any longer,' shouted the other. 'Mail—you know.'

"'Ay! ay! We are all right.'

"'Very well! I'll report you in Singapore... Goodbye!'

"He waved his hand. Our men dropped their bundles quietly. The steamer moved ahead, and passing out of the circle of light, vanished at once from our sight, dazzled by the fire which burned fiercely. And then I knew that I would see the East first as commander of a small boat. I thought it fine; and the fidelity to the old ship was fine. We should see the last of her. Oh, the glamour of youth! Oh, the fire of it, more dazzling than the flames of the burning ship, throwing a magic light on the wide earth, leaping audaciously to the sky, presently to be quenched by time, more cruel, more pitiless, more bitter than the sea—and like the flames of the burning ship surrounded by an impenetrable night.[3]

---

1 come along: make haste 赶快。

2 look out: take care 当心。有这么一个笑话，说一个人坐火车，当火车快走进隧道时，看见一个牌子写着 look out，他以为是叫他伸头，于是大好头颅蹾成为五瓣梅花了。

3 这是指青春的火焰一消灭后，前途永是黑暗，绝不能大地春回，所以好像沉于个无时日的漫漫长夜。

包。我一定带你们同你们的小船到新加坡去。'

"'谢谢你!不!'我们船主说。'我们一定要看这条船的究竟。'

"'我不能再在你们旁边了,'那个人喊道。'邮包——你们知道。'

"'是!是!我们没有危险。'

"'好罢!我到新加坡时替你们报告……再见!'

"他挥手告别。我们这班人们悄悄地落下手里的包裹。汽船向前驶去,走出光圈,我们立刻看不见它了,因为我们眼睛给燃烧得很凶猛的火弄眩了。然后,我晓得我第一次瞧见东方时,我将是个小艇的总指挥。我想这真妙;我们这样忠于老船,我觉得也很妙。我们将看见它的究竟。呵,青春的魔力!呵,青春的火焰,比着火的船的火焰更来得令人目眩,射出有魔力的光辉到大地上,大胆地跳到天上去,很快就给'时间'湮没了,那是比海更残酷,更无怜悯,更苛刻——跟着火的船的火焰一样,被坚不可破的黑夜吞没进去了。

"The old man warned us in his gentle and inflexible way that it was part of our duty to save for the under-writers as much as we could of the ship's gear. Accordingly we went to work aft, while she blazed forward to give us plenty of light. We lugged out a lot of rubbish. What didn't we save? An old barometer fixed with an absurd quantity of screws nearly cost me my life; a sudden rush of smoke came upon me, and I just got away in time. There were various stores, bolts of canvas, coils of rope; the poop looked like a marine bazaar, and the boats were lumbered to the gunwales. One would have thought the old man wanted to take as much as the could of his first command with him. He was very, very quiet, but off his balance[1] evidently. Would you believe it? He wanted to take a length of old stream-cable and a kedge-anchor with him in the long-boat. We said. 'Ay, ay, sir,' deferentially, and on the quiet[2] let the things slip overboard. The heavy medicine-chest went that way, two bags of green coffee, tins of paint—fancy, paint! —a whole lot of things. Then I was ordered with two hands into the boats to make a stowage and get them ready against[3] the time it would be proper for us to leave the ship.

---

1 to be off one's balance: to be mentally upset 心神纷乱。
2 on the quiet: clandestinely 秘密地；偷偷地。
3 against: in anticipation of 预备，逆料。

"老头子用他那温和而固执的口吻警告我们,这是我们责任的一部分,尽力替保险商救出船上的东西。于是乎我们到船尾去工作,它就在船头大放光明,足以照我们做事情。我们拖出一大堆废物。有什么我们不拿呢?一只陈旧的寒暑表,没有道理地钉了无限多的钉子,几乎要了我的命:一阵烟忽然冲来,我刚来得及躲开。这里有许多的物品,好几捆的帆布,好几圈的绳子,船尾甲板看起好像海洋物品的市场,小艇堆得满到船沿。人们会以为这个老头子想从他第一次领的船尽力带走许多东西。他是非常,非常镇静,但是分明是糊涂了。你们会相信吗?他要拿很长的旧水线同一把小锚到他的长艇里去。我们恭敬地答道,'是的,是的,先生,'暗地里让这些东西溜到海里去。一只沉重的医药箱也这样子消失了,还有两袋绿咖啡,许多罐油漆——你们想一想,油漆!——以及许多其它东西。然后,我得到命令,同两个水手到这几只小艇去装货,把它们弄好,预备我们该离大船的时候。

We put everything straight, stepped[1] the long-boat's mast for our skipper, who was to take charge of her, and I was not sorry to sit down for a moment. My face felt raw, every limb ached as if broken, I was aware of all my ribs, and would have sworn to a twist in the back-bone. The boats, fast astern, lay in a deep shadow, and all around I could see the circle of the sea lighted by the fire. A gigantic flame arose forward straight and clear. It flared fierce, with noises like the whirr of wings, with rumbles as of thunder. There were cracks, detonations, and from the cone of flame the sparks flew upwards, as man is born to trouble, to leaky ships, and to ships that burn.

"What bothered me was that the ship, lying broad-side[2] to the swell and to such wind as there was—a mere breath—the boats would not keep astern where they were safe, but persisted, in a pig-headed[3] way boats have, in getting under the counter and then swinging alongside. They were knocking about dangerously and coming near the flame, while the ship rolled on them, and, of course, there was always the danger of the masts going over the side at any moment. I and my two boat-keepers kept them off as best we could, with cars and boat-hooks; but to be constantly at it became exasper-

---

1 to step: to set up 竖起。
2 broad-side: ship's side 船旁。
3 pig-headed: obstinate 顽梗。

"我们把一切东西装好,替我们船主把长艇的桅竿竖起,这条艇是将归他去负责的,我坐下憩息一会儿,觉得松活一下。我的脸孔肿痛,四肢疼得有如折断了,我感到一切肋骨的不舒服,敢赌咒我的脊骨扭歪了。小艇紧靠在船尾,躺在浓影之中,四面我看得见一大圈海给火照亮。一阵巨大的火焰从船前面清澈壁直地上升。它很猛烈地闪燃,声音响得像羽翼的拍拍,还有像雷声的霹雳。此外杂有噼啪同轰发的声音,火花就从这个圆锥形的火焰生出来望〔往〕上飞,正像人为将来的灾难,为漏水的船,为着火的船而生的那样。

"使我麻烦的是大船船舷朝着滚来的浪,对着那时所有的风——一些的微风——以至小艇不肯安居船尾,那里却是安全的地方;它们像小艇们通常那种顽梗的样子,一定要跑到船尾突出部的下面,然后摆到旁边去。它们危险地碰来撞去,走近火焰,大船在它们上面滚转,自然时时刻刻又有桅樯倒下的危险。我同两个守船的人用船桨同船钩极力设法使它们离开大船;但是老是卖这种力气真够令人忿怒,因为我们没有可以滞留的

ating, since there was no reason why we should not leave at once. We could not see those on board, nor could we imagine what caused the delay. The boat-keepers were swearing feebly, and I had not only my share of the work but also had to keep at it[1] two men who showed a constant inclination to lay themselves down and let things slide.

"At last I hailed, 'On deck there, ' and someone looked over. 'We're ready here, ' I said. The head disappeared, and very soon popped up again. The captain says, 'All right, sir, and to keep the boats well clear of the ship. '

"Half an hour passed. Suddenly there was a frightful racket, rattle, clanking of chain, hiss of water, and millions of sparks flew up into the shivering column of smoke that stood leaning slightly above the ship. The coat-heads had burned away, and the two red-hot anchors had gone to the bottom, tearing[2] out after them two hundred fathom of red-hot chain. The ship trembled, the mass of flame swayed as if ready to collapse, and the fore top-gallant-mast fell. It darted down like an arrow of fire, shot under, and instantly leaping up within an oar's-length of the boats, floated quietly, very black on the luminous sea. I hailed the deck again. After some time a man in an unexpectedly cheerful but also muffled tone, as though he had

---

1 to keep at it: hard at work 勤作，奋斗。

理由。我们不能看见船上的人们,也想不出什么产生了这耽搁。守船那两个人轻轻地发誓,我不单有我分下的工作,还得注意这两个人工作,他们常常表示出躺下让小艇顺流溜去的倾向。

"末了,我喊道,'在船面的人们,'有一个人望〔往〕下瞧。'我们这里预备好了,'我说。那个头看不见了,很快又露出来。船主说,'很好,先生,不要使小艇靠近大船。'

"半点钟过去了。忽然间有一阵可怕的嘈杂,刮辣的声音,铁链的琅珰声,水的咝声,无数万的火花飞上,到颤动的烟柱里,那是稍微比船高一些,斜倚在那儿。徽章烧掉了,两个烧得通红的锚也跑到海底去了,扯着烧得通红的二百呯铁链跟它下去。整个船颤动,那一团火挥舞,好像将塌陷,船首的上樯也就倒下了。它火箭似的投下,射到海里去,立刻跳出来,同小船只有一桨之距,安详地浮着,在明亮的海上显得非常黑。我又向船上喊。过了一会儿,一个人用一种出乎意料地高兴的,但是好像他想闭着嘴说话地那样消沉的口吻告诉我,"立刻就

---

2 tearing:此字读作 tar,跟眼泪的 tear 声音不同。

been trying to speak with his mouth shut, informed me, 'Coming directly, sir, ' and vanished. For a long time I heard nothing but the whirr and roar of the fire. There were also whistling sounds. The boats jumped, tugged at the painters; ran at each other playfully, knocked their sides together, or, do what we would, swung in a bunch against the ship's side. I couldn't stand[1] it any longer, and swarming[2] up a rope, clambered aboard over the stern.

"It was as bright as day. Coming up like this, the sheet of fire facing me was a terrifying sight, and the heat seemed hardly bearable at first. On a settee cushion dragged out of the cabin, Captain Beard, his legs drawn up and one arm under his head, slept with the light playing on him. Do you know what the rest were busy about? They were sitting on deck right aft, round an open case, eating bread and cheese and drinking bottled stout.

"On the background of flames twisting in fierce tongues above their heads they seemed at home like salamanders, and looked like a band of desperate pirates. The fire sparkled in the whites of their eyes, gleamed on patches of white skin seen through the torn shirts. Each had the marks as of a battle about him—bandaged heads, tied-up arms, a strip of dirty rag round a knee—and each man had a bottle between his legs and a chunk of cheese in his hand. Mahon

---

1 to stand: to suffer 忍受。

来,"看不见了。有许久时间,我只听到火的呼呼声同咆哮声。还有呜呜声。小船跳动着,拖拉它们的船缆,开玩笑地冲来冲去,船舷相碰,无论我们怎么办,总是一大堆摆到大船旁边。我不能再忍了,攀登一根绳子,从船尾爬到船上去。

"船面明亮得同白天一样。这样爬上去,对着我的这一片火光看起来真是可怕,那股热气起先好像几乎无法忍受。一只有背睡椅的垫子,那是从房里拖出的,卑尔船主坐在上面,他的双腿弯起,一只臂给头枕着,正睡着,火光对着他闪烁。你们知道其它人们忙着什么吗?他们坐在船尾,围着一只打开的箱子,吃面包同酪饼,喝瓶装的黑麦酒。

"凶猛火舌绞扭着在他们头上,他们对于这样的背境觉得很舒适,同火蛇一样,活像一班不顾性命的强盗。火在他们眼睛的白部发光,射到他们破内衣所露出的一块一块白皮肤上。个个人身上好像都有战争的痕迹——绷带缚着的头,扎起来的手臂,一条龌龊的破布围着膝部——个个人有一瓶酒夹在腿上,

---

2 swarming:climbing 爬。

got up. With his handsome and disreputable head, his hooked profile, his long white beard, and with an uncorked bottle in his hand, he resmbled one of those reckless sea-robbers of old making merry amidst violence and disaster. 'The last meal on board,' he explained solemnly. 'We had nothing to eat all day, and it was no use leaving all this.' He flourished the bottle and indicated the sleeping skipper. 'He said he couldn't swallow anything, so I got him to lie down,' he went on; and as I stared, 'I don't know whether you are aware, young fellow, the man had no sleep to speak of [1] for days—and there will be damned[2] little sleep in the boats.' 'There will be no boats by-and-by if you fool about much longer,' I said, indignantly. I walked up to the skipper and shook him by the shoulder. At last he opened his eyes, but did not move. 'Time[3] to leave her, sir,' I said quietly.

"He got up painfully, looked at the flames, at the sea sparkling round the ship, and black, black as ink farther away; he looked at the stars chining dim through a thin veil of smoke in a sky black, black as Erebus[4].

"'Youngest first,' he said.

---

  1 to speak of: worth mention 值得一提的。
  2 damned: very; deplorably 非常，可怜地。
  3 (it is) time to leave her.
  4 Erebus: dark region between earth and Hades 世界与地狱交界处的漆黑地方。

一厚块酪饼在手里。马洪站起来。他那美丽而下流的头，那钩形的侧面，那雪白的长胡子，他手里打开橡皮塞的瓶子，这几点使他像古代不顾死生的海盗，在残忍同蹂躏之中作乐。'我们在船上最后的一餐，'他严重地声明。'我们整天没有东西吃，这些食物都留下也是没有用的。'他挥舞他的瓶子，指着睡正浓的船主。'他说他吃不下什么东西，所以我弄他去躺下，'他继续说；当我直着眼睛看他，'我不知道你晓得不晓得，年青的人，这个老头子有好多天没有睡了——将来在小艇里睡的机会也少得该咒。''将没有小艇了，若使你们再胡闹下去，'我生气地说。我走向船主，推他的肩膀。最后，他睁开眼睛，但是并不动。'已到离开它的时候，先生，'我镇静地说道。

"他满身疼痛地站起，看看火焰，看一看船四围发光的海，和再远黑得同墨水一样的海；他望一望星群，那是在黑得像地狱门的天空里一层稀薄的烟雾中蒙昧发光。

"'最年青的先离船，'他说。

"And the ordinary seaman, wiping his mouth with the back of his hand, got up, clambered over the taffrail, and vanished. Others followed. One, on the point of going over, stopped short to drain his bottle, and with a great swing of his arm flung it at the fire. 'Take this!' he cried.

"The skipper lingered disconsolately, and we left him to commune alone for a while with his first command. Then I went up again and brought him away at last. It was time[1]. The ironwork on the poop was hot to the touch.

"Then the painter of the long-boat was cut, and the three boats, tied together, drifted clear of the ship. It was just sixteen hours after the explosion when we abandoned her. Mahon had charge of the second boat, and I had the smallest—the 14-foot thing. The long-boat would have taken the lot of us; but the skipper said we must save as much property as we could—for the underwriters—and so I got my first command. I had two men with me, a bag of biscuits, a few tins of meat, and a breaker of water. I was ordered to keep close to the long-boat, that in case of[2] bad weather we might be taken into her.

"And do you know what I thought? I thought I would part company[3] as soon as I could. I wanted to have my first command all to

---

1 time: proper time 适当的时候。
2 in case of: in the event of 若使有……事。

"普通水手用手背揩嘴，站起，爬过船尾栏杆，看不见了。别人跟着走。有一个正要跨过去，站住喝干他的酒瓶，手臂一挥，扔到火里去。'把这个也拿去罢，'他喊道。

"船主悲哀地滞在后面，我们让他独自跟他第一次带的船默语一会儿。然后我又上去，末了把他引下。这真是该离船的时候了。船尾铁的东西触着感到火热。

"然后长艇的船缆割断，三只小船缚在一起，飘走远离大船了。我们舍弃它刚在它爆发后十六钟头。第二条小艇归马洪负责，我管最小那一条——十四呎长的小艇。本来长艇就够载我们全部的人；但是船主说我们必得尽力救起船上财产——替保险商——这样子我第一次得到指挥权。我有两个人同我一起，一袋饼干，几罐肉，一小桶水。我得到命令，叫我紧靠着长艇，为的是天气恶劣时我们可以收留到长艇里去。

"你们知道我想什么吗？我想只要办得到，我就要同他们分手。我要独自占有这第一次得到的指挥权。假使有独自航行的

---

3 to part company：to cease to be together 不再在一块儿。

myself. I wasn't going to sail in a squadron if there were a chance for independent cruising. I would make land[1] by myself. I would beat the other boats. Youth! All youth! The silly, charming, beautiful youth.

"But we did not make a start at once. We must see the last of the ship. And so the boats drifted about that night, heaving and setting on the swell. The men dozed, waked, sighed, groaned. I looked at the burning ship.

"Between the darkness of earth and heaven she was burning fiercely upon a disc of purple sea shot by the blood-red play of gleams; upon a disc of water glittering and sinister. A high, clear flame, an immense and lonely flame, ascended from the ocean, and from its summit the black smoke poured continuously at the sky. She burned furiously; mournful and imposing like a funeral pile kindled in the night, surrounded by the sea, watched over by the stars.[2] A magnificent death had come like a grace, like a gift, like a reward to that old ship at the end of her laborious days. The surrender of her weary ghost to the keeping of stars and sea was stirring like the sight of a glorious triumph. The masts fell just before daybreak, and for a moment there was a burst and turmoil of sparks that seemed to fill

---

1 to make land: to discover land as the ship approaches 看见陆地，当船走近的时候。

机会，我是不肯整队前进的。我要凭着自己的本领把它带领靠岸。我要比其它船都走得快。青春！这全是青春！愚蠢的，可爱的，美丽的青春。

"但是我们并不立刻出发。我们一定要看这只船的究竟。于是小艇那晚上就在旁边飘荡，随着浪涌而浮定。人们微睡，醒来，叹息，呻吟。我就望着火烧的大船。

"夹于海天的黑暗之中，它猛烈地烧着，在一圈给跳跃着的血红火光照成紫色的海面上；在一圈灿烂而阴险的水面上。一条明亮的高飞火焰，一条寂寞的极大火焰，由海里上升，从它的高颠有黑烟不断地向天空冲去。它暴怒地烧着；悲哀庄严得像火葬的积薪在夜里点燃，大海围绕着，星群注视着。一个堂皇的死仪像一个恩典，像一份礼物，像一件奖品，给这条老船，在她辛苦生涯的这个末日。它这疲劳的灵魂付给星群同大海去安排，这正同光荣的凯旋同样地感动人们。天刚将破晓时候，

---

2 古时最隆重的葬礼是将尸体放在船上，船望〔往〕海外驶时，把船点燃，于是绝世英雄就在茫茫沧海里火光冲天中净化得无影无踪了。这段隐含有此意。

with flying fire the night patient and watchful, the vast nigth lying silent upon the sea. At daylight she was only a charred shell, floating still under a cloud of smoke and bearing a glowing mass of coal within.

"Then the oars were got out, and the boats forming in a line moved round her remains as if in procession—the long-boat leading. As we pulled across her stern a slim dart of fire shot out viciously at us, and suddenly she went down, head first, in a great hiss of steam. The unconsumed stern was the last to sink; but the paint had gone, had cracked, had peeled off[1], and there were no letters, there was no word, no stubborn device that was like her soul, to flash at the rising sun her creed and her name.

"We made our way[2] north. A breeze sprang up, and about noon all the boats came together for the last time. I had no mast or sail in mine, but I made a mast out of a spare oar and hoisted a boat-awning for a sail, with a boat-hook for a yard. She was certainly over-masted[3], but I had the satisfaction of knowing that with the wind aft I could beat[4] the other two. I had to wait for them. Then we all had a look at the captain's chart, and, after a sociable meal of hard bread

---

1 to peel off: to come off in flakes 一片片脱落。
2 to make one's way: to proceed 前进。
3 over-masted: with too tall or heavy masts 桅太高或太重。
4 to beat: to overcome in a contest 比赛的胜利。

船桅倒下了，一下子火花四散乱飞，好像使耐心的，留神的夜，静默地卧在大海上的空旷的夜，满是飞火。天亮时，它只是一只烧焦的外壳，安详地在一阵烟云之下飘游，里面载有一堆白热的煤块。

"然后，船桨拿出来，小船成一条线围着它的遗留绕行，好像列队送葬——长艇带领着。当我们驶过它船尾时，一朵苗条的火焰刻毒地向我们射来，它忽然间沉下，倒栽的，蒸气很响地嗞一声。尚未毁坏的船尾最后沉下去；但是油漆已经没有了，爆裂了，剥落了，船尾没有字母，没有什么话了，没有恍惚是它的灵魂的那倔强的铭语，对着上升的太阳，闪出它的信条同它的名字。

"我们望〔往〕北走去。一阵微风吹起，将到中午时候，一切小艇最后聚会一下子。我的小艇没有桅，也没有帆，但是我拿一根多余的桨做一只桅，挂上一个布帐当船帆，拿船钩做船桁。她的桅樯的确太重了，但是我心里高兴，知道靠着从船尾吹来的风，我能够追过其它两只船。我得等候它们。然后，我们看一下船主的地图，大家感情融洽地吃一顿硬面包同水，听

and water, got our last instructions. These were simple: steer north, and keep together as much as possible. 'Be careful with that jury-rig[1], Marlow,' said the captain; and Mahon, as I sailed proudly past his boat, wrinkled his curved nose and hailed, 'You will sail that ship of yours under water, if you don't look out, young fellow.' He was a malicious old man—and may the deep sea where he sleeps now rock him gently, rock him tenderly to the end of time![2]

"Before sunset a thick rain-squall passed over the two boats, which were far astern, and that was the last I saw of them for a time[3]. Next day I sat steering my cocklesheel—my first command—with nothing but water and sky around me. I did sight in the afternoon the upper sails of a ship far away, but said nothing, and my men did not notice her. You see I was afraid she might be homeward bound, and I had no mind to turn back from the portals of the East. I was steering for Java—another blessed name—like Bankok, you know. I steered many days.

"I need not tell you what it is to be knocking about in an open

---

1 jury-rig: the rig for temporary use 暂时用的樯。
2 这里轻轻地暗示马洪最终是淹死的。
3 for a time: for a certain period 暂时。

到最后的训令。那是很简单的:望〔往〕北走,尽力聚在一起行驶。'当心那个假桅,马罗,'船主说;马洪,当我骄傲地驶过他的小艇时候,皱起他那弯曲的鼻子,喊道,'你将在水底行舟,假使你不小心,年青的人。'他是个苛刻的老头子——希望他现在所长眠的大海轻轻地摇荡他,慈爱地摇荡他,一直到宇宙的末日!

"黄昏之前,一阵密密的暴风雨降到那两只小艇,它们是远在我这小船的后面,这次看见后,我就没有见到它们了,一直有好久时候。第二天,我坐着驶我这海壳般的轻舟——我第一次带领的船——四围没有别的,只是水天茫茫。下午我的确看见远处一只大船的上帆,但是我不则一声,我的水手没有注意到。你们看我心里怕它是一只归帆,我却不想转身回去,没有进东方的大门。我是向爪哇驶去——那也是个快乐的名字——同盘谷一样,你们知道。我驶了许多日子。

"我用不着告诉你们在一只空船里颠簸是怎么样子。我记得

boat. I remember nights and days of calm¹, when we pulled, we pulled, and the boat seemed to stand still, as if bewitched within the circle of the sea horizon. I remember the heat, the deluge of rain-squalls that kept us baling for dear life (but filled our water-cask), and I remember sixteen hours on end² with a mouth dry as a cinder and a steering-oar over the stern to keep my first command head on³ to a breaking sea. I did not know how good a man I was till then. I remember the drawn faces, the dejected figures of my two men, and I remember my youth and the feeling that will never come back any more—the feeling that I could last for ever, outlast the sea, the earth, and all men; the deceitful feeling that lures us on to joys, to perils, to love, to vain effort—to death; the triumphant conviction of strength, the heat of life in the handful of dust, the glow in the heart that with every year grows dim, grows cold, grows small, and expires—and

---

1 nights and days of calm 从前行船靠帆，狂风当然不妙，若使一丝风都没有，那么船也无法前进。浪漫派诗人 Coleridge 在他那首长篇杰作 *The Rime of Ancient Mariner* 有底下这一段：

Down dropt the breeze, the sails dropt down,
'Twas sad as sad could be,
And we did speak only to break
The silence of the sea!

很能描写这种情形。全首诗有许多描状海洋的妙句，最好读者拿来跟这篇比较一下。

许多日子整天整夜的全然无风,我们划桨,我们划桨,船却好像站住,仿佛给魔力迷惑了,不能走出水平线做成的这一圈海面。我记得酷热,暴风雨的泛滥,那使我们为着救这可爱的生命不断地用桶将船里的水汲出(但是灌满了我们的水瓶),我还记得接连十六钟头口渴干得焦渣,一只舵桨在船尾上使我这第一次带领的船还能头朝着来浪山崩的大海。在那时候以前,我不知道我自己是个多么有本领的汉子。我记得我两个水手瘦长的脸孔同憔悴的样子,我记得我的青春,同那永不会再回来的感觉——当时我觉得我能够永久维持下去,比海,天,和一切人们都更耐久;就是这么一种骗人的感觉,引诱我们到欣欢,到危险,到爱情,到白费的努力——最后到死的途上去;这是优胜者对于自己力量的深信不疑,这是在这盈握的尘土做成的躯体里面的生命热气,这是我们心中的闪烁火光,那却随年时而暗淡,而冷却,而消沉,终于熄灭了——熄灭得真是太早,

---

2 on end: continuously 接连。
3 head on: with the front, pointing directly towards an object 头直向。

expires, too soon, too soon—before life itself. [1]

"And this is how I see the East. I have seen its secret places and have looked into its very soul; but now I see it always from a small boat, a high outline of mountains, blue and afar in the morning; like faint mist at noon; a jagged wall of purple at sunset. I have the feel of the oar in my hand, the vision of a scorching blue sea in my eyes. And I see a bay, a wide bay, smooth as glass and polished like ice, shimmering in the dark. A red light burns far off upon the gloom of the land, and the night is soft and warm. We drag at the oars with aching arms, and suddenly a puff of wind, a puff faint and tepid and laden with strange odours of blossoms, of aromatic wood, comes out of the still night—the first sigh of the East on my face. That I can never forget. It was impalpable and enslaving, like a charm, like a whispered promise of mysterious delight.

"We had been pulling this finishing spell for eleven hours. Two pulled, and he whose turn it was to rest sat at the tiller. We had made out[2] the red light in that bay and steered for it, guessing it must mark some small coasting port. We passed two vessels, outlandish and high-sterned, sleeping at anchor, and, approaching the light, now very dim, ran the boat's nose against the end of a jutting wharf. We

---

1 这真是哀莫大于心死，虚有其表，在宇宙里当一个活尸，然而世上一大半的中年人都是如此。

2 to make out: to observe 看出。

真是太早——还在生命熄灭之前。

"这是我怎样见到东方。我曾经看见过它秘密的地方,曾经深悉它的灵魂;但是现在我对于东方的印象总是从一只小艇,对面是一列高山,在晨曦里蓝色的,远远的;在中午时像一层薄雾;在落照之下变成为紫色的凸凹不一的长墙。我手里好像有一只桨,眼中好像看到灼热的碧海。我还看见一个海湾,一个广阔的海湾,玻璃一样地平,结冰一样地滑,在黑暗中发微光。一盏红灯远在陆地的幽暗里燃烧着,夜是温柔的,暖和的。我们用酸痛的手臂荡桨,忽然间一阵风,一阵带有花卉同香木的馨气的温暖微风,从静寂的夜里吹来——这是东方向我第一下的叹息。这是我永不会忘却的。这是不可捉摸的,迷人的,像一种魔力,像向我们耳语,暗地里允许了神秘的欣欢。

"我们这最后一次的荡舟一共花了十一钟头。两人划船,那个轮到去休息的人就坐在舵杠旁边。我们看出海湾里那朵红光,向它驶去,猜它一定指出某一个泊船的小港。我们驶过两只船,异乡情调的,船尾很高的,抛锚睡着;当我们走近那现在是朦

were blind with fatigue. My men dropped the oars and fell off the thwarts as if dead. I made fast to a pile. A current rippled softly. The scented obscurity of the shore was grouped into vast masses, a density of colossal clumps of vegetation, probably—mute and fantastic shapes. And at their foot the semicircle of a beach gleamed faintly, like an illusion. There was not a light, not a stir, not a sound. The mysterious East faced me, perfumed like a flower, silent like death, dark like a grave.

"And I sat weary beyond expression, exulting like a conqueror, sleepless and entranced as if before a profound, a fateful enigma.

"A splashing of oars, a measured dip reverberating on the level of water, intensified by the silence of the shore into loud claps, made me jump up. A boat, a European boat, was coming in. I invoked the name of the dead; I hailed: 'Judea ahoy!' A thin shout answered.

"It was the captain. I had beaten the flagship by three hours, and I was glad to hear the old man's voice again, tremulous and tired. 'It it you, Marlow?' 'Mind the end of that jetty, sir,' I cried.

"He approached cautiously, and brought up[1] with the deep-sea

---

1 to bring up: to come to a stop 使停住。

胧的红光，我们小艇的船头碰到一只突出码头的末端。我们疲倦得瞎了眼睛了。我的水手放松船桨，从坐板上摔下，仿佛死了。我把船系在一根大桩上。一阵潮流轻轻地潺潺着。岸上芬芳的黑暗集成庞大的一堆一堆，那是密生的大丛植物，也许是——寂然的，古怪的东西。在它们脚下，半圆形的海滨微微闪光，像一番幻梦。绝无灯光，绝无动弹，绝无声响。神秘的东方对着我，它是香得像一朵花，静得同死一样，暗得同坟一样。

"我是坐着，疲倦得不能以文字形容，狂欢有如一个战胜者，睡不着，神魂颠倒，好像当前有一个深奥的，命运攸关的谜。

"桨溅水的声音，水面回响的有规律的打水声，给〔跟〕岸的寂静相比变为大声的拍拍，使我跳起来。一只小艇，一只欧洲的小艇，驶进来。我呼唤已死者的名字；我喊：'犹太！'一个细邈的喊声回答。

"这是船主。我比主艇先到三点钟；我很高兴，再听到老头子颤动的，疲累的声音。'是你吗，马罗？''当心码头的末端，先生，'我喊。

"他小心地走近，用深海的铅线把船弄靠岸，这些线我们救

lead-line which we had saved—for the underwriters. I eased my painter and fell alongside. He sat, a broken figure at the stern, wet with dew, his hands clasped in his lap. His men were asleep already. 'I had a terrible time of it,' he murmured. 'Mahon is behind—not very far.' We conversed in whispers, in low whispers, as if afraid to wake up the land. Guns, thunder, earthquakes would not have awakened the men just then.

"Looking round as we talked, I saw away at sea a bright light travelling in the night. 'There's a steamer passing the bay,' I said. She was not passing, she was entering, and she even came close and anchored. 'I wish,' said the old man, 'you would find out whether she is English. Perhaps they could give us a passage somewhere.' He seemed nervously anxious. So by dint of[1] punching and kicking I started one of my men into a state of somnambulism, and giving him an oar, took another and pulled towards the lights of the steamer.

"There was a murmur of voices in her, metallic hollow clangs of the engine-room, footsteps on the deck. Her ports shone, round like dilated eyes. Shapes moved about, and there was a shadowy man high up on the bridge. He heard my oars.

"And then, before I could open my lips, the East spoke to me,

---

1 by dint of: by means of 靠着。

出来——为着保险商。我放宽我的船缆,落到同它一排。他坐在船尾,一个精神涣散的人,沾着露水,他的双手叉在怀中。他的水手都已睡着了。'我受了许多辛苦困难,'他低声说。'马洪在后面——没有隔多远。'我们说话是用耳语,低声的耳语,好像只怕扰醒这片大陆。至于水手,那时炮声,雷声,地震都不能把他们弄醒。

"我们谈时,向四面望,我看见一盏明灯在夜的海里航行。'那里有一只汽船走过海湾,'我说。它不是过路,它是进口,它甚至于走近泊下。'我希望,'老头子说,'你去打听它是否英国船。也许他们能够带我们到别地方去。'他好像焦急得神经很受震动。于是靠着拧同踢,我把我的一个水手弄到睡游的状态,给他一个桨,自己另拿一把,向汽船的灯光划去。

"船上有喋喋的说话声,机器房金属家伙空洞的铿锵声,甲板上的脚步声。它的舷侧门发光,圆得像睁大的眼睛。人影在船上走动,有一个模糊人形高高地站在舰桥上。他听到我的划桨声音。

"然后,在我能够开口之前,东方向我说话,但是用的是西

but it was in a Western voice. A torrent of words was poured. into the enigmatical, the fateful silence; outlandish, angry words, mixed with words and even whole sentences of good English, less strange but even more surprising. The voice swore and cursed violently; it riddled the solomn peace of the bay by a volley of abuse. It began by calling me Pig, and from that went crescendo into unmentionable adjectives—in English. The man up there raged aloud in two languages, and with a sincerity in his fury that almost convinced me I had, in some way, sinned against the harmony of the universe. I could hardly see him, but began to think he would work[1] himself into a fit.

"Suddenly he ceased, and I could hear him snorting and blowing like a porpoise. I said—

"'What steamer is this, pray?'

"'Eh? What's this? And who are you?'

"'Castway crew of an English barque burnt at sea. We came here tonight. I am the second mate. The captain is in the long-boat, and wishes to know if you would give us a passage somewhere.'

"'Oh, my goodness! I say... This is the Celestial from Singapore on her return trip. I'll arrange with your captain in the morning... and, ... I say, ... did you hear me just now?'

---

1 to work: to excite 激动。

方的口腔。 大阵的话倾注到谜一般的，命运也似的静默里去；异乡情调的怒语，杂有几个字，甚至于整句的发音清晰的英文，这虽然没有那么异乡的，可是更令人惊奇。这个人拼命地赌咒发誓；用一串连珠的毁骂使海湾严重的静默变成莫名其妙。起先叫我做猪，于是步步上升，说出不能出口的形容字——用英文说的。站在上面的人用两种语言大声怒骂，气得那么真挚样子，几乎使我相信我有些冒犯了大宇宙的和谐。我差不多看不见他，但是开始想他将气得晕倒了。

"忽然间他停住，我能听到他鼻孔喷气同喘息像一只海豚。我说：

"'这是什么汽船？'

"'唉？怎么样？你是谁？'

"一只在海上着火的英国帆船的飘零水手。我们今晚来到这里。我是二副。船主在长艇里，想知道你肯不肯带我们到别地方去。"

"'啊，我的天呀！我说……这是"天国"从新加坡回去。早上我将同你船主商量……还有……我说……你刚才听见我说话没有？'

"'I should think the whole bay heard you.'

"'I thought you were a shore-boat. Now, look here —this infernal lazy scoundrel of a caretaker has gone to sleep again—curse him. The light is out, and I nearly ran foul[1] of the end of this damned jetty. This is the third time he plays me this trick. Now, I ask you, can anybody stand this kind of thing? It's enough to drive a man out of his mind[2]. I'll report him... I'll get the Assistant Resident to give him the sack[3], by...[4]! See—there's no light. It's out, isn't it? I take you to witness the light's out. There should be a light, you know. A red light on the—'

"'There was a light.' I said, mildly.

"'But it's out, man! What's the use of talking like this? You can see for yourself it's out—don't you? If you had to take a valuable steamer along this Godforsaken[5] coast you would want a light, too. I'll kick him from end to end of his miserable wharf. You'll see if I don't. I will—'

"'So I may tell my captain you'll take us?' I broke in.

---

1 to run foul: to collide 撞。

2 out of one's mind: distracted 胡涂了；疯了。

3 to give one the sack: to dismiss one 斥退；辞却。

4 by... 咒骂的话多半是用by字开头的，这里因为他说的话太下流，所以不写出来。

5 Godforsaken: dismal 悲惨的；黯淡的。

"'我想海湾里所有的人们都听到你的话了.'

"'我以为你是一只本地的船。现在,你看——这个该死的懒流氓,这个看守者又去睡了——真是该咒。灯光又灭了,我几乎撞着这可恶的码头。这是第三次他跟我开这玩笑,现在我问你,有谁能够忍受这种事情吗?这足够叫人气疯了。我要把他报告上去。……我要使驻外外交副代表把他开除,我敢赌……!你看——那里并没有亮。已经灭了,是不是?我要你做见证,那个亮是灭了。那里应当有个亮,你知道。一盏红灯在……'

"'那里起先有个亮,'我温和地说。

"'但是它灭了,汉子!这样谈论有什么用呢?你自己能够看见它是灭了——你看得见吗?若使你领一艘宝贵的汽船,走过这个上帝所弃的海岸,你也会要一盏灯。我将把这流氓从他这可怜的码头这一头踢到那上头。你看我会不会放松他。我一定——'

"'那么我可以告诉我的船主你肯带我们走?'我打断他的话。

"'Yes, I'll take you. Good-night,' he said, brusquely.

"I pulled back, made fast again to the jetty, and then went to sleep at last. I had faced the silence of the East. I had heard some of its language. But when I opened my eyes again the silence was as complete as though it had never been broken. I was lying in a flood of light, and the sky had never looked so far, so high, before. I opened my eyes and lay without moving.

"And then I saw the men of the East—they were looking at me. The whole length of the jetty was full of people. I saw brown, bronze, yellow faces, the black eyes, the glitter, the colour of an Eastern crowd. And all these beings stared without a murmur, without a sigh, without a movement. They stared down at the boats, at the sleeping men who at night had come to them from the sea. Nothing moved. The fronds of palms stood still against the sky. Not a branch stirred along the shore, and the brown roofs of hidden houses peeped through the green foliage, through the big leaves that hung shining and still like leaves forged of heavy metal. This was the East of the ancient navigators, so old, so mysterious, resplendent and sombre, living and unchanged, full of danger and promise. And

"'是的,我将带你们一同走。再见,'他粗鲁地说道。

"我划回去,又把船缚在码头旁边,于是最后去睡觉。我会面对东方的静默了。我会听到它的一些语言了。但是当我再睁开眼睛,它的静默是这么完整,仿佛从来没有破坏过。我是躺在大光明底下,天空从来没有像这么辽远,这么高朗。我睁开眼睛,毫不动弹地躺着。

"然后我看见东方的人们——他们望着我。码头上满是人。我看棕色的,青铜色的,黄色的脸孔,黑眼睛,一队东方群众的灿烂夺目,色调辉煌。这班人眼睛钉〔盯〕着我们,没有一点说话的声音,没有一声的叹息,没有丝毫的转动。他们直着眼睛看下面的小艇,看夜里从海外来到他们这儿这几个睡着的人们。一切东西都是静的。棕树的叶子安详地站着,天空衬在后面。沿岸的树林没有一枝摇动,隐着瞧不见的屋子的棕色屋顶偷偷地现在绿荫之中,现在发光挂着,静止得有如重铁铸成的大叶子之中。这是古代航海家的东方,这么古老,这么神秘,灿烂而忧郁,虽然生气勃勃,却永远不变,满是危险同希望。

these were the men. I sat up suddenly. A wave of movement passed through the crowd from end to end, passed along the heads, swayed the bodies, ran along the jetty like a ripple on the water, like a breath of wind on a field—and all was still again. I see it now—the wide sweep of the bay, the glittering sands, the wealth of green infinite and varied, the sea blue like the sea of a dream, the crowd of attentive faces, the blaze of vivid colour[1]—the water reflecting it all, the curve of the shore, the jetty, the high-sterned outlandish craft floating still, and the three boats with the tired men from the West sleeping, unconscious of the land and the people and of the violence of sunshine. They slept thrown across the thwarts, curled on bottom-boards, in the careless attitudes of death. The head of the old skipper, leaning back in the stern of the long-boat, had fallen on his breast, and he looked as though he would never wake. Farther out old Mahon's face was upturned to the sky, with the long white beard spread out on his breast, as though he had been shot where he sat at the tiller; and a man, all in a heap[2] in the bows of the boat, slept with both arms embracing the stem-head and with his cheek laid on the gunwale. The East looked at them without a sound.

"I have known its fascination since; I have seen the mysterious shores, the still water, the lands of brown nations, where a stealthy

---

1 这里是指东方人爱鲜色的衣服，辉煌夺目，有如火焰。
2 all in a heap: all in a mass 一堆。

这班就是东方的人们。我忽然坐起来。群众里有一个波动从这头一直达到那头，大家的头都向一边倾，大家的身体都这么摆动，这个激动像水面的波纹，田中的微风——一下子大家又归于静止。想起来如在目前——一大片的海湾，闪烁的沙滩，庞杂的，无限的绿色世界，蓝得像梦里海洋的大海，一群注视的脸孔，鲜艳颜色的衣服跟火焰一般——这些全被水反映出来，还有一弯的海岸，码头，恬静地浮在水面的船尾很高的异乡船只，载着从西方来睡着的疲劳的人们的三条小船，这几个人完全不觉得这个国土，这里人民同太阳的猛烈。他们熟睡，有的横躺在坐板上面，有的蜷伏在船底板子上面，那种不在乎的态度简直同死一样。肯倚着长艇船尾的船主的头垂到他的胸际，看起来他好像永不会醒来。再远一些，马洪脸朝着天，白色的长须摊在他胸前，好像他坐舵杠旁被人枪射了；还有一个人，弯成一团在船首，睡时双臂抱着龙骨，他的脸颊放在船沿。东方没有声音地望着他们。

"此后我知道了它的魔力；看见了神秘的海岸，静止的水，棕色人种的国土，那里有一个阴险的'报复之神'埋伏着，追

Nemesis[1] lies in wait, pursues, overtakes so many of the conquering race, who are proud of their wisdom, of their knowledge, of their strength. But for me all the East is contained in that vision of my youth. It is all in that moment when I opened my young eyes on it. I came upon it from a tussle with the sea—and I was young—and I saw it looking at me. And this is all that is left of it! Only a moment; a moment of strength, of romance, of glamour—of youth?... A flick of sunshine upon a strange shore, the time to remember, the time for a sigh, and—good-bye! —Night—Good-bye[2]... !"

He drank.

"Ah! The good old time—the good old time. Youth and the sea. Glamour and the sea! The good, strong sea, the salt, bitter sea, that could whisper to you and roar at you and knock your breath out of you."

He drank again.

"By all that's wonderful it is the sea, I believe, the sea itself—or is it youth alone? Who can tell?But you here—you all had something out of life: money, love—whatever one gets on shore—and, tell me, wasn't that the best time, that time when we were young at

---

1 Nemesis: an ancient goddess of retributive justice 古代司天罚之女神。
2 这是指死的永诀,所以用大写,以表严重之意。

赶,袭击这许多来征服的种族,这些种族却自令他们的聪明,他们的知识,他们的力气。但是对于我,整个东方是包括在我年青时这一瞥眼。这完全是在我向他睁开我年少眼睛的那一刹那。我从同海恶斗一场来到它这里——我正年青——我看它望着我。这就是它所留下的惟一印象!只一刹那;具有魅力,浪漫性,魔力——青春的一刹那?……阳光突然射到异乡的海岸,值得记忆的时候,引起一声长叹的时候,于是就是——再见!——毁灭后的沉沉黑夜——永诀……!"

他喝酒。

"啊,从前良好的时光——从前良好的时光。青春同海。魔力同海!良好的,有力的大海,咸味的,刻毒的大海,它能够向你细语,向你咆哮,把你打得没有气。"

他喝酒。

"最奇怪却是海,我相信,是海——或者是青春?谁知道?但是你们诸位——你们从人生都得到一些东西:金钱,爱情——无论你在岸上得到了什么东西——请告诉我,那是不是

sea; young and had nothing, on the sea that gives nothing, except hard knocks—and sometimes a chance to feel your strength—that only—what you all regret?"

And we all nodded at him: the man of finance, the man of accounts, the man of law, we all nodded at him over the polished table that like a still sheet of brown water reflected our faces, lined, winkled; our faces marked by toil, by deceptions, by success, by love; our weary eyes looking still, looking always, looking anxiously for something out of life, that while it is expected is already gone[1]—has passed unseen, in a sigh, in a flash—together with the youth, with the strength, with the romance of illusions.

---

1 这几句话可以概括整个人生，有那个人不感到这个惆怅，读者大概会为之掩卷深思吗？

绝妙的时光,当我们年青在海上飘游;年青,什么东西都没有,在海上,那是什么东西都不给的,除开猛烈的打击——有时给你们一个感到自己力气的机会——惟有这个——是你们所不能忘怀的吗?"

我们都向他颔首:理财家,会计员,律师,我们都向他颔首,对着这明亮的桌子,它像一片棕色的止水反映出我们画有线的,满是皱纹的脸孔;我们被劳工、欺骗、成功、爱情加上标志的脸孔;我们疲倦的眼睛还是,永远是,焦急地想从人生里得到某件东西,那当我们期望时候,已经逃掉了——不知不觉之间消灭了,一声叹息,一下闪光之间没有了——连同青春,魅力,同幻境的浪漫情调。

The Constant Lover
忠心的爱人
（英汉对照）

St. John Hankin　著
梁遇春　译注

"英文小丛书"之一，上海北新书局，1931年4月付排，1931年5月初版

St. John Hankin

(1869—1909)

他是牛津大学出身的,后来当新闻记者。他主要的戏剧是:*The Two Mr. Wetherbys*,*The Return of the Prodigal*,*The Charity that Began at Home*,*The Cassilis Engagement*等。

他的喜剧同王尔德的唯美派戏剧一样,是从一个新的观察点去欣赏人生。他们的态度既不是道德的(moral),也不是不道德的(immoral),却是没有含有道德的成分(non-moral),仿佛世上并没有那些观念,我们享乐时尽可以放手做去。若使我们把世俗的道德观念扔在一边,那么我们也许会觉得他们所说的刁钻古怪的话是最真实的真理。实在说起来,我们平时一举一动,甚至于念头的起伏,都是受conventionality的支配,何妨暂时松活一下呢?这些戏剧就是我们在这个乌烟瘴气的环境里的一服清凉剂。

他的喜剧又有些像萧伯纳(Bernard Shaw)的作品。他们用唐突奇怪的结构同对话来说他们自己严重的主张。其实,喜剧恐怕是最严重的东西,莫里哀(Moliere)的神品有那一篇不是隐含有无限的教训。但是就是猜不出那哑谜的人们也觉得他的戏是极有趣味的,这样子能够使雅俗共赏,每个观众都有所获得，这才可以算个成功的作品，古今伟大的戏剧都是如此。有人说，戏剧是低能的东西，因为它的目的是博一群无聊观众的欢心；但是在满足群众的欲望之外，还能够有一个更深邃的境界让识者去领略，这却是戏剧的艺术高明的地方。这种亭亭玉立，濯污泥而不染的神情是个个有本领的编剧家都具有的，我们现在读的这位作家也是一个例子。

The Constant Lover

A Comedy of Youth in One Act

Characters

Evelyn Rivers, eighteen or twenty

Cecil Harburton, twenty-five

Before the curtain rises the orchestra will play the Woodland Music (cuckoo) from *Hansel and Gretel*[1], and possibly some of the Grieg[2] Pastoral Music from *Peer Gynt*[3], or some Gabriel Fauré.[4]

---

1 *Hansel and Gretel*：这是德国当代音乐家Engelbert Humperdinck的杰作，是谈神仙故事的歌舞剧。Hansel同Gretel这两个兄妹住在森林旁边，到林中采果，遇到女妖，后来靠着他们的智慧将自己同许多其他受难的孩子们都解脱出来，反把女妖烧成一块大饼。

2 Grieg：Edvard Hagerup Grieg（1843—1907）是挪威有名的编曲家，他的乐曲有一种缥缈甜蜜的情调。

忠心的爱人
一幕青春的喜剧

剧中人物

厄味宁·利维斯，十八岁或二十岁

塞西尔·哈堡顿，二十五岁

在开幕之前，乐队奏《罕塞尔同格勒忒午》里面的《林地曲》（杜鹃曲），也可以奏格黎格所编的《皮耳·真提》里面的牧曲，或者迦伯列·福耳所编的歌曲。

---

3 *Peer Gynt*：易卜生（Ibsen）的一本戏剧，Grieg 曾为它编出一部绝妙的乐曲，那使他成为近代一个大音乐家。

4 Gabriel Fauré（1845—1924），法国的作曲家。

SCENE: A glade in a wood. About C[1], a great beech-tree, the branches of which overhang the stage, the brilliant sunlight filtering through them. The sky, where it can be seen through the branches, is a cloudless blue.

When the curtain rises Cecil Harburton is discovered sitting on the ground under the tree, leaning his back against its trunk and reading a book. He wears a straw hat and the lightest of grey flannel suits. The chattering of innumerable small birds is heard while the curtain is still down, and this grows louder as it rises, and we find ourselves in the wood. Presently a wood pigeon coos in the distance. Then a thrush begins to sing in the tree above Cecil's head and is answered by another. After a moment Cecil looks up.

Cecil   By Jove[2], that's jolly! [Listens for a moment, then returns to his book.]

[Suddenly a cuckoo begins to call insistently. After a moment or two he looks up again.]

Cuckoo too! Bravo[3]! [Again he returns to his book.]

[A moment later enter Evelyn Rivers R[4]. She also wears the lightest of summer dresses, as it is a cloudless day in May. On her head is a shady straw hat. As she approaches the tree a twig snaps

---

1 C：Center舞台的中心，在剧本中通常只写C字。

2 By Jove：Jove是罗马人所崇奉的天帝名字，就是希腊的Jupiter或Zeus.据说生下来时命里带这个星宿的人是心境快乐的，jovial, joviality这

布景：森林中的一块空旷草地。近于中央有一棵大榉树，它的枝叶覆盖舞台，明亮的太阳光就经过这些枝叶渗透下来。天，从叶的空隙所望得见的，是无云的一片蓝色。

当开幕时候，我们看见塞西尔·哈堡顿坐在树下地上，背靠着树干，正在看一本书。他戴一顶草帽，穿一套最鲜明的灰色法兰绒衣服。当幕还是闭着时候，已可以听到无数小鸟的呢喃，开幕时声音更大了，我们看到眼前是一座森林。不久有一只斑鸠在远处作鸪鸪声。然后一只画眉在塞西尔头上的树里开始歌唱，有另一个画眉和着。过一会儿塞西尔抬起头。

塞西尔　哈哈，这真妙！（听一会儿，然后又继续看书。）

（忽然间一只杜鹃开始坚决地啼唤。过一下子他又抬起头。）

杜鹃呀！好！（他又继续看书。）

（不久厄味宁·利维斯从右边进来。她也是穿一套颜色极鲜明的夏衣，因为这是五月里一个无云的日子。她头上戴一顶有荫的草帽。当她走近大树时候，她的脚踏到一个小树枝，发出

几个字也都是从这个字变化出来。所以 by Jove 是高兴时所发的感叹辞。

3　Bravo：Good excellent！好！妙！

4　R：right 舞台的右边，参看296页注1。

under her foot and Cecil looks up. He jumps to his feet[1], closing book, and advances to her, eagerly holding out his right hand, keeping the book in his left.]

[Reproachfully.] Here you are at last!

Evelyn   At last?

Cecil   Yes. You're awfully late! [Looks at watch.]

Evelyn   Am I?

Cecil   You know you are. I expected you at three.

Evelyn   Why? I never said I'd come at three. Indeed, I never said I'd come at all.

Cecil   No. But it's always been three.

Evelyn   Has it?

Cecil   And now it's half-past. I consider I've been cheated out of[2] a whole half-hour.

Evelyn   I couldn't help it. Mother kept me. She wanted the roses done in the drawing-room.

Cecil   How stupid of Mrs. Rivers!

Evelyn   Mr. Harburton[3]!

Cecil   What's the matter?

---

1 to jump to one's feet: to stand up suddenly 突然站起；跳起来。

2 to cheat out of: to get by fraud out of (person) 从（某人）那里骗去。

3 Mr. Harburton: 听到他骂她的母亲，她很惊讶，所以喊他的名字，仿佛说："你怎么说这样话？"带有责备的意思。

一下轻脆的声音，塞西尔就抬起头。他立刻站起来，把书合起，向她走去，热烈地伸出他的右手，左手拿着他的书。）

（责备的。）你到底也来了！

厄味宁　到底？

塞西尔　是的。你的确来得太迟！（看表。）

厄味宁　真的吗？

塞西尔　你知道是真的。我从三点钟起就期待着你。

厄味宁　怎么？我绝没有说我三点钟会来。真的，我简直就没有说我会来。

塞西尔　不。但是照例总是三点钟时候。

厄味宁　真的吗？

塞西尔　现在是三点半了。我认为我被骗去整整半个钟头。

厄味宁　我没有办法。妈妈把我留着。她要把客厅的玫瑰花弄好。

塞西尔　利维斯太太多么傻呀！

厄味宁　哈堡顿先生！

塞西尔　什么事？

Evelyn I don't think you ought to call my mother stupid.

Cecil Why not—if she is stupid? Most parents are stupid, by the way[1]. I've noticed it before. Mrs. Rivers ought to have thought of the roses earlier. The morning is the proper time to gather roses. Didn't you tell her that?

Evelyn I'm afraid I couldn't very well. You see, it was really I who ought to have thought of the roses! I always do them. But this morning I forgot.

Cecil I see. [Turning towards the tree.] Well, sit down now you are here. Isn't it a glorious day?

Evelyn [Hesitating.] I don't believe I ought to sit down.

Cecil [Turns to her.] Why not? There's no particular virtue about standing, is there? I hate standing. So let's sit down and be comfortable.

[She sits, so does he. She sits on bank under tree, left of it. He sits below bank to right of tree.]

Evelyn But ought I to be sitting here with you? That's what I mean. It's—not as if I really know you, is it?

Cecil Not know me? [The chatter of birds dies away.]

---

1 by the way: formula introducing digression 通常谈话时，忽然牵连到别的不大相干的事情上时，常用这句话做引子，或者放在后面做个解释。这样说到支节上去，好像人们走路中途转弯入小径，所以叫做 by the way。

厄味宁　我觉得你不该说我的母亲傻。

塞西尔　为什么不该——假使她真是傻？其实，天下的父母多半都是傻的。这一点我从前已经看到了。利维斯太太应当早些想起玫瑰花。早晨是采玫瑰花适当的时候。你告诉她过没有？

厄味宁　恐怕我不大配说这句话。你看，实在是我应当想起玫瑰花！一向都是我去采玫瑰花。但是今天早上我忘记了。

塞西尔　是的。（脸转过来朝着树。）你现在来了，请坐下罢。今天天气不是很好吗？

厄味宁　（迟疑着。）我不知道我该不该坐下。

塞西尔　（脸向着她。）为什么不该？站着并没有什么特别好处，你看有没有？我讨厌站着。让我们坐下，舒服些罢。

（她坐下，他也坐下。她坐在树下土坡上，在树的左边。他坐在土坡下，在树的右边。）

厄味宁　但是我该不该在这里同你一块儿坐着呢？这是我的意思。这样——仿佛我真认识了你，是不是？

塞西尔　不认识我？（小鸟的呢喃声消灭了。）

Evelyn Not properly—we've never even been introduced. We just met quite by chance here in the wood.

Cecil Yes. [Ecstatically.] What a glorious chance!

Evelyn Still, I'm sure Mother wouldn't approve.

Cecil And you say Mrs. Rivers isn't stupid!

Evelyn [Laughing.] I expect most people would agree with her. Most people would say you oughtn't to have spoken to a girl you didn't know like that.

Cecil Oh, come, I only asked my way back to the inn.

Evelyn There was no harm in asking your way, of course. But then we began talking of other things. And then we sat down under this tree. And we've sat talking under this tree every afternoon since. And that was a week ago.

Cecil Well, it's such an awfully jolly tree.

Evelyn I don't know what Mother would say if she heard of it.

Cecil Would it be something unpleasant?

Evelyn [Ruefully.] I'm afraid it would.

Cecil How fortunate you don't know it, then.

Evelyn [Pondering.] Still, if I really oughtn't to be here... Do you think I oughtn't to be here?

Cecil I don't think I should go into[1] that if I were you. Sensible

---

1 to go into: to discuss minutely 详细讨论。

厄味宁　没有正式地——没有人替我们彼此介绍过。我们完全是出于偶然在这里林中相遇。

塞西尔　是的。(狂欢的样子。)多么好的一个偶然呀！

厄味宁　但是，我相信妈妈不喜欢我这样。

塞西尔　你还说利维斯太太不傻！

厄味宁　（大笑。）我预料大多数人们会同她的意见一致。大多数人们会说你对于一个你不认得的女子不该像那样子讲话。

塞西尔　呵，来，我那次只是问回到旅馆的路。

厄味宁　问路当然是无害。但是我们却谈起别的事情了。然后我们坐在这棵树底下。从此我们天天下午坐在这树下谈天。这已经有一星期了。

塞西尔　不错，这是这么妙的一棵树。

厄味宁　我不知道妈妈听到这事会说什么话。

塞西尔　那会是听起来使人不高兴的话吗？

厄味宁　（悲伤的。）我恐怕那会是。

塞西尔　那么，幸而你不知道。

厄味宁　（沉思的。）然而，假使我真不该在这儿……你想我该不该在这儿？

塞西尔　我想我不会顾虑这么多，假如我是你。聪明的人

people think of what they want to do, not of what they ought to do, otherwise they get confused. And then of course they do the wrong thing.

Evelyn   But if I do what I oughtn't, I generally find I'm sorry for it afterwards.

Cecil   Not half so sorry as you would have been if you hadn't done it. In this world the things one regrets are the things one hasn't done. For instance, if I hadn't spoken to you a week ago here in the wood I should have regretted it all my life.

Evelyn   Would you? [He nods.] Really and truly?

Cecil   [Nods.] Really and truly. [He lays his hand on hers for a moment, she lets it rest there. Cuckoo calls loudly once or twice—she draws her hand away.]

Evelyn   There's the cuckoo. [Cecil rises and sits up on bank R of her, leaning against tree.]

Cecil   Yes. Isn't he jolly? Don't you love cuckoos?

Evelyn   They are rather nice.

Cecil   Aren't they! And such clever beggars. Most birds are fools—like most people. As soon as they're grown up they go and get married, and then the rest of their lives are spent in bringing up herds of children and wondering how on earth to pay their school-

们只想他们爱干的是什么，不去想他们该干的是什么，否则他们弄胡涂了。那么当然做出错事了。

厄味宁　但是若使我干了我不该干的事情，我后来总免不了追悔。

塞西尔　假使你没有干，那么你会加一倍地追悔。在这个世界里人们所惋惜的是他们所没有干的事情。譬如，前一星期在这林中我没有同你说话，那么我一生都会追悔这个当面错过。

厄味宁　你会吗？（他点头。）真的吗，的的确确吗？

塞西尔　（点头。）真的，的的确确的。（他把他的手放在她手上一会儿，她也让它停在那儿。杜鹃大声地啼了两下——她把她的手缩去。）

厄味宁　那儿有杜鹃。（塞西尔起来，坐在土坡上她的右边，背靠着树。）

塞西尔　是的。他妙不妙？你喜欢杜鹃吗？

厄味宁　他们都还有意思。

塞西尔　可不是吗！他们又是这么聪明的叫花子。大多数的鸟是傻子——同大多数的人们一样。他们一长大，就跑去结婚，此后的岁月就全花在养大一大群的小孩子，不知道在人世里怎样付他们小孩子们学堂里种种的费用。你们的杜鹃看出了

bills[1]. Your cuckoo sees the folly of all that. No school-bills for her! No nursing the baby! She just flits from hedgerow to hedgerow flirting with other cuckoos. And when she lays an egg, she lays it in some one else's nest, which saves all the trouble of housekeeping. Oh, a wise bird!

Evelyn [Pouting, looking away from him.] I don't know that I do like cuckoos so much after all. They sound to me rather selfish.

Cecil Yes. But so sensible! The duck's a wise bird too in her way. [She turns to him.] But her way's different from the cuckoo's. [Matter-of-fact.] She always treads on her eggs.

Evelyn Clumsy creature!

Cecil Not a bit. She does it on purpose[2]. You see, it's much less trouble than sitting on them. As soon as she's laid an egg she raises one foot absent-mindedly and gives a warning quack. Whereupon the farmer rushes up, takes it away, and puts it under some wretched hen, who has to[3] do the sitting for her. I call that genius!

Evelyn Genius!

Cecil Yes. Genius is the infinite capacity for making other people take pains.

Evelyn How can you say that?

---

1 school-bills: 学校于学期终止时向家长要各种费的账。
2 on purpose: intentionally 故意。
3 to have to: to be obliged to 不得不。

这类举动的愚蠢。她用不着担忧怎样付学费！也用不着看护小孩子！她只是从这个篱笆飞到那个篱笆，同别个杜鹃调情。当她下卵时候，她下在别个鸟的窝里，这就省了一切料理事务的麻烦。啊，真是一只聪明鸟！

厄味宁　（努唇，脸转过去不看他。）我疑惑我到底有没有那么喜欢杜鹃。据我看起来，他们有些自私。

塞西尔　是的。但是这么聪明！鸭子也是一只聪明鸟，有她的办法。（她转过脸向他。）但是她的办法与杜鹃的办法不同。（平淡的。）她总是践踏她生下的卵。

厄味宁　笨畜生！

塞西尔　一点也不。她故意这样干。你看，这比坐在上面孵卵省事得多了。她每次生下一个卵，就胡涂地举起一只脚，喊出一声警告。于是乎农夫赶紧跑来，把卵拿开，放在某一个可怜的母鸡底下，她就得替她去孵了。我认为这是天才！

厄味宁　天才！

塞西尔　是的。天才无非是具有叫人去受苦的极大本领。

厄味宁　你怎么会说这种话。

Cecil I didn't; Carlyle[1] did.

Evelyn I don't believe he said anything of the kind. And I don't believe ducks are clever one bit. They don't look clever.

Cecil That's part of their cleverness. In this world if one is wise one should look like a fool. It puts people off their guard. That's what the duck does.

Evelyn Well, I think ducks are horrid, and cuckoos too. And I believe most birds like bringing up their chickens and feeding them and feeding them and looking after[2] them.

Cecil They do. That's the extraordinary part of it. They spend their whole lives building nests and laying eggs and hatching them. And when the chickens come out the father has to fuss round finding worms. And the nest's abominably overcrowded and babies are perpetually squalling, and that drives the husband to the public-house, and it's all as uncomfortable as the devil—

Evelyn Mr. Harburton!

Cecil Well, I shouldn't like it. In fact, I call it fatuous.

[Evelyn is leaning forward pondering this philosophy with a slightly puckered brow. A slight pause.]

---

1 Thomas Carlyle（1795—1881），英国近代大思想家，他主张英雄崇拜论。他所谓英雄多半是能够领袖人群，驾驭别人的英才，所以塞西尔开玩笑说喀来儿认为凡能与人以麻烦者皆是天才。

2 to look after：to take care of 照呼〔拂〕；看护。

塞西尔　这不是我说的，是喀来儿说的。

厄味宁　我不相信他说过这类话。我也不相信鸭子有一点儿聪明。看起来他们并不像聪明样子。

塞西尔　这也是他们聪明的一点。在这个世界里，若使一个人真是聪明，那么外面看起来他该像个傻子。这才可以叫人们不提防。鸭子就是如此。

厄味宁　我觉得鸭子是可怕的，杜鹃也是可怕的。我相信大多数的鸟儿喜欢养育他们的小鸟，饲养他们，看护他们。

塞西尔　他们是如此。这在他们生活里占非常重要的地位。他们一生都费在筑巢，下卵同孵卵。当小鸟出来后，做父亲的得忙于到处找小虫了，窝是挤得要命的，小孩子永远乱啼着，这就把丈夫赶到酒馆里去了，这些事都是不舒服得有如魔鬼——

厄味宁　哈堡顿先生！

塞西尔　唔，我不喜欢这类事。真的，我认为这是愚笨。

（厄味宁稍微皱着眉头身体向前倾斜，默思这个哲学。大家无言片时。）

I say, you don't look a bit comfortable like that. Lean back against the tree. It's a first-rate tree. That's why I chose it.

Evelyn　[Tries and fails.] I can't. My hat gets in the way[1].

Cecil　Take if off, then.

Evelyn　I think I will. [Does so.]That's better. [Leans back luxuriously against the trunk; puts her hat down on bank beside her.]

Cecil　Much better. [Looks at her with frank admiration.] By Jove, you do look jolly without your hat!

Evelyn　Do I?

Cecil　Yes. Your hair's such a jolly colour. I noticed it the first time I saw you. You had your hat off then, you know. You were walking through the wood fanning yourself with it. And directly[2] flush on your cheeks, and your eyes were soft and shining—

Evlyn　[Troubled.] Mr. Harburton, you mustn't say things to me like that.

Cecil　Mustn't I? Why not? Don't you like being told you look jolly?

Evelyn　[Naively.] I do like it, of course. But ought you...?

---

1 to get in the way: to cause inconvenience 阻碍着。
2 directly: as soon as 一……，立即……

我说，这样子你一点也不舒服。背靠着这棵树罢。这是个再好没有的树。所以我特地拣选它。

厄味宁　（试一试，没有靠好。）我办不到。我的帽子挡着。

塞西尔　那么，把它取下罢。

厄味宁　我想我要取下。（取下帽子。）好得多了。（畅快地靠在树干上；将她的帽子放在身旁土坡上。）

塞西尔　好得多了。（坦白地现出赞美的神气望着她）。哈哈，你不戴帽子更显得漂亮！

厄味宁　真的吗？

塞西尔　是的。你的头发有这么妙的颜色。我第一次瞧到你时，就看出这一点了。你在林中走着，用帽子扇自己。我一看到你，太阳就出来，简直是把你的头发浸在阳光里。你双颊上有最可爱的红潮，你的双眸是温柔明媚——

厄味宁　（烦恼的。）哈堡顿先生，你不该对我说这类的话。

塞西尔　我真不该吗？为什么不该？你不爱听人家说你长得漂亮吗？

厄味宁　（天真地。）我自然爱听。但是你该……？

Cecil　[Groans.] Oh, it's that again.¹

Evelyn　I mean, it's not right for men to say those things to girls.

Cecil　I don't see that—if they're true. You are pretty and your eyes are soft, and your cheeks — why, they're flushing at this moment! [Triumphant.] Why shouldn't I say it?

Evelyn　Please!...[She stops, and her eyes fill with tears.]

Cecil　[Much concerned.] Miss Rivers, what's the matter? Why, I believe you're crying!

Evelyn　[Sniffing suspiciously.] I'm... not.

Cecil　You are. I can see the tears. Have I said anything to hurt you? What is it? Tell me. [Much concerned.]

Evelyn　[Recovering herself by an effort.] It's nothing. Nothing really. I'm all right now. Only, you won't say things to me like that again, will you? Promise. [Taking out handkerchief.]

Cecil　I promise... if you really wish it. And now dry your eyes and let's be good children. That's what my nurse used to² say when my sister and I quarrelled. Shall I dry them for you? [Takes her handkerechief and does tenderly.]

Evelyn　[With a little gulp.] Thank you. [Takes away handker-

1　厄味宁总是顾虑该不该，塞西尔却只想自己喜欢不喜欢干，从这可以看出两人性格的不同：一个是被世俗无聊的道德观念（conventionality）束缚住，一个是能够乐天地享受人生。

2　used to: be accustomed 常常；惯于。

塞西尔　（呻吟。）啊，又是那一套话了。

厄味宁　我的意思是，男人们对于女人们不该说这类话。

塞西尔　我却不以为然——若使这类话是真的。你的确长得美丽，你的眼睛是温柔的，你的双颊——嗳吓，它们此刻正涨着红潮！（得意的。）那么，我为什么不该说呢？

厄味宁　请你！……（她停了，她的眼睛满是清泪。）

塞西尔　（很关心的。）利维斯小姐，什么事？嗳呀，我相信你哭起来了！

厄味宁　（带有嫌疑地歔气着。）我……没有。

塞西尔　你是哭了。我能看见眼泪。我说了什么话伤了你吗？是什么话呢？请告诉我。（很关心的。）

厄味宁　（用一下劲恢复原状了。）没有事。的确没有事。我现在好了。只是，请你不再对我说这类话，可以吗？请答应我。（拿出手巾。）

塞西尔　我答应……若使你真要我这样。现在擦干你的眼睛，让我们做好孩子。这是我的保姆常说的话，当我的姊妹同我吵架。我替你擦干吗？（拿她的手巾，温柔地替她擦干。）

厄味宁　（吞下一口气。）谢谢你。（把手巾拿开。）你多么

chief.] How absurd you are! [Puts it away.]

    Cecil   Thank you!

[Evelyn moves down, sitting at bottom of bank, a little below him.]

    Evelyn   Did you often quarrel with your sister?

    Cecil   Perpetually. And my brothers. Didn't you?

    Evelyn   I never had any.

    Cecil   Poor little kid. You must have been rather lonely.

    Evelyn   [Matter-of-fact.] There was always Reggie.

    Cecil   Reggie?

    Evelyn   My cousin, Reggie Townsend. He lived with us when we were children. His parents were in India.

    Cecil   [Matter-of-fact.] So he used to quarrel with you instead.

    Evelyn   [Shocked.] Oh, no! We never quarrelled. At least, Reggie never did. I did sometimes.

    Cecil   How dull! There's no good in quarrelling if people won't quarrel back.

    Evelyn   I don't think there's any good in quarrelling at all.

    Cecil   Oh, yes, there is. There's the making it up[1] again.

    Evelyn   Was that why you used to quarrel with your sister?

    Cecil   I expect so, though I didn't know it, of course—then. I

---

1 making it up: reconciliation 和解；修好。

胡闹！（把手巾藏起。）

　　塞西尔　谢谢你！

（厄味宁移动一下，坐在土坡下，比他低一点儿。）

　　厄味宁　你常同你姊妹吵架吗？

　　塞西尔　永远是吵架。还同我的兄弟吵架。你呢？

　　厄味宁　我压根儿没有兄弟姊妹。

　　塞西尔　可怜的孩子。你一定有些寂寞。

　　厄味宁　（平淡的。）勒吉总是同我在一起。

　　塞西尔　勒吉？

　　厄味宁　我的表兄弟，勒吉·坦增德。当我是个小孩子时候，他同我们住在一块儿。那时他的父母在印度。

　　塞西尔　（平淡的。）那么他常来同你吵架。

　　厄味宁　（惊愕。）啊，不！我们绝不吵架。最少，勒吉不吵架。我偶然到〔倒〕有。

　　塞西尔　多么无聊！若使人家不来对吵，吵架就没有好处了。

　　厄味宁　我不觉得吵架会有什么好处。

　　塞西尔　啊，有好处。有言归于好的好处。

　　厄味宁　那么，你跟你姊妹吵架就是为这个缘故吗？

　　塞西尔　我希望是，我那时当然不知道。我记得，我常同

used to tease her awfully. I remember, and pull her hair. She had awfully jolly hair. Like yours—oh! I forgot, I mustn't say that. Used you to pull Reggie's hair?

Evelyn [Laughing.] I'm afraid I did sometimes.

Cecil I was sure of it. How long was he with you?

Evelyn Till he went to Winchester. And of course he used to be with us in the holidays after that. And he comes to us now whenever he can get away for a few days. He's in uncle's office in the city. He'll be a partner some day.

Cecil Poor chap!

Evelyn Poor chap! Mother says he's very fortunate.

Cecil She would. Parents always think it very fortunate when young men have to go to an office every day. I know mine do.

Evelyn Do you go to an office every day?

Cecil No.

Evelyn [With dignity.] Then I don't think you can know much about it, can you?

Cecil [Carelessly.] I know too much. That's why I don't go.

Evelyn What do you do?

Cecil I don't do anything. I'm at the Bar[1].

---

1 at the Bar: a lawyer 律师。Bar 的本来意思是法庭里被告者所站地方旁边的栅栏,后来转变为"法律""律师职业"这些意思。

她捣乱捣得很凶,抓她的头发。她有极妙的头发。像你的这样——啊!我忘却了。我不该说这话。你常抓勒吉的头发吗?

厄味宁　(大笑。)我恐怕我有时抓他的头发。

塞西尔　我早已猜出了。他同你一起住多久?

厄味宁　一直到他到温撒斯特去。此后放假时他当然常来同我们一起住。现在只要他能有几天闲暇,总是来到我们这儿。他在京城里他叔父的公司里办事。将来他可以成为一个股东。

塞西尔　可怜的孩子!

厄味宁　"可怜"的孩子!母亲说他是"很幸运的"。

塞西尔　她当然会这样说。做父母的总认为那是很幸运的,当年青的人天天得到办公室去。我知道我的父母是这样的。

厄味宁　你天天到一个办公室去吗?

塞西尔　不。

厄味宁　(俨然。)那么,我看你恐怕不大懂得这类事情,你懂得吗?

塞西尔　(不在乎的样子。)这类事情我懂得太多了。所以我不去。

厄味宁　你干什么呢?

塞西尔　我什么也不干。我是一个律师。

Evelyn If you're at the Bar, why are you down here[1] instead of up in London[2] working?

Cecil Because if I were in London I might possibly get a brief. It's not likely, but it's possible. And if I got a brief I should have to be mugging in chambers, or wrangling in a stuffy court, instead of sitting under a tree in the shade with you.

Evelyn But ought you to waste your time like that?

Cecil [Genuinely shocked.] Waste my time! To sit under a tree—a really nice tree like this—talking to you. You call that wasting time!

Evelyn Isn't it?

Cecil No! To sit in a frowsy office adding up figures when the sky's blue and the weather's heavenly, that's wasting time. The only real way in which one can waste time is not to enjoy it, to spend one's day blinking at a ledger and never notice how beautiful the world is, and how good it is to be alive. To be only making money when one might be making love, that is wasting time!

Evelyn How earnestly you say that!

[Cecil leans forward—close to her.]

Cecil Isn't true?

---

1 down here：他们现在谈话的地方是乡"下"，跟伦敦相比，就用down字。

2 up in London：这个up字的意义同我们说"上"城去的上字一样。

厄昧宁　假使你是个律师，你为什么不上城去工作，却在这儿乡下呢？

塞西尔　因为若使我在伦敦，我也许会得到一个案子。大概是不会的，但是可能的。假使我得到一个案子，我就得在房里赶紧预备，或者到个气闷的法庭用劲辩论，不能同你坐在这棵树的凉荫下面了。

厄昧宁　但是你可以这样浪费了你的光阴吗？

塞西尔　（真是惊愕了。）"浪费"我的光阴！坐在树下——一棵像这样真好的树——同"你"闲谈。你认为这是"浪费光阴"吗？

厄昧宁　这还不是吗？

塞西尔　不！坐在一间恶臭的办公室里算帐目，当天是蔚蓝色，天气是天堂般的，"这"才是浪费时光。一个人浪费光阴的惟一办法是不去享受这时光，整天向一本帐簿霎眼，绝没有去注意世界是多么美丽，活在世上是多么好。当一个人可以去恋爱时候，却只去挣钱积钱，"这"才算做浪费时光！

厄昧宁　你多么正经地讲这些话呀！

（塞西尔身向前倾——同她很接近了。）

塞西尔　这些话不是真的吗？

Evelyn   [Troubled.] Perhaps it is. [Looks away from him.]

Cecil   You know it is. Every one knows it. Only, people won't admit it. [Leaning towards her and looking into her eyes.] You know it at this moment.

Evelyn   [Returning his gaze slowly.] I think I do.

[For a long moment they look into each other's eyes. Then he takes her two hands, draws her slowly towards him, and kisses her gently on the lips.]

Cecil   Ah! [Sigh of satisfaction. He releases her hands and leans back against the tree again.]

Evelyn   [Sadly.] Oh, Mr. Harburton, you oughtn't to have done that!

Cecil   Why not?

Evelyn   Because... [Hesitates.] Because you oughtn't... Because men oughtn't to kiss girls.

Cecil   [Scandalized.] Oughtn't to kiss girls! What non-sense! What on earth were girls made for if not to be kissed?

Evelyn   I mean they oughtn't... unless... [Looking away.]

Cecil   [Puzzled.] Unless?

Evelyn   [Looking down.] Unless they love them.

Cecil   [Relieved.] But I do love you. Of course I love you. That's why I kissed you.

厄味宁　（烦恼的。）也许是。（脸不看着他，向别处望了。）

塞西尔　你知道这些话是真的。个个人都知道。只是，人们不肯承认。（身子向她倾斜，望着她的眼睛。）你此刻就晓得这些话是真的了。

厄味宁　（慢慢地报答他的凝视。）我想我知道。

（有许多时间他们互相凝视。然后他拉她的双手，慢慢地把她拖过来，温柔地吻她的嘴唇。）

塞西尔　呀！（满意的叹息。他松开她的手，身子又靠着树。）

厄味宁　（悲哀地。）哈堡顿先生，你不该干这样事！

塞西尔　为什么不该呢？

厄味宁　因为……（犹豫。）因为你不该……因为男人不该吻女人。

塞西尔　（生气的。）不该吻女人！多么不通的话！女人不让人吻，那么她们在世上有何用处呢？

厄味宁　我的意思是他们不该……除非是……（脸望别的地方。）

塞西尔　（莫名其妙的。）除非什么？

厄味宁　（垂头。）除非他们"爱"她们。

塞西尔　（高兴起来了。）但是我"的确"爱你。我当然是爱你。所以我才吻你。

[A thrush is heard calling in the distance.]

Evelyn   Really? [Cecil nods. Evelyn sighs contentedly.] That makes it all right, then.

Cecil   I should think it did. And as it's all right I may kiss you again, mayn't I?

Evelyn   [Shyly.] If you like.

Cecil   You darling! [Takes her in his arms and kisses her long and tenderly.] Lean your head on my shoulder, you'll find it awfully comfortable. [He leans back against the tree.]

[She does so.] There! Is that all right?

Evelyn   Quite. [Sigh of contentment.]

Cecil   How pretty your hair is! I always thought your hair lovely. And it's as soft as silk. I always knew it would be like silk. [Strokes it.] Do you like me to stroke your hair?

Evelyn   Yes!

Cecil   Sensible girl! [Pause; he laughs happily.] I say, what am I to call you? Do you know, I don't even know your Christian name[1] yet?

Evelyn   Don't you?

---

1 Christian name: name given at christening 受洗礼时所给的名字,就是我们中国人所谓名字。他们寻常所谓 name 常是指 surname(姓)。

（远处有一只画眉唱着。）

厄味宁　真的吗？（塞西尔点头。厄味宁心满意足地叹一口气。）那么就对了。

塞西尔　我想是对的。既然是对的，我可以再吻你了，可以吗？

厄味宁　（害羞地。）若使你高兴。

塞西尔　你这可爱的人儿！（拥着她，温柔地同她吻了许久。）把你的头靠在我肩膀上，你会觉得那是非常舒服的事情。（他背靠着树。）

（她也这样做。）你看！好不好？

厄味宁　很好。（满意的叹息。）

塞西尔　你的头发"多么"美丽呀！我总是觉得你的头发可爱。那是同丝一样的软。我早就知道那是跟丝一样的。（抚摩她的头发。）你喜爱我抚摩你的头发吗？

厄味宁　我喜欢！

塞西尔　聪明的女孩子！（彼此不说话一会儿；他快乐地大笑。）我说，我怎样喊你？你知道吗，我到现在还不晓得你的名字？

厄味宁　你不晓得吗？

Cecil　No, you've never told me. What is it? Mine's Cecil!

Evelyn　Mine's Evelyn.

Cecil　Evelyn? Oh, I don't like Evelyn, It's rather a stodgy[1] sort of name. I think I shall call you Eve[2]. Does anyone else call you Eve?

Evelyn　No.

Cecil　Then I shall certainly call you Eve. After the first woman man ever loved.[3] May I?

Evelyn　If you like—Cecil.

Cecil　That's settled, then.

[He kisses her again. Pause of utter happiness, during which he settles her head more comfortably on his shoulder, and puts arm round her.]

Isn't it heavenly to be in love?

Evelyn　Heavenly!

Cecil　There's nothing like it in the whole world. Love is the most beautiful thing in the whole world! Say so.

---

1 stodgy: stuffed; crammed; sticky 充塞的；黏性的。这里是说这个字念起满口都是音，缠不清的。

2 Eve：外国人喊亲爱的人们时，常将他的名字任意缩短，以表亲昵之意。

3 《圣经》里说上帝创造的人第一个是亚当 Adam，他的妻子是夏娃 Eve。

塞西尔 不，你从来没有告诉我过。是什么呢？我的名字是塞西尔。

厄味宁 我的名字是厄味宁。

塞西尔 厄味宁？啊，我不喜欢厄味宁这个字。那是属于念起满口都是声音的那类名字。我想我将叫你做夏娃。有别人叫你做夏娃吗？

厄味宁 没有。

塞西尔 那么我一定叫你做夏娃。照男人所爱的第一个女人的名字。我可以吗？

厄味宁 若使你高兴这样——塞西尔。

塞西尔 那么，这算决定了。

（他又吻她。彼此无言，浸在极端的快乐之中，在那时间里他把她的头更舒服地放在他肩膀上，将他的手臂圈着她。）

恋爱岂不是天堂般的生活吗？

厄味宁 真是天堂般的生活！

塞西尔 全世界上什么都比不上它。恋爱是全世界里最美丽的东西！你也这样说罢。

Evelyn   Love is the most beautiful thing in the whole world.

Cecil   Good girl! There's a reward for saying it right. [Kisses her.] [Pause of complete happiness for both.]

Evelyn   [Meditatively.] I'm afraid Reggie won't be pleased.

[The chatter of sparrows is heard.]

Cecil   [Indifferently.] Won't he?

Evelyn   [Shakes her head.] No. You see, Reggie's in love with me too. He always has been in love with me, for years and years. [Sighs.] Poor Reggie!

Cecil   On the contrary. Happy Reggie!

Evelyn   [Astonished.] What do you mean?

Cecil   To have been in love with you years and years. I've only been in love with you a week... I've only known you a week.

Evelyn   I'm afraid Reggie didn't look at it like that.

Cecil   [Nods.] No brains.

Evelyn   You see, I always refused him.

Cecil   Exactly. And he always went on loving you. What more could the silly fellow want?

Evelyn   [Shyly, looking up at him.] He wanted me to accept him, I suppose. [The bird chatter dies away.]

厄味宁　　恋爱是全世界里最美丽的东西。

塞西尔　　好姑娘！说得不错，给你一个奖品。（吻她。）（两人默默地在完满的幸福之中。）

厄味宁　　（沉思地。）我恐怕勒吉会不高兴。

（麻雀的呢喃又听得见。）

塞西尔　　（冷淡地。）他不会吗？

厄味宁　　（摇头。）不。你看，勒吉也爱着我。他爱着我已经有许多年了。（叹气。）可怜的勒吉。

塞西尔　　不能这样说。应该说快乐的勒吉！

厄味宁　　（惊异的。）你是什么意思？

塞西尔　　跟你恋爱了许多年，这岂不是幸福吗？我才同你恋爱了一星期……我才认得你一星期。

厄味宁　　我恐怕勒吉不作这样想。

塞西尔　　（点头。）没有脑筋。

厄味宁　　你看，我总是拒绝"他"。

塞西尔　　对的。他就总是爱着你。这个傻家伙还要什么呢？

厄味宁　　（害羞地，抬头看看他。）他"要"我答应嫁他，我想大概是。（小鸟呢喃的声音消灭了。）

Cecil   Ah! .... Reggie ought to read Keats's[1] *Ode to a Grecian Urn*[2]. I say, what jolly eyes you've got! I noticed them the moment we met here in the wood. That was why I spoke to you.

Evelyn   [demurely.] I thought it was to ask your way back to the inn.

Cecil   That was an excuse. I knew the way as well as you did. I'd only just come from there. But when I saw you with the sunshine on your pretty soft hair and lighting up your pretty soft eyes. I said I must speak to her. And I did. Are you glad I spoke to you?

Evelyn   Yes.

Cecil   Glad and glad?

Evelyn   Yes.

Cecil   Good girl! [Leans over and kisses her cheek.]

---

1 John Keats（1795—1821），英国浪漫派的诗人。不幸短命而死，有人说他是被人骂死的，有人说他是因为失恋而死的，而且说像他感情这么热烈的人是应该失恋的。

2 *Ode to a Grecian Urn*：这是济慈杰作之一。他歌颂一只希腊的古瓶，上面画有男女嬉戏之图。他的诗里有一段说：

Ah, happy, happy, boughs! that cannot shed

Your leaves, nor ever bid the Spring adieu;

And, happy melodist, unwearied,

For ever piping songs for ever new;

More happy love! more happy, happy love!

For ever warm and still to be enjoyed,

For ever panting, and for ever young;

塞西尔　呀！……勒吉应该念济慈的《希腊古瓮颂》。……我说，你有一副多么妙的眼睛！我从前在林中碰到你，就看出了。所以我同你说话。

厄昧宁　（佯为端严地。）我想那是问回到你旅馆的路。

塞西尔　那是一个藉口。我知道那条路不下于你。我那时刚从那儿来。但是当我看见太阳光晒着你那美丽温柔的头发上，照亮你那美丽温柔的眼睛，我对自己说我非跟你说话不可。我说话了。你现在觉得高兴吗，我那天向你说话？

厄昧宁　是的。

塞西尔　真真高兴吗？

厄昧宁　是的。

塞西尔　好姑娘！（身向她斜倾，吻她的面颊。）

All breathing human far above,
That leaves a heart high-sorrowful and cloyed,
A burning forehead, and a parching tongue.
"呀，快乐，快乐的绿枝！你们不会落叶，也从不和春天告别；还有快乐的音乐家，不倦地永久吹出永久是新鲜的调子；更快乐的爱情！更快乐的爱情！永久是热烈的，始终是可乐的，永久恋慕着，永久是青春；远胜过人间世一切的热情，那只留下个悲伤厌倦的心境，发烧的额头同一个干燥的苦舌。"全诗及译文见拙编《英文诗歌选》。

Evelyn   [Sigh of contentment; sits up.] And now we must go and tell Mother.

Cecil   [With a comic groan.] Need we?

Evelyn   [Brightly.] Of course.

Cecil   [Sigh.] Well, if you think so.

Evelyn   [Laughing.] You don't seem to look forward to it much[1].

Cecil   I don't. That's the part always hate.

Evelyn   Always? [Starts forward and looks at him puzzled.]

Cecil   [Quite unconscious.] Yes. The going to the parents and all that. Parents really are the most preposterous people. They've no feeling for romance whatever. You meet a girl in a wood. It's May. The sun's shining. There's not a cloud in the sky. She's adorably pretty. You fall in love. Everything heavenly! Then—why, I can't imagine—she wants you to tell her mother. Well you to tell her mother. And her mother at once begins to ask you what your profession is, and how much money you earn, and how much money you have that you don't earn[2]—and that spoils it all.

Evelyn   [Bewildered.] But I don't understand. You talk as if you had actually done all this before.

Cecil   So I have. Lots of times.

---

1 to look forward to it much: to anticipate it with much pleasure 很高兴地期望着。

2 这是指家产。

厄味宁　（满意的叹息；坐起来。）我们现在必得去告诉妈妈。

塞西尔　（带一种滑稽的呻吟。）我们必得去吗？

厄味宁　（高兴地。）当然。

塞西尔　（叹气。）好罢，若使"你"觉得该去。

厄味宁　（大笑。）你仿佛不大切望走这个步骤。

塞西尔　我不。这是我素来痛恨的步骤。

厄味宁　"素来？"（吓了一跳，身体向前倾，糊涂地望着他。）

塞西尔　（完全不觉得。）是的。到爱人的父母那儿，以及种种事情。父母真是天地间最荒谬的人们。他们对于"浪漫情调"绝无感觉。你在林中碰到一个姑娘。正是春天。太阳照耀着。青天无片云。她是美丽得值得赞美。你恋爱上了。一切事情恍如天上神仙的！然后——为什么呢，我想不出来——她要你去告诉她的母亲。你向她的母亲说了。她母亲立刻开始问你操什么职业，你每月挣多少钱，你有多少不是你自己挣来的钱——这把一切都弄窘了。

厄味宁　（莫名其妙了。）但是我不大懂你的话。你说得好像这些事你实在都干过了。

塞西尔　我是干过了。而且有许多次了。

Evelyn   Oh! [Jumps up from ground and faces him, her eyes flashing with rage.]

Cecil   I say, don't get up. It's not time to go yet. It's only four. Sit down again.

Evelyn   [Struggling for words.] Do you mean to say you've been in love with girls before? Other girls?

Cecil   [Apparently genuinely astonished at the question.] Of course I have.

Evelyn   And been engaged to them?

Cecil   Not engaged. I've never been engaged so far. But I've been in love over and over again[1].

[Evelyn stamps her foot with rage—turning away from him.]

My dear girl, what is the matter? You look quite cross. [Rises.]

Evelyn   [Furious.] And you're not even ashamed of it?

Cecil   [Roused to sit up by this question.] Ashamed of it? Ashamed of being in love? How can you say such a thing! Of course I'm not ashamed. What's the good of being alive at all if one isn't to be in love? I'm perpetually in love. In fact, I'm hardly ever out of love—with somebody.

Evelyn   [Still furious.] Then if you're in love, why don't you

---

1 over and over again: many times 许多次。

厄味宁　啊！（从地上跳起来，脸对着他，她的眼睛因为生气闪动发光。）

塞西尔　我说，不要站起来。这还不是站起来的时候。现在才四点哩。再坐下来罢。

厄味宁　（气得说不出话。）你的意思是不是说从前你跟女子恋爱过？许多别个女子？

塞西尔　（分明真真是很惊讶这个问题。）我当然有过。

厄味宁　同她们订婚了没有？

塞西尔　没有订婚。一直到现在我还没有订婚过。但是我却一再恋爱了许多次。

（厄味宁气得顿足——掉过头不看他。）

我亲爱的姑娘呀，什么事？看起来你很不高兴的样子。（站起。）

厄味宁　（大怒。）你一点儿都不觉得不好意思吗？

塞西尔　（听到这句问话，惊奇得坐起来。）不好意思吗？因为恋爱，觉得不好意思吗？你怎么会说这样的话！我当然不会不好意思。一个人没有恋爱，活着还有什么好处呢？我永远是恋爱着的。真的，我几乎没有跳出恋爱圈外——总是跟人恋爱着。

厄味宁　（还是大怒。）你既然是恋爱了，为什么不订婚

get engaged? A man has no business[1] to make love to a girl and not be engaged to her. It's not right.

Cecil [Reasoning with her.] That's the parents' fault. I told you parents were preposterous people. They won't allow me to get engaged.

Evelyn Why not?

Cecil Oh, for different reasons. They say I'm not serious enough. Or that I don't work enough. Or that I haven't got enough money. Or else they simply say they "don't think I'm fitted to make their daughter happy." Anyhow, they won't sanction an engagement. They all agree about that. Your mother would be just the same. [Impatient exclamation from Evelyn.] I don't blame her. I don't say she's not right. I don't say they haven't all been right. In fact, I believe they have been right. I'm only explaining how it is.

Evelyn [Savagely.] I see how it is. You don't really want to be married.

Cecil Of course I don't want to be married. Nobody does unless he's perfectly idiotic. One wants to be in love. Being in love's splendid. And I dare say being engaged isn't bad—though I've had no experience of that so far. But being married must be simply hateful.

Evelyn [Boiling with rage.] Nonsense! How can it be hateful

---

1 business: right to do something 做某一件事情的权利。

呢？一个人不该同一个女子恋爱，而不同她订婚。这是不对的。

塞西尔　（跟她辩论。）这是父母的错处。我早就告诉你了，父母是荒谬的人们。他们不肯让我订婚。

厄味宁　为什么呢？

塞西尔　啊，有各种理由。他们说我的态度不够严重。或者说我工作太少。或者说我钱挣得不多。有时他们只说他们"看我不能够使他们的女孩快乐。"总而言之，他们不肯答应订婚。这是他们意见一致的地方。你的母亲也正是这样。（厄味宁发出不耐烦的感叹声音。）我并不骂她。我并没有说她不对。我没有说她们都是不对。其实，我相信她们都是对的。我单是解释我为什么没有订婚。

厄味宁　（野蛮地。）我看出你为什么没有订婚。你实在不想结婚。

塞西尔　我当然不想结婚。谁也不想，除非他是个完全傻子。人们只想恋爱，恋爱是绝妙的事情。我敢说订婚也不坏——虽然到现在止我关于这件事还没有过经验。但是结婚一定简直是可恨的事情。

厄味宁　（盛怒。）瞎话！恋爱既是绝妙的事情，结婚怎

to be married if it's splendid to be in love?

[The cuckoo is heard.]

Cecil   Have you forgotten the cuckoo?

Evelyn   Oh!!!

Cecil   No ties, no responsibilities, no ghastly little villa with children bellowing in the nursery. Just life in the open hedgerow. Life and love. Happy cuckoo!

Evelyn   [Furious.] I think cuckoos detestable. They're mean, horrid, disgusting birds.

Cecil   No, No. I can't have you abusing cuckoos. They're particular friends of mine. In fact, I'm a sort of cuckoo myself.

Evelyn   [Turning on him.] Oh, I hate you! I hate you! [Stamps her foot.]

Cecil   [With quiet conviction.] You don't.

Evelyn   I do!

Cecil   [Shaking his head.] You don't. [Quiet gravely.] One never really hates the people one has once loved.

[He looks into her eyes. For a moment or two she returns his gaze fiercely. Then her eyes fall and they fill with tears.]

Evelyn   [Half crying.] How horrid you are to say that!

Cecil   Why?

Evelyn   Because it's true, I suppose. Oh, I'm so unhappy! [Begins to cry.]

会是可恨的事情呢?

(杜鹃的啼声可以听得到。)

塞西尔　你忘却杜鹃吗?

厄味宁　啊!!!

塞西尔　没有束缚,没有责任,没有小孩子在养婴房里乱啼着的鬼气森森的小屋子。生活和爱情。快乐的杜鹃呀!

厄味宁　(大怒。)我觉得杜鹃是可恨的。他们是下流的,可怕的,讨厌的鸟。

塞西尔　不,不。我不能让你毁骂杜鹃。他们是我的好朋友。其实,我自己就是一种杜鹃。

厄味宁　(脸向着他。)啊,我恨你!我恨你!(顿足。)

塞西尔　(带着沉静的自信。)你没有。

厄味宁　我是恨你!

塞西尔　(摇头。)你没有。(十分严重地。)一个人绝不会真真恨一个人曾经爱过的人。

(他望着她的眼睛。她起先凶猛地报答他的凝视。然后她眼睛下垂,满是眼泪了。)

厄味宁　(半哭着。)你说这话多么可怕呀!

塞西尔　为什么呢?

厄味宁　因为那是真话,我想。啊,我是这么伤心呀!(哭起来。)

Cecil [Genuinely distressed.] Eve! You're crying. You mustn't do that. I can't bear seeing people cry. [Lays hand on her shoulder.]

Evelyn [Shaking it off.] Don't. I can't bear you to touch me. After falling in love with one girl after another like that. When I thought you were only in love with me.

Cecil So I am only in love with you—now.

Evelyn [Tearfully.] But I thought you'd never been in love with anyone else. And I let you call me Eve because you said she was the first woman man ever loved.

Cecil But I never said she was the only one, did I? [Argumentatively.] And one can't help[1] being in love with people when one is in love, can one? I couldn't help falling in love with you, for instance, the moment I saw you. You looked simply splendid. It was such a splendid day, too. Of course I fell in love with you.

Evelyn [Slightly appeased by his compliment, drying her eyes.] But you seem to fall in love with such a lot of people.

Cecil I do. [Mischievously.] But ought you to throw stones at me[2]? After all[3], being in love with more than one person is no worse than having more than one person in love with you. How about Reggie?

---

1 to help: to avoid; to prevent 避免；阻止。
2 to throw stones at me: 这是用《圣经》里的典故，见《约翰福音》第八章。人们带一个行淫时被拿着的妇人，来问耶稣他们该不该用石头打死这妇人，耶稣说："你们中间谁是没有罪的，谁就可以先拿石头打她。"

塞西尔　（真真焦急了。）夏娃！你哭着。你千万不要哭。我不能忍看别人哭。（手放在她肩膀上。）

厄味宁　（摆开。）不要这样。我不能忍让你碰我。你这样子同这个又同那个女子恋爱。我起先还以为你只爱着我。

塞西尔　我是只爱着你——此刻。

厄味宁　（满眼的眼泪。）但是我以为你绝没有爱过别人。我让你叫我做夏娃，因为你说她是男人所爱的第一个女人。

塞西尔　但是我绝没有说她是男人惟一的爱人，我说过吗？（辩论的神气。）当一个人在恋爱之中时候，他免不了爱着人，他能够不爱吗？比如，我一看见你时候，我不能不爱你。看起来，你简直是漂亮极了。那天又是这么漂亮的日子。我当然跟你恋爱起来了。

厄味宁　（听到他恭维的话，气稍平些，就擦干她的眼睛。）但是你仿佛爱上了这许多人。

塞西尔　我是。（捣乱的样子。）但是你该向我掷石子吗？实在说起来，爱上了一个以上的人并不坏过于有一个以上的人爱你。勒吉不是也爱你吗？

(He that is without sin among you let him first cast a stone at her。)

3　After all：never the less；not with standing 其实。

Evelyn   Reggie?

[The sparrows' chatter starts again.]

Cecil   [Nods.] Reggie's in love with you, isn't he? So am I. And both at once too! I'm only in love with one person at a time.

Evelyn   [Rebelliously.] I can't help Reggie being in love with me.

Cecil   And I can't help my being in love with you. That's just my point. I knew you'd see it.

Evelyn   I don't see it at all. Reggie is quite different from you. Reggie's love is true and constant...

Cecil   Well, I'm a constant lover if you come to that.

Evelyn   You aren't. You know you aren't.

Cecil   Yes, I am. A constant lover is a lover who is constantly in love[1].

Evelyn   Only with the same person.

Cecil   It doesn't say so. It only says constant.

Evelyn   [Half laughing.] How ridiculous you are! [Turns away.]

Cecil   [Sigh of relief.] That's right. Now you're good-tempered again.

---

1 a constant lover 是一个有恒心的爱人，所以这句直译起来是："一个有恒心的爱人是一个恒在爱情之中的人。"

厄味宁　勒吉？

（麻雀的噪声又起来了。）

塞西尔　（点头。）勒吉爱着你，是不是？我也爱着你。两人而且是同时的！我每次却只爱着一个人。

厄味宁　（反抗的样子。）勒吉要爱我，我没有办法。

塞西尔　我要爱你，我也没有办法。这是我的论点。我知道你会看出。

厄味宁　我一点儿也看不出。勒吉跟你大不相同。勒吉的爱情是真的，他是忠心的……

塞西尔　可是，若使你谈到这点，我也是一个忠心的爱人。

厄味宁　你不是。你知道你不是。

塞西尔　是的，我是。一个忠心的爱人是一个忠于爱情的人。

厄味宁　只跟同一个人。

塞西尔　这个定义不这样说。它只说忠心。

厄味宁　（半笑。）你多么可笑呀！（脸向别处。）

塞西尔　（放心了，叹一口气。）好了。现在你癖〔脾〕气又好起来了。

Evelyn   I'm not.

Cecil   What a story[1]!

Evelyn   I'm not. I'm very, very angry.

Cecil   That's impossible. You can't possibly be angry and laugh at the same time, can you? No one can. And you did laugh. You're doing it now.

[She does so unwillingly.]

So don't let's quarrel any more. It's absurd to quarrel on such a fine day, isn't it? Let's make it up, and be lovers again.

[The sparrows die away.]

Evelyn   [Shaking her head.] No.

Cecil   Please!

Evelyn   [Shaking her head.] No.

Cecil   Well, you're very foolish. Love isn't a thing to throw away. It's too precious for that. Love is the most beautiful thing in the whole world. You said so yourself not ten minutes ago.

Evelyn   I didn't. You said it. [Looking down.]

Cecil   But you said it after me. [Gently and gravely.] Eve, dear, don't be silly. Let's be in love while we can. Youth is the time to be in love, isn't it? Soon you and I will be dull and stupid and middle-aged like all the other tedious people. And then it will be too

---

1 story: a lie 一句谎言。

厄味宁　并没有。

塞西尔　多么大的谎呀！

厄味宁　我没有扯谎。我是非常，非常生气。

塞西尔　这是不可能的。你不能够同时生气又大笑，你办得到吗？谁也做不到。而你的确大笑了。你现在还笑着。

（她不愿意地笑了。）

好罢，我们不要再吵架了。这样的佳日吵嘴真是无谓，是不是？让我们言归于好，再做爱人们罢。

（雀噪的声音停了。）

厄味宁　（摇头。）不。

塞西尔　请！

厄味宁　（摇头。）不。

塞西尔　唉，你真傻。爱情不是随便可以扔去的东西。它太贵重了，不该受如此看待。爱情是世上最美丽的东西。还没有十分钟以前，你自己不是说过吗。

厄味宁　我没有说。你说了。（眼望着地上。）

塞西尔　但是你跟着我说了。（温柔地，严重地。）夏娃，亲爱的人，别做个傻子。让我们及时恋爱。年青是恋爱的时光，是不是？不久，你我都变成迟钝，愚蠢，中年了，像一切那班

late. Youth passes so quickly. Don't let's waste a second of it. They say the May-fly only lives for one day. He is born in the morning. All the afternoon he flutters over the river in the sunshine, dodging the trout and flirting with other May-flies. And at evening he dies. Think of the poor May-fly who happens to be born on a wet day! The tragedy of it!

    Evelyn   [Softly.] Poor May-fly.

    Cecil   There! You're sorry for the May-fly, you see. You're only angry with me.

    Evelyn   Because you're not a May-fly.

    Cecil   Yes, I am. A sort of May-fly.

    Evelyn   [With suspicion of tears in her voice.] You aren't. How can you be? Besides, you said you were a cuckoo just now.

    Cecil   I suppose I'm a cuckoo-May-fly. For I have wet days. And if you're going to cry again, it might just as well be wet, mightn't it? So do dry your eyes like a good girl. Let me do it for you. [Does it with her handkerchief.]

    [She laughs ruefully.]

    There, that's better, And now we're going to be good children again, aren't we?

    Evelyn   [Giving in.] Yes.

    Cecil   [Holding out hand.] And you'll kiss and be friends?

    Evelyn   I'll be friends, of course. [Sadly.]But you must never

讨厌的人们。到那时已经是太迟了。青春消逝得这么快。让我们不要虚费一秒的时光。人们说蜉蝣只有一天的生命。他早上生下来，整个下午他在河上太阳中飞翔，躲避鳟鱼，跟别个蜉蝣调情。黄昏时候他死了。想一想刚好在一个潮湿日子生下的可怜蜉蝣！那种的悲剧！

厄味宁　（曼声地。）可怜的蜉蝣。

塞西尔　哈哈！你看，你为着那蜉蝣伤心。你只是跟我闹气。

厄味宁　因为你不是一个蜉蝣。

塞西尔　是的，我是。一种蜉蝣。

厄味宁　（声音里含有泪声。）你不是。你怎么会是？而且，你刚才说你是一只杜鹃。

塞西尔　我想我是一只杜鹃蜉蝣。因为我有我潮湿的日子。若使你再哭起来，那简直是潮湿日子了，是不是？擦干你的眼泪，像个好孩子罢。让我替你擦。（用她的手帕擦。）

（她悲伤地笑了。）

呀，好多了。我们现在再当好孩子吗？

厄味宁　（让步。）是。

塞西尔　（伸出手。）你肯接吻，做好朋友吗？

厄味宁　我当然肯做好朋友。（悲哀地。）但是你永远不该

kiss me again.

Cecil   What a shame! Why not?

Evelyn   Because you mustn't.

Cecil   [Cheerfully.] Well, you'll sit down again anyhow, won't you? Just to show we've made it up. [Moves towards tree.]

Evelyn   [Shakes head.] No.

Cecil   [Disappointed; turns.] Ah... Then you haven't really made it up.

Evelyn   Yes, I have. [Picks up her hat.] But I must go now. Reggie's coming down by the five o'clock train; and I want to be at the station to meet him. [Holds out hand.]Good-bye, Mr. Harburton.

Cecil   [Taking hand.] Eve! You're going to accept Reggie! [Pause.]

Evelyn   [Half to herself.] I wonder.

Cecil   And he'll have to tell your mother?

Evelyn   Of course.

Cecil   [Drops her hand.] Poor Reggie! So his romance ends too!

Enelyn   It won't. If I marry Reggie I shall make him very happy.

Cecil   Very likely. Marriage may be happiness, but I'm hanged if it's romance!

Evelyn   Oh! [Exclamation of impatience.]

再吻我了。

塞西尔　多么不成话！为什么不该？

厄味宁　因为你不应当。

塞西尔　（高兴地。）好罢，无论如何，你总可以坐下来，你坐下吗？也总可以表示我们是言归于好了。（向树林移动。）

厄味宁　（摇头。）不。

塞西尔　（失望了；脸转过去。）唉……那么，你实在并没有言归于好。

厄味宁　是的，我跟你和好了。（检〔捡〕起她的帽子。）但是我现在一定要走。勒吉乘五点钟的火车来；我想到火车站接他。（伸出手。）再见，哈堡顿先生。

塞西尔　（握手。）夏娃，你将答应嫁给勒吉了！（两人默然。）

厄味宁　（一半对她自己说。）也许。

塞西尔　那么他得去向你母亲说？

厄味宁　当然。

塞西尔　（放松她的手。）可怜的勒吉！他的浪漫情调也就这样结束了！

厄味宁　不会。假使我嫁给勒吉，我将使他非常快乐。

塞西尔　很可能的。结婚也许是快乐的事情，但是我愿意绞死，若使那是浪漫的事情！

厄味宁　啊！（不耐烦的感叹声。）

[She turns away and exits R.]

[Cecil watches her departure with a smile, half amused, half pained, till she is long out of sight. Then with half a sigh turns back to his tree].

Cecil   [Reseating himself.] Poor Reggie! [Reopens his book and settles himself to read again.]

[A cuckoo hoots loudly from a distant thicket, and is answered by another. Cecil looks up from his book to listen as the curtain falls.]

CURTAIN[1].

---

1 curtain: the curtain drops 闭幕。

（她转身走开，从右边下。）

（塞西尔含一种半乐半苦的微笑看她走去，一直等到她久已走出舞台了。然后，稍微叹一口气，转过脸，向着树。）

塞西尔　（自己坐好。）可怜的勒吉！（重新打开他的书，又归心看书了。）

（从远处的小丛林一只杜鹃大声啼着，另一只和着。塞西尔不看他的书，抬起头去听，幕就渐渐下来了。）

闭幕。